About Time

To the memory of

Colin Haycraft

1929 – 1994

Nullum quod tetigit non ornavit

About Time

a work of fiction

by

Rodney Dale

Fern House

An original paperback
first published in 1995 by Fern House
19 High Street, Haddenham, ELY, Cambs CB6 3XA
01353 741229

A catalogue record for this book is available
from the British Library

ISBN 0 9524897 0 8

Jacket by Chris Winch Design
Printed by Antony Rowe Ltd, Chippenham

Acknowledgements

As always, I am indebted to my wife Judith,
and sons Timothy, Henry & Malcolm.

My thanks also to many people who have contributed – wittingly or
otherwise – to this work, including:

Jacintha Alexander	Beryl Bainbridge
Gillian Booth	Rob Cameron
Frances Chetwynd	Prof Christopher Cook
Frank Cook	Sara Cornthwaite
Len Douglas	John Farrow
Carole Fraser	Michael Grosvenor Myer
Valerie Grosvenor Myer	Janet Hales
Prof Stephen Hawking	Anna Haycraft
Colin Haycraft	Dr Sheila Lachmann
Chris Lakin	Pam Lakin
Nick Langley	Nicholas Leonard
George Melly	Trish Morris
Tom Rosenthal	Tony Short
Steve Temple	Clive Treacher
Loz Weaver	Rebecca Weaver
Nick Webb	Janet Whelan
Chris Winch	Cathy Young

And particularly Gina Keene for her help with production and distribution.

Some comments on *About Time*:

You're very good at conversations . . .   Beryl Bainbridge

I was extremely impressed! . . . the tone is so confident I can see no way it can
falter . . . splendid, original, *etc*.   George Melly

The essentially schematic nature of the book is too intrusive upon the reader's
well being.   Tom Rosenthal

Other works by Rodney Dale include

Biography

Louis Wain – the man who drew cats
(William Kimber 1968, Michael O'Mara 1991)
Catland (Duckworth 1977)
The Sinclair Story (Duckworth 1985)
From Ram Yard to Milton Hilton (CCL 1979; 1982)

Technology

British Library CD–ROM *Inventors & Inventions* (1994)
British Library Discoveries & Inventions series (1992–4)
    Timekeeping, Early Railways, Early Cars
With Henry Dale
    The Industrial Revolution
With Rebecca Weaver
    Machines in the Home, Machines in the Office,
    Home Entertainment

With Ian Williamson
    BASIC Programming (Cambridge Learning 1979)
    Understanding Microprocessors (Macmillan 1980)
    The Myth of the Micro (Star 1980)

Medicine – with Dr John Starkie
    Understanding AIDS (CA; Hodder & Stoughton 1988)

Careers
    Becoming an Architect (RIBA 1983)

Folklore – urban myths
    The Tumour in the Whale (Duckworth; Star 1978)
    It's True . . . it happened to a friend (Duckworth 1984)
    Det är sant . . . en god vän berättade (Mimer 1985)

Music
    The World of Jazz (Phaidon 1980)
    A History of Jazz (Jade Books 1983)

Cosmology – with George Sassoon
    The Manna Machine (Sidgwick & Jackson 1980)
    The Kabbalah Decoded (Duckworth 1978)

Author's preface

Said Benjamin Disraeli: 'When I want to read a novel, I write one.' That was how *About Time* came into being – I wrote the sort of work of fiction that I'd like to read. And writing it forced me to crystallise my ideas about so many things.

The central figure of *About Time* is Chaite (pronounced with a hard 'CH', and to rhyme with 'mighty') who is killed in a car accident on Wednesday 16 July 1986, the day after her twenty-eighth birthday. And here is a clue to the title, for the book is indeed 'about time' – on the one hand the time fixed by the precise dates which are necessary for the coincidence and synchronicity and sequentiality of life; on the other the timelessness of attitudes and conversations.

Through description and conversation the book observes and explores many topics: from the building of Stonehenge to the afterlife; from the birth of a child to the nature of God; from crematorial ceremony to the loss of a limb.

In *About Time* we recognise both our importance and our insignificance; things cannot happen other than the way they do. The work recounts Chaite's relationship with Colley, the technical director of a small electronics company. We see them through a window, as others see us in our environment. We can but speculate (if we so wish) on their existence outside the confines of the book – Bishop Berkeley lives.

About Time is constrained between Thursday 30 July 1987 and Cup Final Saturday 21 May 1983, in that order. It is thus 'about time' in another sense – time turned about. A further constraint is that we are in the world of the 1980s; the behaviour and language are those of those times. But as well as being constrained, the book is timeless; here are the hopes and insights and blind spots of Chaite and Colley; they are as human as the fictional Charles Pooter and the very real Samuel Pepys – two others about whom we both know and don't know a great deal. 'There's no such thing as the present: it's merely the interface between the past and the future.' No wonder the more things change, the more they remain the same.

The work has already drawn much interesting and perceptive comment. Tom Rosenthal's observation ('The essentially schematic nature of the book is too intrusive upon the reader's well being') encapsulates what I look upon as success – I'm not seeking to provide an easy read – at least in a philosophical sense. But perhaps Tom was following Colin Haycraft's dictum: 'Sometimes make a friend of an author; never make an author of a friend.' Or, to quote another Haycraftism: 'The easiest thing to say [as a publisher, to someone submitting a book] is "no" – it saves you a lot of trouble, and it seldom turns out that you were wrong.'

I should mention two innovations. First, I have introduced certain typographical devices for setting conversations and thoughts therein – on which much of the book depends. Second, there is an 'interactive index', which provides a literary game, linking allusions (in the text) to their sources (in the index).

Finally, I know that there is an apparent preoccupation with food and drink, but one does spend a lot of one's life considering, preparing and enjoying it.

I hope that you find none of this too intrusive upon your well being.

Rodney Dale
Fern House, Haddenham
February 1995

Contents

1

Thursday 30 July 1987

30 July; half past two. Colley was thinking of Chaite.
He had just seen a cherished number for sale – KYT15.
Suitably arranged, this would have looked good on Chaite's car –
KYT1'5 – a bolt, perhaps, performing the office of apostrophe. It would
have helped those who had a problem pronouncing her name as well.

His telephone rang.
'2307'
'I ... I just thought I'd give you a ring'
A shot of adrenaline; Colley's heart leapt.
It was Chaite's voice. But it couldn't be – exactly a year ago, he'd been
at Chaite's funeral.
He had to say something:
'Mercia! – Where are you?'
'Here, of course ... [it *was* Mercia] ... but I'm planning to be there'
This was not altogether true. Acting on an impulse one year on, Mercia
was telephoning the man her elder sister had loved; now on an impulse
she decided that she wanted to see him again.
'When?'
Colley was interested. Very interested. That voice awakened so many
memories; so much pleasing pain.
'I've got to come over on business ... [please don't ask me what business]
... some time in the next few days. Perhaps we could meet for a drink.
I've got some photos you might like to ...'
'Perhaps we could meet for lunch. I'm free on Friday ... and Tuesday and
Wednesday next week ...'
'Friday would be fine ... [the sooner the better] ... where do you suggest?'
'Can you make The Unicorn at about midday? It's in Thundermold
Street'
'Thundermold Street? I don't believe it; in fact, I never have, but I know
exactly where it is, and I'm looking forward to seeing you. Twelve
o'clock on Friday'
Colley sensed that she was in a hurry to go.
'Fine. How are you, by the way?'
'Fine. I'll tell you on Friday'
'I'll look forward to it. Bye'
'Bye'

1

Colley put down the handset and stared at the telephone. 'With twenty-six soldiers of lead I will conquer the world' he said to himself. 'With combinations of ten spring-loaded digits I can speak to anyone, anywhere within reason. But not to Chaite'

Mercia, wherever she was, had pressed a sequence of digits and spoken clearly to Colley in direct voice on the electrical telephone.
'What will I be doing in forty-eight hours?' Colley asked himself. Would history repeat itself? Forgetting that he wouldn't want it to, even if it could, Colley rather hoped it would.

2
Thursday 16 July 1987

16 July; nine-thirty in the morning.
Colley sat at his desk contemplating his calendar.

It was exactly a year since he had heard that Chaite had been killed. But what does 'exactly a year' mean? Colley wondered. What about 29 February? 'They' gave us leap seconds to tidy up nature; and what is it measured relative to? Is the earth a little in front of where it was, or a little behind?

And now he was standing outside the solar system, seeing the earth with a thin line indicating its elliptical orbit, basking in a busy flurry of man-made satellites, the moon calmly controlling the tides, the other planets dimly unimportant.

Colley's time manifested itself as a solid mechanical model in which he fitted firmly in place, a player in a desmodromic drama, the great celestial wheels synchronised by the connecting rods of Chronos, a cerulean symphony, an orchestrated orrery – he could almost hear the music of the spheres. Now his thoughts somehow controlled the earth; he saw it oscillate uncertainly on its line, not knowing how to run.

Then, in a dizzy swoop as instantaneous as it was everlasting his extraterrestrial self crossed that great void and entered his corporeal body with an almost palpable jolt, and there he was sitting at his desk, contemplating his calendar.

Whatever the mechanism, Colley concluded, it was at about this time on this day last year that I heard that Chaite had crashed her car ... the day after her twenty-eighth birthday.

He drew forth the drawer where he kept his Chaiteana – a few notes, holiday postcards – all in Chaite's hand ('not so much spidery; more harvest manic' he'd said); a G-string (guitar!); some little rubber bands; a picture of Chaite whom he had loved luxuriously – never uxoriously – mock schmock, innocuous worse luck, held back by tact, restrained by training.

Chaite ... how he had missed her ... how he had felt the void that Chaite, killed, had filled. So Colley turned over the ana he knew so well, over which he had lingered less as the months passed, Chaite crystallising in his mind's eye in idealised form, a cerebral shade as the terrible ache in his bereaved body slowly subsided.

For Colley, Chaite would always be twenty-eight years old, although it was thirty years since she had been born. A Chaite older than twenty eight could now never be; it was inconceivable. He recalled a paragraph he had seen in the paper that very morning:

SKELETON DATED
The skeleton found last week by workmen excavating in Market-street, Addercote, has been examined by pathologists at St Mary's hospital. A spokesp-erson said today that the skeleton was of a woman of about thirty, and was over 2,000 years old.

Ambivalently, that woman was both thirty and two thousand years old. Had Chaite lived, thought Colley – were we both to have lived – she would have been sixty when I was seventy. And yet, when I'm seventy, Chaite will still be twenty eight.

The day after Chaite's death, Colley had been tortured by the thought that 24 hours before he could have called Chaite; spent the day with her – perhaps averted her death by doing so.

Each day of the following week he had lived its previous week's counterpart, when Chaite had been so alive; weeks became months and the relation between his BC and AD – Before Crash and After Death – became blurred; memories emerged and merged at random, we did this or that, the past and the present no longer distinguishable.

Colley had forgotten how unsatisfactory their relationship had become in its final throes; just as the summers of childhood are perpetually sunny, so all he chose to remember was the good. It never occurred to him that, had Chaite never met him, she would probably still be alive –

even he was not so tortured or tortuous as to need to extract mileage from that.

'Perhaps it's as well we can't see into the future ... [Colley had said, in one of his interminable conversations with Chaite during the pleasing pain of his obsession] ... and yet ... time cannot run in two directions at once. In the world in which we find ourselves, the cup falls from the table; from our past experience of falling cups we suspect it will shatter on the floor, but sometimes we catch it; sometimes it bounces; then we are surprised and amused – perhaps because it has defied the norm'
Chaite thought about that one: 'So ... were time to run the other way, "shattered" pieces would assemble themselves on the floor and rise to the table. And yet, when the pieces started to assemble, we could never be sure what they would become – we wouldn't always know what they were "meant" to be. Once again, our experience might lead us to suspect what'd happen, but time would have to advance before we could be sure'
Colley became excited: 'Does this imply some sort of reverse gravity – enabling things to rise to some level (such as the table) after assembly? In our present system, Mother Geonature (she of things inanimate) is busy increasing the entropy; Mother Bionature (she of animals and plants) is busy defying her sister'
'Isn't it all this that makes life seem so improbable? All the millions of ways things *could* be, and yet they've chosen one – or one has been chosen – which has enabled them to reproduce themselves and to evolve until they've produced what seems to be that pinnacle of creation – man – who is (presumably) nearer to understanding what it's all about than is any other type of living creature'
'So ... plants and animals developed hand in hand (as it were), the forces driving them enabling the evolution of structures whose purpose couldn't possibly be known until they were up and running ...'
'Yes ... unless by some divine plan'
'Is it right to question this? Does the whole unlikely saga of evolution – or perhaps it's special creation? – speak for the existence of God?'
Chaite thought: 'Well ... only this pinnacle of creation could begin to appreciate God ... so perhaps God after all did create man in His own image as a ready-made fan club? Or has evolution taken its course and presently reached a being which has the nous to suss out what's happening – and postulate God?'
'All right then ... but man apparently worshipped God long before the necessity for Him had become apparent. Or do you think that man's

earlier necessity was for a maker, defender, redeemer and friend rather than a panaceal answer to the meaning of everything?'

They fell silent again. Colley picked up the time theme: 'So time runs in the direction it does, and Bionature defies Geonature; Geonature respects entropy; Bionature scorns it. And if time ran the other way, evolution would become devolution. And what would this do for life?'

'Well ... this could explain the evolution of structures whose purpose couldn't possibly be known until they were up and running. If they *de*volved, of course, their purpose would be plain from the first'

'As things are, birth seems a reasonable starting point; we're born, grow up, and at some usually unpredictable and unspecified time we die. In reverse, how would losing one's experience, getting smaller and smaller, and popping into the womb work?'

'Surely there'd be no surprise there? ... But I bet you'd have the same sense of loss at a birth. Anyway ... you'd get used to the continual stream of coffins emerging from crematorium and graveyard, being opened ...'

'By overgivers?'

'... and "giving birth" – or perhaps "taking death"? And would we increte food and exgest it? ...'

'It sounds disgusting ...'

'... and think of the scene in the pub on a Saturday night ...'

'I don't want to ... ugh!'

Colley thought again: 'All right, then ... what about the dustmen bringing bags of what *we* call rubbish every week, to be unpacked ... you'd need selective reverse gravity there, to get the tea-leaves out ...'

'I still don't like it very much. Can't you think of something nice?'

'Well ... concerts would be rather fun, wouldn't they? And motor racing?'

'What about benefactors arriving at banks and safe deposits in fast cars, and rushing in with sacks of money and valuables ... coming home and finding that you had a television and video, and that your jewellery box was filled?'

'Ah ... but what would you think about phobanthropists ... taking all that money from hospices, and universities, and the third world in order to reconstruct their millions?

'Surgeons standing by waiting for the excinerator to produce diseased organs to incise?'

'Hedgehogs – rabbits – cats on the roads ...'

'Still not very nice. I suspect that a great deal of what might happen backwards *isn't* very nice ... as far as our way of looking at things is concerned. Now, does that reflect our present way of looking at things

(which wouldn't hold good in "reverse" time), or does it mean that lots of things that happen now are "nice"?'
'Do we have to think of everything "happening backwards"? ... will people walk and talk backwards ... would it be exactly like running a film backwards ... or ... ?'
That gave them some food for thought.

So they had carried on. And yet ... could they have seen into the future? Could they have analysed what they were saying and become prescient? What about the manner of Chaite's death – was that pure coincidence in the light of another conversation they had had? Or is it just that so many things happen that it would be odder still if there were no coincidences?

They had been talking about the chances of things happening, and Colley had introduced personal and statistical ways of looking at things.
'How do you mean?' asked Chaite.
'Well, suppose you're invading the Normandy Beaches, tumbling out of personnel carriers, running up to your first position, guns firing at you from all around'
'Not from all around, surely? ... [literal Chaite] ... Your own people wouldn't be firing up the beach at you, would they?'
'No – but you know what I mean. You're under fire, shells bursting all around – it's all like stock footage on the telly. Now, if you think that one of the projectiles has your name written on it, you'll be scared fartless'
'Well?'
'Well, if you look at it that only 30 per cent of your force will be hit (or whatever the statistic is), and that therefore 70 per cent will get through and you're more likely – *ipso facto* – to be in that 70 per cent; if, in other words, you flip from the personal to the statistical point of view it ought to make you feel a lot better'
'How do you know?'
Colley tried to imagine himself in battle: 'I don't – I just said you *ought* to feel better. If only you can remember to think that way in the heat of the moment. I've always thought that if I had to go into battle that's what I'd think. It's like bravery'
'What do you mean, it's "like bravery"?'

'When you do something and everyone says "how brave" because they're looking at it from the outside. But while it's going on you're just doing what you've got to do ...'

'A man's got to do what a man's got to do?'

'Exactly – people laugh at that phrase because it's become a cliché, but it's what I'm talking about. But of course the borderline between bravery and foolhardiness is very unclear – I bet more people get medals for unthinking foolhardiness than for conscious bravery'

'It's all to do with being in the right place at the right time – or the wrong place at the wrong time ...'

'Or the right place at the wrong time or the wrong place at the right time'

'That's enough place and time – Ed'

Colley thought about place and time. Then: 'There can't be anything "right" or "wrong" about the place and the time. You are where you are because of where you were just before. If you're moving, your speed and direction determine where you're going to be. And if you're stationary, that's where you are'

'In which case it's only the time dimension which is moving on'

'Precisely. So as far as two objects meeting is concerned ... the bullet *does* have your name written on it, doesn't it? Yes ... so far, I've only thought of this in connection with accidents'

Chaite was curious: 'What sort of accidents?'

'Travelling – road – accidents. I sometimes think of two – or even more – people setting out from different places at different times, and they're set to crash into one another but of course they don't know it'

'You're thinking of one starting from Newcastle and the other from Carlisle and they meet on the A69?'

'Yes, that's the sort of thing'

'But most crashes aren't like that – head on – surely there are crashes at T-junctions ... and when someone runs into the back of the car in front ... and lorries toppling on top of you ...'

'Well, I'm sure my principle still holds good. If someone chooses to pull out from a T-junction when someone else is on a collision course that's very much an example of the place where you're going to be being governed by the place where you were'

'It doesn't seem as dramatically inevitable as the Newcastle–Carlisle crash'

'No. But if one of the crashers had set off a little earlier or a little later ... but they couldn't have done – it's not *any* crash that's inevitable, it's the crash they actually have'

'What happens if someone crashes into a stationary object. A lorry ... or a wall ... or a tree?'
'I suppose that, as far as the stationary object is concerned, it must be all in time rather than in space. The object's just standing there waiting – without knowing, of course. But you've chosen three interesting things there. The lorry presumably was driven to where it is, and is expecting to drive away again. So it's only temporary. The wall is presumably built for a purpose – someone has chosen where to put it to make a boundary, or to be aesthetically pleasing, or to be part of a house. Its presence is more permanent – a different sort of chance'
'And the tree may be where a bird happened to drop its seed, or it got carried there in the mud on someone's wellies, or whatever'
'Yes – and its survival is threatened at every stage – being eaten as a seed, or a tender sapling, or uprooted to make way for the wall, or knocked over by the lorry. But it's this statistical thing again. Fish lay millions of eggs in order to ensure that there'll go on being enough fish. You can't say *which* eggs will survive – just that it's one in a million or whatever it is. But the strange thing is that there seems to be some force which ensures that the appropriate number gets through'
'It happens in all sorts of apparently less critical circumstances – leaves falling off trees, bubbles going up in fizzy drinks, customers visiting a cafeteria. I think there must be some sort of overall controlling force. If we think about it, we'll see that it governs ... probably everything ... if not directly, then at second hand. The driving force of the universe. And it must be amazingly accurate in its timing – think of radioactive half-life, for example'

Later, Colley had come across a question posed by Arthur Koestler:
'How does a radioactive element know what its half-life is?'
He fell to thinking about this statistically at the atomic level, and was drawn to the conclusion that the passage of time is somehow a sub-atomic phenomenon. Atomic masers keep time (at 1.42GHz) correct to one second in 1.7 million years. How you measured this, he didn't know. Once again, he had the feeling that he was on the threshold of a complete understanding of the universe ... and once again the secret eluded him.

Time fast, time slow.
Chronos and Kairos; the classical Greek conceptions of time – Chronos constant as the clepsydra; Kairos the correct, the appropriate, time. And yet, experience showed that there was a variable time: 'Where's

the morning gone?' ... 'This week seems to have been going on for ever' ...
'Hours crawl; years fly' – Old Chinese proverb.

Time getting faster as you get older ... Colley had found the secret of
that one: assume that you develop full awareness at the age of two; then
when you are six, you have four years to remember ... so the year
between six and seven is one quarter of your aware life. The year
between 32 and 33 is one thirtieth of your aware life. The year between
62 and 63 is one sixtieth of your aware life. And so on ... no wonder that
the years roll by – on ever-better-lubricated bearings.

Hours don't seem to suffer from this problem ... [Chaite had said] ... and
what about the slow-motion timing of an accident – you know what's
going to happen, and yet you're powerless to do anything about it'

This was yet to happen to Chaite. What a mercy she could not know –
she'd *still* have been powerless to do anything about it.

3
Saturday 7 February 1987

Just where was Chaite now?

Colley remembered one of their conversations about the afterlife – if
heaven was all sweetness and light, just niceness going on and on and on
and on and on for ever, was it not going to be more like hell?

What was heaven like? Were people in heaven freer to move about
than they had been when earthbound? Could they move across the
boundaries of time as well as space?

Did Mozart spend all his time at the pool table ... playing Jelly
Roll Morton? Did he sit at the piano and play Jelly Roll Morton too?
Did they respect one another's music; learn from one another? On earth,
Morton knew of Mozart, but did Mozart in heaven know of Morton?

What did the Bach family make of Scott Joplin? What did Claude
Debussy and Bix Beiderbecke have to say to one another?

'Alors!! *Dans une Brume* – c'est formidable'
'Merci, Claude'
'Ma foie'
'Quel fromage'

Colley saw heaven as a sort of open-plan office area of infinite extent,
bathed in a white light which stopped just short of harshness. There
were shoulder-high partitions as far as the eye could see in every

direction; everyone clean and wholesome, each in his or her little cubicle, ever open for discourse, a perpetual perambulation of visits and converse ... and there, above it all, was a dimly-perceived structure something like the organ in the Royal Festival Hall with banked choirs of angels and God busy doing nothing – and everything.

Free as the social intercourse in Colley's heaven was, it was clinical and admitted of no frailty. Chaite's heaven, on the other hand, was more like an infinite Bartholomew Fair; if the inmates of Colley's heaven were clad in innocuous robes, Chaite's were much more colourful and flamboyantly dressed, a continual surge of jostling humanity going nowhere in particular, yet moving all the time, laughing and joking, processions, street parties; there was no loneliness – in Chaite's heaven, you couldn't be lonely, even if you wanted to be.

Was there a language barrier? Could they all understand one another? Did those in heaven know what was happening on earth? And because so much was happening all at once, how could they find out what was on, let alone tune into it? Or was time such that the idea of simultaneity was meaningless? Much the same as the concept of time starting – the creation of matter – of the world. How can we possibly comprehend it?

And did they have access to anything they wanted in heaven? Suppose Oliver and Armstrong wanted to hear what they'd recorded in 1923, could they call up records and equipment? Could Dan Leno enjoy Charlie Chaplin movies? Or perhaps he'd seen them already – watched them being made, even.
'Interesting – we've had music and clowning – universal languages. What about mathematics? Another universal language'
'God yes; Euclid, Newton, Euler, Fermat ...'
'Will everything be "known" in heaven? No mystery to Fermat's last theorem?'
'Surely, the only mysterious thing about Fermat's last theorem is that it *is* his last, and that he himself hinted that he had a "marvellous" proof. I side with Gauss, who pooh-poohed it, saying that he could easily lay down a multitude of such propositions "which one could neither prove nor dispose of"'
'Well, now he can reveal his "marvellous proof"; he can challenge Gauss'
'Wait. Since Gauss knew "more" than Fermat – in the sense that he lived later – how does Fermat catch up? How do Euclid and Archimedes catch up, for that matter?'

'Interesting. Given that they all had about the same orders of magnitude of thought-hours at their disposal in life, what can we conclude about the quantity that one person can learn or develop in a lifetime? After all, what took Euclid a lifetime to develop can actually be assimilated very rapidly once someone else (*ie* Euclid) has done it'
'Well ... if everyone knows everything – has access to everything – there can be no language barriers after all. So how will one know which language to use to communicate. Or is it done by telepathy?'
'Shurely the mishtake we're making is that we're not thinking of any of these as whole-life people – we're just looking at a few moments of their lives – a few achievements – that we happen to know about, recorded on paper, or film, or canvas, or tape, or whatever. Just how are we to know about – let alone recount – whole lives? It takes longer to explain what you're doing than to do it – an optical illusion, a flower arrangement, a haiku'
'Well, then ... do you think that all the hundreds of people we've heard of – and the millions we haven't – all know each other, have access to each other, get on with each other?'
'Will everyone be happy all the time? And healthy?'
'Will people who have lost bits be restored?'
'I'm sure they will. But will everything be restored? Missing limbs, perhaps ... but what about appendixes – to name but one bit that might have been removed? And if that, what about hair, nails, teeth ...? And how old will they be?'
'As old as they were when they died'
'But suppose they were infirm and senile?'
'Then they'll ... well, they'll be whole, and age doesn't matter anyway'
'There must be a plethora of babies in heaven. What about foetuses? Where do we draw the line?'
'What about people who were born imperfect?'
'Physical imperfections are only one sort. People aren't equally brainy, or dextrous, or good at maths, languages, sport ... or needlework, or paperhanging ... who's to decide what's imperfect?'
'You see? We're trying to fit heavenly bodies into an earthly Procrustean bed'
And there they had left it.

Colley couldn't help feeling that, if Chaite were 'alive' somewhere, she would have come back to him. For a while, he felt cabined, cribb'd, confined in a cube of concrete, much as he thought Chaite would feel if she *were* alive and *couldn't* come back.

And yet he shouldn't, as they had put it, 'try to fit heavenly bodies into an earthly Procrustean bed'. If time were so different where Chaite was, perhaps the idea of 'coming back' never occurred to her, even if she could. Suppose a year to him were but a nanosecond to her.

A thousand ages in thy sight are but an evening gone – Colley became fascinated with that: where had Isaac Watts got his insight from? He looked it up. Easy – Psalm 90, verse 4: *for a thousand years in thy sight are but a yesterday* ... hold on – 2 Peter; chapter 3, verse 4: *But, beloved, be not ignorant of this one thing, that one day is with the Lord as a thousand years, and a thousand years as one day.*

Once again Colley had a feeling that ancient man – certainly the witnesses of the Old Testament – knew something that we, with all our knowledge, were failing to recognise.

There'd have to be some time compression in heaven if there were to be 'enough' time for everybody to do everything. Perhaps Chaite *did* come back in picosecond bursts; with 31.5 million seconds in an earth year, it would be quite long enough for her – who had to pack so much into her new life – but too fleeting for him.

This way lay ... madness? Or could it be the secret of the universe? For a picosecond burst – and not for the first time – Colley fancied that he had actually grasped the secret of time: with blinding clarity he saw and understood; then the omniscience dissolved from his comprehension, leaving him utterly frustrated.

It was impossible to comprehend every thought and fact and memory that had been extinguished and obliterated in the moment of Chaite's death. Some of what was lost was trivial, the detritus of life – that the pepper was in the corner cupboard, that the seam of the tartan shirt was pulling away, that the hyacinth in the amber bulb glass was going to be blue.

Anyone who looked in the corner cupboard would see at a glance that the pepper was pepper, and that a great deal more besides was there, to be used or disposed of as the decider decided.

The tartan shirt had been wrested from a wire basket outside a cheapo-cheapo shop at the seaside; a split seam was par for the course and anyone who might think of wearing the shirt would pull it contemplatively from hand to hand – this was Chaite's; she was about my size – perhaps examining (in vain) the left sleeve for some clue to the mystery of Chaite's accident ... but then again that shirt might be used as a duster, or thrown away, and no one would ever know about the seam.

Would anyone throw a hyacinth away? One would surely wait for it to burgeon, becoming blue, something seemingly springing from nothing, fed but by water and air, owing its life to Chaite who had chosen and nurtured it and now wasn't there to enjoy what was continuing as best it could in its plantly way as an extension of she who had set it up.

This sort of knowledge was little loss – what was so obvious was hardly knowledge. Some of Chaite's memories lost were scarcely less trivial and just as irretrievable; nobody knew of her recollection of an image of the moon through a stand of beeches as an owl hooted, to be answered by another, distant; the evocative smell of dry dust that had always reminded her of a cupboard in a childhood house where she had delightedly discovered a trunk full of granny's garments – and why had her mother seemed so put out at the discovery? – a tableau she had seen from a train of a girl in an apron about to feed a flock of eager geese, shades of white and brown and green, a grassy slope, a tumbledown of corrugated iron, memorable in its powerful inconsequentiality.

Much later, Chaite had read:
> Four ducks on a pond,
> A grass-bank beyond,
> A blue sky of spring,
> White clouds on the wing;
> What a little thing
> To remember for years –
> To remember with tears.

She knew exactly what William 'Up-the-airy-mountain' Allingham had felt; from such a stream of oubliobilia, uncommunicable to others yet so meaningful to ourselves, are our memories made – sometimes we want to tell people about them because they mean so much to us; the moments seem somehow to encapsulate universal truths, yet always frustrate us as we learn again that they are uncommunicable.

So did the shades of Chaite's knowledge pass from the retrievable the obvious and the unmemorable, to the irretrievable the obscure and the important; relating the seemingly unrelated, juxtaposing facts gleaned from her browsing; serendipitous snippets. The popular (and generally forgotten) artists and novelists spanning the century or so before she had been born had been her passion, cherished in her mind, knowledge for the sake of knowledge. Anyone who wanted to know about Cecil Aldin, or Hall Caine, or Harry Furniss, or Dornford Yates or a host of others could ask Chaite.

But even Colley was more interested in the fact that she had the knowledge than in what that knowledge was: '*A man will turn over half a library to make one book* ... [he had quoted, and] ... *Knowledge is of two kinds; we know a subject ourselves, or we know where we can find information upon it.* You know so much about these people; you ought to write it down ... Before it's too late' he had added.

Neither had seen anything prophetic in that; there was plenty of time ... wasn't there? If you thought about all the possible implications of what you were saying you'd never say anything lest it should touch some raw spot of the past or presage some psychic lesion of the future. The present, reasoned Colley, did not exist; rather was it an interface between the past and the future. The present, like the point of Euclidean geometry, had position, but no dimension. And yet, like the point, it had not only no dimension, but every dimension. For the future, you could not always be worrying about 'before it's too late'; everyone had to go sometime.

As for the past ... he remembered going into Sibson's office breezily one morning, to find him grimly tidying his desk: 'What a beautiful morning – full of the joys of spring, eh Sib? What's making *you* tidy up at last?'
'Er ... my mother's just died, so I'm going over to Oswestry for a couple of weeks to sort things out'
A cement-mixer effect in Colley's head thought it had instructed his voice to say: 'I'm so sorry ... I didn't mean ... Is there anything ...?'
It had come out as 'Aarrgh-gurgle-grunt-psshh-huhummmm' as Colley had backed out of Sibson's office. Never having cared much for Colley, Sibson carefully concealed that both for him and for his mother, prematurely senile and painfully ill, it was the proverbial merciful release.

And never since had Colley – whose low opinion of Sibson had been largely the cause of his original false geniality – said anything to him without weighing every word with such care that subsequent communication between them – such as it was – became stilted, to say the least.

14

4

Wednesday 30 July 1986 and before

The mourners filed slowly out of the crematorium chapel into the bright sunlight, blinking. The women had no particular problems with their hands – they had umbrellas and hand-bags to hold – but the men felt constrained to clasp their hands before them as if the duty minister – whom they had never seen before, and would probably never see again – might be planning some dastardly attack on their persons.

Trying to be inconspicuous, shy, self-effacing, Colley was among the last to leave; his elaborate politeness on these occasions was of the kind which would attempt to promote chivalry by holding open a revolving door. He shook hands with the cherubic priest as he passed through the portals – MORS JANVA VITÆ.

The hearse was just pulling out of the gates with its living cargo to collect another dead one; to them it was a job; a way of life. 'I spose it's a way of life ... [people would say to them in the pub, adding] ... or death, more like – hahaha'

The funeral director had already ushered the first mourners into the Garden of Remembrance, where they now stood in knots, talking in subdued tones, eyes watery, smiles brave. The floral tribulations – the most consistently troublesome part of a funeral director's work – were tastefully laid out, Chaite's fresh and colourful in contrast to those wilting from previous days – a teddy bear constructed entirely of chrysanthemums; a motorcycle of lilies: *From his Mate's* – a masterpiece of the florist's art; a triumph of incongruous medium over illiterate message:

With uncouth rhymes and shapeless sculpture deck'd
  Implores the passing tribute of a sigh.

Somewhat condescending of Gray, thought Colley, not pausing to wonder whether it was perhaps not somewhat condescending of *him* to think it.

Colley's heart had leapt when he saw the girl in the front pew. That coppery, sphinx-like hair ... it *was* Chaite. But it couldn't be – Chaite was in the coffin. Yet as she turned round it *was* Chaite ... and then it wasn't. It must be Chaite's younger sister, Mercia. Colley had heard about her, but had never met her; all he knew was that she was unmarried, was a geographer – what did they do? He had a vague picture of a geographer standing on a peak in Darien, trying to control and orient a flapping map – had recently returned from an assignment abroad, lived in Little Bygrave ... and it was her with whom Chaite had recuperated after her accident.

Next to Mercia was Chaite's elder sister, Cepha, and her husband Rupert; 'too young for funerals', Chaite's nephews and nieces were at school. Cepha & Co had been the last people to see Chaite alive. For that, Colley could not forgive them; *he* should have been the last person to see Chaite alive; perhaps if he had she wouldn't be dead. Though illogical, the thought made him angry.

Now they were all outside. Colley wanted to meet Mercia, but not Cepha & Co. Feeling like a sheepdog he quickened his pace, surreptitiously trying to separate Mercia from the flock without anyone else noticing. He awarded himself full points for the outrun, but dropped more and more on the fetch; panic rose ... where was she? Not gone, surely?

He found the shedding ring; she was standing by a little group of soi-disant uncles and aunts, almost defying anyone to talk to her. He stalked her, sidled up to her, held out his hand – not in the open 'look-I'm-not-carrying-a-sword' way, but more covert, like a cowboy preparing to shoot from the hip: 'I'm Colley ... you must be Mercia' He'd been practising the line since he'd espied her. He hoped it sounded spontaneous; that the effort needed to utter it didn't show.
'Colley ... You don't look like your picture'
That voice ... it was Chaite's. They shook hands. It was not like selecting a herring.
'*That* picture? I'm the rider. Cardophagus is the donkey. I don't ride. Normally'
He wondered if this were too obscure; too flippant, even, for Mercia at her sister's funeral.
'You're just like Chaite said to talk to'
'I haven't said much yet'
'You've said enough ... [Colley's heart sank; she noticed] ... I mean, you've said enough for me to know you're the Colley Chaite talked about'
'She talked about ME?'
'Of course. She was very much in love with you'
Colley burst into tears. He had never been sure. Now it was too late.

People had come from all over the country for Chaite's funeral.
Magnetic funeral; relations who did not normally exchange so much as a Christmas card with one another converged for Chaite from Abram, and Cubert, and Mutford, and Westenhanger, and other places of which only

they had heard; colleagues from workplaces; friends from the village; friends from college; friends; all gathered. Chaite's sisters Mercia and Cepha. Cepha's family. Even Chaite's ex-husband Roy and his subsequent, the lovely Lavinia. No one talked to them. No one could imagine why Roy had come after what he'd done to Chaite. They didn't know the whole story. Now Chaite could not tell, and Roy had no reason to. No one would ask him.

Jesus said, I am the resurrection, and I am the life; he who believes in me, though he die, yet shall he live, and whoever lives and believes in me shall never die.

Here is to be noted ... [read Colley in the Book of Common Prayer to which he steadfastly clung] *... that the Office ensuing is not to be used for any that ... have laid violent hands upon themselves.*

Had Chaite laid a violent hand upon herself? The Church had obviously been guided by the Coroner's verdict – or did people worry that much about such things nowadays?

Perhaps it was different for cremations. He found it hard to concentrate on the Duty Minister's words of comfort – *our dear departed sister* (who, in our case, we did not know).

And why did people try to sing hymns whose tunes nobody knew? What comfort was that? Something rousing and unequivocal – that was what was wanted. He'd have suggested *O God, our help in ages past* – but then ... nobody had asked him.

Dog Colley got back into his manger – there was no reason why he *should* have been consulted. Nobody knew about him and Chaite (he thought). Did he have some greater right to her than did her family? A jumble of thoughts and emotions jostled through his mind.

He had wanted to see Chaite just once more, to say good-bye to her 'properly', to say things he couldn't've said to her in life – especially after the nature of their parting. He had called the undertakers to ask if he could visit Chaite ...

'I'm sorry, sir, but the coffin has been sealed'

Undertakers' jargon – the lid had been screwed down ... but then Chaite was no longer a pretty sight.

And that admixture of anger, self-pity and frustration which is grief envelops Colley.

Let us commend our sister Chaite to the mercy of God our Maker and Redeemer ...

And now Colley imagines Chaite in her coffin, isolated and alone.

Heavenly Father, by your mighty power you gave us life, and in Your love you have given us new life in Jesus Christ ...

And now Colley imagines Chaite somehow floating above the congregation, gratified that there are so many people.
We entrust Chaite to your merciful keeping, in the faith of Jesus Christ your Son our Lord, who died and rose again to save us, and is now alive and reigns with you and the Holy Spirit in glory for ever.
AMEN.
And Colley himself experiences some momentary gratification that there should be so many people.
May God in his infinite love and mercy bring the whole church, living and departed in the Lord Jesus, to a joyful resurrection and the fulfilment of his eternal kingdom.
AMEN.
And now Chaite turns into Lizzie Siddall, to be buried in Highgate Cemetery with the volume of Dante Gabriel Rossetti's poems entwined in her hair.
Man born of woman has but a short time to live ...
And now, Lizzie Siddall is to be exhumed, in order to retrieve the poems.
Like a flower he blossoms ... [Blossoms – Albert Moore] *... and then withers; like a shadow he flees ...* [great fleas have lesser fleas ...] *... and never stays.*
And why hadn't DGR kept a copy of the poems?
In the midst of life we are in death; to whom can we turn for help, but to you, Lord, who are justly angered by our sins?
And what difference had the ghoulish manner of the renaissance of those poems made to their sale?
Lord God, holy and mighty ... [mighty Chaite] *... holy and immortal, holy and most merciful Saviour, deliver us from the most bitter pains of eternal death ...*
And anyway, Chaite's not to be buried, she's to be cremated, which reduces the opportunity for funerary artefacts.
You know the secrets of our hearts: in your mercy, hear our prayer, forgive us our sins, and at our last hour let us not fall away from you ...
And an artificial limb would be the ultimate in funerary artefacts ... wouldn't it? ... but Chaite in heaven will be whole again ... won't she?
We have entrusted our sister Chaite to God's merciful keeping, and we now commit her body to be cremated in sure and certain hope of the resurrection to eternal life through our Lord Jesus Christ, who died, was buried, and rose again for us. To Him be glory for ever and ever.
Colley subsides, quiescent, into his handkerchief. And the Duty Minister surreptitiously presses the button, and the heavy velvet

curtains enclose the coffin containing Chaite, and time and the crowd of mourners stand still for her moment of finality. And nobody knows why Chaite died. And nobody will ever know for certain.

That the coffin would be wound through the doors, and manhandled on to a bier to await its turn in the fiery furnace; that the 99 per cent of Chaite that was volatile would ascend from the crematorium chimney as vapour – to fall on their lawns as dew, even; that the osseous remains of Chaite would be raked out and fed through the cremulator for scattering in due time; all these were facts of the process yet to come which were not foremost in the mourners' minds.

For Chaite was dead, flattened in her car as it had decelerated from 68mph to zero in less than a second against the stag-headed oak which had stood at a bend in the road through Marby for well over 250 years.

It was 1727. On the day that George I had died, nobody in Marby – or anywhere else for that matter – knew that a squirrel was burying an acorn which was destined not to perish as would all its fellows, but to live and grow and influence the lives of men and women.

Quercus robur marbiensis would pass from insignificant shoot, to seedling, to sapling; it would grow and become a landmark, and when man's greed, man's desire for destruction, man's ruthless legalised vandalism had threatened it, it would be subject to a preservation order, a public enquiry, and a purchase for the people in perpetuity by an anonymous philanthropist.

So it is that all about us stand potential deodands; we cannot know that this or that will cause death – our death – and Chaite had admired *Quercus robur marbiensis* scores of times as she had driven past it to or from one or other of her sisters. And now that acorn buried in 1727 had worked out some purpose.

> *Alien they seemed to be:*
> *No mortal eye could see*
> *The intimate welding of their later history ...*

Thus had Thomas Hardy written; at Harland and Wolff thousands of men were fashioning the SS *Titanic*; up in the Arctic, God was singlehandedly fashioning the iceberg.

The Marby Oak had been mature enough for the emerging cart-track to divert itself round it; the track whose line had become immutable as it gained importance and became Main Street, Marby, so that it was now possible for the likes of Chaite to travel it – or not, as the case might be – heedless of the speed limit, at 68mph.

As the Marby Oak had grown, generations of birds nesting in its branches had seen all: the construction of the canal basin at the termination of the Marby Arm of the Grand Union Canal; they had seen Marby grow, encouraged by its canal, until it attracted the attention of the railway company – and had not Robert Stephenson himself surveyed the line, selected the site for the station, spoken for the shareholders in that very Town Hall that the birds could see from the branches of the Marby Oak?

Generations of birds had seen the rise of the railway, and the decline of the canal, the basin falling into disuse and decay until the enthusiasts came and put it in order; then was the long-lost bustle of business replaced by the busyness of holiday hire.

And then they had seen the railway decline, diesel supplant steam, diesel depart, disuse and decay, until the enthusiasts came and put it in order; then was the bustle of business, so long absent from the station, replaced by week-ends steeped in the nostalgia of steam. The birds, and the now stag-headed Marby Oak, had seen it all.

And Chaite's car, the metallic mauve Metro automatic, 897kg – including the 53kg Chaite, and her luggage – had been effortlessly decelerated from 68mph to zero by the Marby Oak, the object to all intents and purposes immovable, the force far from irresistible: kinetic energy turned to heat, and noise, and death.

Oddly enough, Chaite had not minded running into the Marby Oak when she had seen that there was absolutely nothing she could do about it. Time was so drawn out that her 68mph was a snail's pace. She thought, careful Chaite, of all her affairs in order; she thought of her tidy flat, cushions puffed and diamonded, the lid of the lavatory lowered; she thought of her life insurance maturing and her beneficiaries smiling through their tears; she thought of Roy – and what he had made her do – with a diminishing anger, for it didn't matter now; she thought of Colley with the love she'd never allowed herself to show him; there was so much time to think and so much to think about that it was unbearable; the bonnet of the metallic mauve Metro crumpling so very slowly, little cracks gradually appearing in the windscreen and growing, the whole vehicle heaving and erupting; she thought of her sisters, and her mother and father whom she had loved so – indeed, they were looming large, and coming to greet her, arms outstretched, and she extended hers, noting what seemed to be her restored form with some interest, and less surprise, experiencing an overwhelming regret that she could not tell Colley about it, as her time ground to a halt in heat, and noise, and a great blinding light, as every thought and fact and memory in her brain was extinguished and obliterated for ever.

Datta
> *Dayadhvam*
>> *Damyata*
Shantih shantih shantih

5

Wednesday 16 July 1986 & after

After the impact, the silence. Then switches clicked, lights lit, sashes squeaked. Several people dialled 999 and called for an ambulance. The ambulance service alerted the police; PC Sanger in a panda car was close by; first on the scene, his aspirations to become a traffic officer evaporated temporarily. He flashed his torch; the young female person in the metallic mauve Metro must be very dead. He radioed HQ, reported the index mark of the vehicle, called for the fire brigade emergency tender, and expected that the duty inspector would be alerted.

The ambulance arrived: Geoff and Keith; however, the control room had warned PC Sanger to make sure that nothing was moved – and so nothing was moved. Next on the scene was a traffic patrol car; Clive and John debouched, exchanged words with PC Sanger, went to see for themselves, busied themselves setting up flood-lights as the fire brigade emergency tender arrived.

Blue lights rotated relentlessly, monotonously, more and more of them. The circumarboreal residents of Marby were nought but human; there was little sleep with all that blue light activity. Some stayed at their windows; others donned déshabillé and appeared in the street 'to see if there was anything they could do' from compassion, helpfulness, or pure curiosity. Those with the right idea supplied the professionals with coffee and biscuits.

The team on the emergency tender put up screens round the mauve Metro, just as the duty inspector – keen from his recent appointment – arrived with the police photographer, who happened to live near him. The photographer set up his equipment; flashes marked the recording of the tableau of Chaite's appointment with the Marby Oak for posterity.

Dr Conway arrived on the scene. His wife had placed his casual trousers in too hot a wash, and his pyjamas protruded colourfully; the fire brigade provided access to Chaite; he pronounced her dead and went back home to bed. The fire brigade finished releasing Chaite; such was her state that it took some time for them to twig that there was no left hand to be found. Chaite was extracted by the ambulance crew:

> Take her up tenderly,
> Lift her with care;
> Fashioned so slenderly,
> Young, and so fair!

Chaite was borne away in the ambulance with PC Sanger to provide evidence of continuity; he signed her over to the hospital mortuary to await identification and the post mortem.

Clive and John gathered and listed Chaite's property from the metallic mauve Metro; they were somewhat taken aback to find Chaite's arm among the detritus on the floor.

The car was lifted on to a HIAB and borne away to the police yard to await daylight examination by an accident investigation officer.

The number of flashing blue lights gradually diminished; the Marby Oak returned to some semblance of normality as dawn broke to the sound of brooms sweeping broken glass. The viewers had long since returned to their beds, but few slept; nevertheless, they reflected not that their lives were a free gift from God ... still believing that accidents happen only to other people.

On interrogation, the police computer traced the metallic mauve Metro to Chaite's address; her landlady was away for the week-end – which was probably just as well. A combination of Chaite's diary and address book led an officer to the more-relevant Cepha and Rupert. Since there was no doubt who the young lady was, and seeing that she was no longer alive, formal identification was deferred until the morning.

Rupert arrived at the mortuary after a desultory non-breakfast, and performed what Colley would have described as 'his mournful duty'. It was an occasion about which he was never to speak.

Soon after, PC Sanger identified Chaite to the pathologist as the young lady who had been removed from the vehicle in Marby the previous night. Then he left to continue his unquiet day off.

The pathologist examined and probed Chaite to no avail; he removed samples for the lab, which couldn't find anything untoward either.

The coroner opened an inquest, and adjourned it for evidence to be gathered; he released Chaite to the undertaker of Rupert's choice.

The accident investigator examined and probed Chaite's car to no avail; there was nothing suspect on which the police lab could conduct further tests. He released the metallic mauve Metro to the garage of Rupert's choice. He recorded the fact that the odometer showed that the car had covered 16786 miles at the time of the crash, but did not, in his report, draw attention to the fact that this happened to be the date. He did, however, mention the coincidence to his fiancée that evening. She laughed at him for taking it so seriously. He became even more serious. As the ensuing row reached its climax, she threw the ring back at him and stormed out of his life.

He poured himself a generous tumbler of neat whisky, and consoled himself that he was well rid of someone with so little imagination, thanking God that he had found out before it was too late. Serious as he was, it never occurred to him to wonder at the chain of events which had led to her departure.

In the Coroner's Court, PC Sanger had his brief moment of glory as the first officer on the scene, and gave evidence that the Chaite who had been removed from the Marby Oak was the Chaite whom the pathologist had examined.

The pathologist reported that he had found no sign of alcohol or drugs, nor pathological condition, nor any other identifiable cause of impairment save the fact that the deceased's left arm had been amputated some fourteen centimetres below the elbow.

Rupert gave evidence that his sister-in-law had a creditable past and a glowing future; that she had lost her left hand in 'a domestic accident' over three years before (and for some reason nobody asked him to elaborate); that she had been driving the Metro for well over a year and he was confident of her absolute competence as a driver – for was she not a member of the Institute of Advanced Motorists? – and, no, he had no reason to believe that she had any worries: she was, in fact, financially well off, and due to start a new job soon.

The accident investigator reported that he had found nothing wrong with the metallic mauve Metro; Clive confirmed that the road surface had been dry and in good condition; that marks on the road suggested that the deceased had been travelling in excess of 60mph – in a restricted area – and that there was no evidence that she had tried to brake to avoid the tree.

After some discursive deliberation, the Coroner returned a verdict of death by misadventure. Outside the court, Rupert and Cepha embraced tightly and wept. They had of course been certain that Chaite had not laid violent hand upon herself; now they could take comfort – by reasoning which they never suspected was spurious – from the fact that the Coroner's verdict corroborated that belief.

6

Saturday 5 – Tuesday 15 July 1986

Chaite had spent her last week with her sister's family; a holiday week during which she had immersed herself in being Auntie Chaite to two nephews and two nieces who loved her (in a John-Frumm-like way) – and her metallic mauve Metro, treating it as an extension to their home; leaving it filled with discarded wrappers and crisps bags and empty Coke cans.

On the last day, they had celebrated Auntie Chaite's twenty-eighth birthday by going to Shalthorpe zoo, and done zooly things: monkeystudy, sealwatching and penguin fancying.

While the children swang on the swings, Chaite had watched the alligators, unchanged in their habits since the days of the dinosaurs, time capsules of reptilian remanence.

Chaite had focused her thoughts on the alligators in their artificial environment, until the panorama changed to a desolate swamp, nothing man made, no humans, no hominids. The chatter of the people became that of pterodactyls; she heard the distant trumpeting of an elephant and the throaty purring roar of a tiger as of feral beasts roaming freely; the hair on her neck bristled. As the only human being in that world, millions of years before her time, Chaite shivered. As long as she kept still and silent, all would be well. It would only be when she moved the slightest muscle that she would have to fend for herself in this hostile world – whether it was the world of the solitary human out of her time faced with survival (and 'survival for what?' asked the Only Girl in the World), or the solitary human in her real here-and-now body, at this moment in sole charge of her family's four representatives of the next generation.

Reality returned with the impact of a niece clasping her legs: 'Auntie Chaite, have you ever seen a dinosaur?'
'Not a real live one – only skeletons, and models, and pictures like you've got in your book'

'Are there any real live ones?'

'Not stegosauruses and diplodocuses and pterodactyls and things like that. But those alligators there have been like that for millions of years'

'Are those alligators millions of years old?'

'Well, *they* aren't, but there have been alligators that look like that for millions of years'

'Do you think they tell stories about what it was like millions of years ago?'

'I expect so. But I expect they haven't seen a lot of change – because they've stayed the same, and crawled about in the water ...'

'Perhaps they tell stories about how man came'

'And what it used to be like when it was all open fields around here'

'Auntie Chaite ...'

'Yes?'

'Did an alligator bite off your hand?'

'Yes ... when I was on a pirate ship on the South China Seas'

Most of the time the children took Auntie Chaite's missing left hand for granted and didn't talk about it. Chaite didn't mind talking about it as long as people didn't ask too many questions about how she had lost it. What she *did* mind was people who elaborately pretended not to notice; it could make them clumsy. Not that everyone did notice; her artificial hand could be gratifyingly lifelike (in a passive sort of way) and most people were singularly unobservant.

'Auntie Chaite ...'

'What now?'

'When will it be time for our sandwiches?'

Chaite looked at her watch: 'It's time now – call the others, and we'll go to the picnic area'

It was a happy meal. It may have been simple and basic, they may have been sitting in a slightly-too-hot sun on a slightly-too-breezeless day, they may have been surrounded by too many people, others' badly-behaved brats entering the amateur walkers' championships, tottering their sticky fingers perilously close to strangers, coming up to peer and stare, caterwauling as they dropped their ice-creams in the fine grey dust; all of this may have been, but it could not detract from the happiness of the meal, as happy as some of the other happy meals engraved on Chaite's mind – salmon sandwiches and champagne out of tooth glasses, an unlikely but delicious buffet in the village hall, that other birthday party twenty-four years before when she had had so many cherished presents, and green jelly and ice cream and the nicest soft banana cake she had ever tasted.

'When are you going away, Auntie Chaite?'

'Tonight. I've got to be at home tomorrow to write some letters, and next week I'm going to look for a job'

'Don't you have a job?'

'Not at the moment. I used to have one, and then I stopped. So I've got to find another'

'What sort of a job are you going to find?'

'I'm not sure' Chaite wasn't giving anything away.

'Will it be a typing job?'

'How do you type with one hand?'

'I'll show you sometime'

'Our Mummy can type'

'Our Mummy does very fast typing'

'Our Mummy doesn't have a job'

'I thought everybody had a job'

'Our Daddy's got a job'

'Yes, Daddy's got a very hard job'

'Why can't you stay some more?'

'When can we go to see a film?'

'I'll take you to see a film next time I come'

'When you've got a job'

Thinking about the job, Chaite fell into conversation with Cepha and Rupert that evening. She could never understand how a sister of hers could have married Rupert. Remembering herself and Cepha – and Mercia – as girls, talking about the men they would marry, never would she have imagined someone as humourless as Rupert. But he was good and kind and solid; it seemed somehow obscene to criticise him for not being what *she* thought he ought to be. After all, she was a fine one to talk; she thought angrily of Roy, and – as she put it to herself somewhat unfairly – what he had done to her. And she thought of Colley; if she hadn't met him as she did, she wouldn't be looking for a job now.

Chaite could have made more of her hopes of returning to Sellis & Co, Auctioneers & Estate Agents, but she felt it was tempting Providence to treat the outcome of her forthcoming interview as cut and dried.

And anyway, discussion would perhaps give her some fresh ideas. Rupert had tried to force her to look at the job hunt objectively; he started by asking her to write down her strengths and weaknesses (he qualified both as 'perceived'). They tried this; if any of them perceived Chaite's enforced right-handedness as a weakness, they didn't let on.

Then Rupert asked her to record her experience (he qualified it as 'practical'). It was here that she started to kick over the traces; she knew he meant his analysis with kindness, but she felt she was being treated as an object – similar to the RAF concept of people. as self-loading freight. Rupert's clinical approach started to annoy her; seeing what was happening, Cepha tried to bring the analysis under control; she started to play it like a game; before long, she and Cepha developed a fit of sisterly giggles and then, predictably, Rupert had become annoyed.

So the attempt had fallen by the wayside for, in spite of the giggles, Chaite could feel her temper rising. She had thought she had conquered it now; knew how to control it – she had cause enough to regret its consequences; its eruption had more than once had a profound effect upon the course of her life. And here it was, irrepressible.

Cepha had never fully understood Chaite's terrible temper; Chaite had left home and married Roy. It had had something to do with Chaite's accident, and later her losing her job; she knew that Chaite hadn't told her the truth, and she could see no way of opening the subject. Mercia knew even less about it than Cepha; Roy had disappeared.

Chaite stood up, voice quivering: 'I think I must go home now'
'You don't have to ... [and you really ought to calm down before you do] ... why not have a good night's rest; take it easy ... anyway, the children will want to see you before you go'
Chaite knew that Cepha was right, but: 'I've said good-bye to them – they're not expecting to see me tomorrow'

She felt that there was nothing she could do other than go upstairs and pack, load her car and, after a perfunctory parting, set off for her appointment with the Marby Oak.

7

Monday 9 June – Friday 4 July 1986

Exactly how it came about that Chaite was departing from WEL she wasn't sure. To say it was a combination of her handing in her notice and Colley asking her to leave was an overstatement. Perhaps it was by mutual agreement. In the nicest possible way. She had rung Colley on the morning he returned from paternity leave: 'Can I come and see you, please?'

'Will it do this at two-fifteen this afternoon?'

Chaite had been winding herself up for this: 'You seek to intimidate me by the use of quarter hours? ... No, it wouldn't'

Something in her voice made him agree: 'Right, come now'

She went along to his office. He waved at her to sit down; in the few seconds between her ringing off and walking along the corridor he had taken another call. Typical! The call ended. Colley smiled charmingly: 'Now, how can I help you?'

He was so formal.

'I know you don' t like talking about ... about *us* in working hours ...'

'No; I've always thought it was better not ... is that what you want to talk about?'

'Yes. I congratulated you on becoming a father. For the third time. Remember?'

'Well?'

'If I thought your marriage was old and tired it would be bad enough, but it isn't. You've just become a father for the third time. Don't you see?'

'See what?'

He was deliberately obtuse; he didn't want to see anything, yet Chaite appeared to be letting him off the hook – he ought to be grateful. Yet now that the moment had come he was less than receptive because *he* hadn't taken the initiative. *He* ought to be asking *her* to leave ... but he would feel such a heel. Double heel: to Genista and to Chaite. Whatever he did would be wrong.

'Colley. I've got to leave WEL'

'Why?'

'Because ... oh, if you can't see why, how can I possibly explain? You and I may think that our friendship is innocent, but ... how can it be? The mere fact that ... look, Genista must know all about it, and she can't like it one little bit, and I don't blame her. Genista's right for you even if you think you need something extra from me. I'm just not going to stay around and wreck your marriage'

'You're not wrecking my marriage'
'You mean to tell me you stay out like you do, and Genista doesn't notice?'
'All right ... [Colley wonders how he can save Chaite; retain her on his shelf] ... we can stop seeing each other ... so much ... but Genista doesn't know about ... you're doing a good job here, and I can see no reason at all why you should give it up'
'There's every reason ... believe me, Colley, I don't want to go, but I'm absolutely sure I must. You're making me feel ... well, sort of hemmed in. Claustrophobia. You're so ... possessive. You ought to go home sometimes and possess Genista. I used to find it fun when we first met ... thrilling ... [so she admits that?] ... but now I've met Genista ... [so *that's* it] ... it makes me feel sort of ... vaguely ... queasy, even if she doesn't know'
Colley can feel Chaite slipping from his grasp. He wants her, but he knows that what his friend Leslie said is true – Chaite is free and independent, and can't magically transfer her qualities to him. 'If you want to go on enjoying her, you must never let on that you want to keep her' Leslie had said. Was it too late to dissuade her?
'When do you want to go?' Was that subtle?
'I've been thinking about that. I've got a possible replacement on my books – she's coming in on Wednesday ... [you seem to have it all worked out] ... fortnight's overlap, I could leave on ... Independence Day'
'You seem to have it all worked out. Suppose your ... replacement doesn't fit? Or won't come?'
'She will. She came in and saw Ted last week ...'
'WHAT?'
'... it's all fixed'
'What can I say ...?' Calm yourself.
'Nothing ... it's *meant*'

The next day, Chaite phoned Cepha: 'Could I come and stay with you for a bit? I've got some holiday'
'That would be smashing – the children keep asking when you're going to come again'
'You and Rupert could go away for a few days. I can look after them'
Cepha wondered – fleetingly, irrationally – if that would be safe:
'Well ...'
'It's no imposition. After all, they're all the family I've got, apart from my sisters'
'If you're sure ... we can talk about it when you come – when *are* you coming, by the way?'

29

'Saturday week; I'll leave in the morning, and be with you around lunch time'

Then Chaite rang directory enquiries: '... It's a firm of house agents: Sellis & Toker'
There was a pause; then: 'I've got a Sellis & Co, Auctioneers & Estate Agents, but no Toker'
Chaite's heart leapt.
'And the number?'
'Is Rusham 29491'
'Thank you very much'
She dialled Sellis & Co, mentally preparing a disguised voice:
'Sellis & Co; can I help you?'
'May I speak with Mr Toker?' She wondered if her assumed American accent sounded as phoney down the line as it did to her.
'I'm afraid Mr Toker has left the firm'
'Oh, can I have you put me into touch with him?'
That sounded clumsy ... but perhaps they talked like that in ...
Bozeman, Montana.
'I'm sorry, he's before my time. I'm sure Mr Sellis will know ... Hello?'
Chaite didn't hear her say 'Hello?' for she had caused the question by cutting off the call. She dialled the number again.
'Sellis & Co; can I help you?'
Chaite assumed as lah-de-dah a voice as she could muster: 'Is it possible to speak to Mr Sellis?'
'Are you the American that rang just now? We got cut off'
'American? Of course not. My name is Chaite; please tell Mr Sellis I would like to talk to him'
There were clicks.
'Chaite – my dear – fancy hearing from you. How are you?'
'I'm fine. As a matter of fact, I could be looking for a job in a few weeks' time. In your area. I just thought ... perhaps ... you might ... know of something?'
'Why don't you come and see me? I had to let Toker go, I'm afraid. You were right about him ... though rather brutal'
'I *was*? I was. Well – anyway, if he's not there, I'll not mind coming to see you. I'll be with my sister at Shalthorpe on Saturday week. Then I'm going to visit Mercia – you remember?'
'Yes, of course. At Little Bygrave. When are you coming up here?'
'The week-end after next. Shall I call in on the Monday after that?'

'That'd be splendid. Come about ... let's see ... come about quarter to one, and we'll have lunch. I'll look very forward to that. Goodbye, my dear'
'Goodbye, Mr Sellis ... and thanks'
'Don't mention it. Goodbye'
'Goodbye'
This could go on for ever; Chaite put the phone down, prepared to face Colley at any time.

Colley had gone home the previous evening in a turmoil of gratitude and despair. Should he mention Chaite's departure to Genista? Suppose Chaite decided for some reason not to go? He decided to wait.

   Little Nikki (as opposed to her aunt, Big Nikki) and Giles were playing in the garden; William was in his pram under the walnut tree. There was an appetising smell wafting through the open back door. He went in: 'Hello – – Genista!'
'Colley! You're early!'
'I know – isn't it nice?'
'It certainly is ... I'll finish what I'm doing, and we can sit in the garden'
'I'll get some chairs'
'And what would you like to drink?'
'G&T'
Genista put her hand on his forehead: 'Are you *sure* you're all right?'
'Of course I am. Why not?'
Genista relaxed: 'It's good to see you, whatever it is'
She kissed him.

With no effort at all, Colley spent an evening of domestic bliss, helping to bathe Nikki, Giles and William, making William comfortable and tucking him up snugly, then looking at *The Boy's Wonder Book of Aeroplanes* he'd had when he was their age (with his imitative scribbles still in it) with the others; then reading *Mr Fork and Curly Fork* for old times' sake before taking them up to their beds and tucking them in.
'Good night, Little Nikki'
'Good night, Daddy. Daddy ... I like it when you come home and read to us'
'Good night, Giles'
'Good night, Daddy. Will you come home early tomorrow like this again?'
'I'll try'

The corners of Colley's eyes burned; he heard strains of heavenly choirs as a fairy swooped in through the window to wand tinkling, twinkling stars on to the children's sleepy heads before swooping out into the night again.

'Too much Walt Disney is bad for you'

'What did you say, Daddy?'

'Nothing. Go to sleep'

There being nothing on the telly, he and Genista went to bed early. And, it being a hot night, he and Genista went to bed naked.

*   *   *   *   *   *   *

'Colley'

'Yes?'

'It's never been as good as that before'

'Do you think we'll have a fourth?'

'If it's meant. Could be rather nice. William'll be about a year old'

'Could you manage four?'

'I could cope with dozens'

'If it goes on like this, you may have to'

'Good night, Colley. And thank you. I love you'

'I love you too. Night'

'Mmmm'

So they had slept. For the first time for a long time, Colley didn't wake early thinking of Chaite. To do so, he realised when she at last swam into his ken, was obscene. She swam away again.

He was married to Genista. He had behaved very badly. She was worth a hundred Chaites (if he were allowed to think of Chaite to compare her).

The week got round to Friday. Colley and Chaite hadn't exactly avoided one another, but it so happened that their paths didn't cross either. That gave the week-end to see whether new leaves stayed turned.

Chaite decided to go and see Mercia. She didn't bother to check if Mercia would be there; she had a key to Mercia's house, so it didn't matter that much. It was a change she wanted primarily; Mercia would be an added delight.

Chaite drove across to Little Bygrave; turned into the pub car park behind Mercia's house. She walked round to the front, only to find that

Mercia was out. She opened the front door, tossed her overnight bag into the hall, re-emerged into the fine summer evening.

Into the pub to see who was there. A couple of couples she knew vaguely as friends of Mercia smiled and nodded, but were obviously interwrapt; the atmosphere within seemed oppressive compared with the exterior summer. She bought herself a pint of shandy and went to sit in the garden so that she could listen to the birds, breathe the tender air, and watch the sunset.

As she listened and watched, its timelessness overcame her. The sun shone on the bench she sat on, like a burnish'd throne; it was made of wood from trees which might have been planted in her great-great-grandfather's time.

But the sound of the birds must have remained unchanged for thousands – tens of thousands? – of years. And the sunset? That must have happened countless millions of times, whether there was anyone there to see it or not. She sat and thought herself back through the centuries ... what could she see? The cars disappeared, the pub disappeared, the landscape became unfamiliar as she thought herself into a forest – changing from oak, beech and hornbeam to more primitive forms until she was surrounded by giant cycads and equisetales. The horizon assumed the guise of an artist's impression of sunset on Mars. 'What a privilege – to be present in the great Carboniferous forest'
'I beg your pardon?'
It was a small man of indeterminate years wearing an obvious wig that looked as though a ginger cat had settled on his head; the effect was heightened by a nose and moustache which looked as though they came off with his spectacles. He was carrying a glass containing a clear liquid with ice floes and lemon; Chaite assumed it was gin, since he was also carrying a bottle of tonic. Unasked, he sat down.
'Oh, I was just musing ... *musing upon the king my brother's wreck*'
There was silence. He broke it: 'You're a bit poetical then? A bit of a poet ... ess, if I may be so forward'
Chaite was benign with the evening, but irritated with the intruder: 'What makes you say that?'
'*Musing upon the king my brother's wreck, And on the king my father's death before him* – The Waste Land'
'Or *The Tempest*?'
'Mr Eliot seemed to think so, but it's a bit far fetched'
Chaite felt even more profoundly irritated that such a weedy interloper should come barging into her Carboniferous forest and start quoting Mr Eliot at her. What could she say?

'Do you understand it?'
Damn. That sounded patronising; she didn't want that.
'Does anyone understand it? Did you know that Eliot himself said:
I wasn't even bothering whether I understood what I was saying? Isn't it
the case that you read it; you declaim it to yourself; it gives you a
feeling that you understand something – whatever it is? And that sort of
oneness is understanding'
Chaite relaxed slightly: 'Oh, you mean it's a bit like *Why do you
picture John of Gaunt as a somewhat emaciated Grandee*??'
'Yes. Exactly. No ... that's humorous. The thing we're talking about is
words washing over you so that you feel refreshed –
 Time present and time past
 Are both perhaps present in time future,
 And time future contained in time past.
 If all time is eternally present
 All time is unredeemable'
'That sums up what I was thinking exactly'
Chaite hoped he wouldn't ask her to elaborate.
'How interesting. Can I get you a drink?'
Chaite didn't want to be indebted to him, but she thought he owed her
something for intruding: 'Thank you. May I have a gin and tonic?'
'Of course, my dear'
It sounded stilted and lecherous. Chaite recoiled. He went away,
carrying the empties. She wondered if she could – should – slip away,
but decided against it. After all, she had nothing else to do;
conversation was now preferable to silence, and it was unlikely that
anyone she could rustle up – even if she felt like making the effort –
would provide better conversation than he. Anyway, she'd never get rid
of him ... and he might live close by; then she'd never dare show her
face again. But why should she write him off because of his
unprepossessing appearance? She realised that she was all too prone to
do this; pigeonhole people because of their appearance. Chaite thought
he looked – and sounded – uneducated, so she felt uneasy that her
constructs – that he must therefore be unintelligent – were apparently
incorrect. Sometimes she hated herself: what would they talk about
next?

 He returned with a tray of drinks; he'd bought some crisps as well.
He tipped tonics into the gins. He passed her a glass; raised his:
'Cheers!'
'Good health!'

It was a double gin – or was it a treble? Whatever it was, it gave Chaite a hefty kick in the throat. She felt tears in her eyes, but resolved not to show that she was discomfited:
'Arrrgh ... delicious' She coughed.
'Would you like some crisps?'
'Yes – thanks'
Without comment, he opened a packet and passed it to her; then:
'Some poems aren't obscure:
   And here on my right is the girl of my choice
   With the tilt of her nose and the chime of her voice ...'
So *that* was why he'd changed position. The devil – how dare he suggest that they should get engaged – if it *was* his suggestion. Perhaps he was just näive. It needed pursuing: 'You're saying I'm the girl of your choice?'
'Yes. I knew it the moment I saw you. And when you started quoting poetry ...'
Chaite; a sudden child; talking to a strange man: 'I think I ought to be going now'
'Please stay – you haven't finished your drink. Anyway, I didn't mean anything'
'Then why did you say it?'
'I ... I just wanted to talk. My wife's just ...'
'Your *wife*?'
'My late wife ... please stay and talk a little'
'All right, but my sister will be coming any minute – and then I'll have to go'
Damn. Why hadn't she said 'my brother'? But then she'd have been tempted to say 'my brother, who's a policeman' and then neither of them would have believed it. Liars ought to have good memories. Tell the truth, and you can't be inconsistent. She hoped Mercia would come. With a man. As she took another sip of G&T she had a sudden, wild, melodramatic fear that he might have drugged it. He spoke: 'What do you do? For a living, I mean'
'Me? I'm a people person – I'm in personnel'
Tell him in bits – it'll spin it out.
'Locally?'
'No ... across at Foxworth – a place called WEL – I don't suppose you've heard of it ... [damn – patronising inflection – try again] ... I don't suppose you've heard of it?'
'Wilkinson Electronics? Yes, I know old Bob Wilkinson ... [Do you? Well, even if I'm leaving, I'd better be careful] ... we're both on the bench'

You on the bench? Well I never. But to question it would seem rude ... as would this pause if it were to last any longer: 'And what do you do ... apart from being on the bench?'

Chaite heard the incredulity in her voice as she said it. But the moment was shattered by the arrival of Mercia, with a man and a woman whom she did not know, the former carrying a tray of drinks.

Mercia rushed forward to embrace Chaite: 'How wonderful to see you – are you staying?'

'Yes – I've put my things in your hall – hope you don't mind'

'Not at all ... I see you've met Hugh'

'Not formally'

'Hugh's Professor of English at the university up the road. I expect he's been keeping you entertained'

With keen interest, Chaite observed her perception of Hugh flip: 'Yes, he's been telling me all about his trip up the Amazon to locate a Lost Tribe of Israel'

'Oh, he's always boring us with that ... [said the man] ... my name's Guthrie, by the way – and this is Alice, Hugh's wife'

Chaite couldn't carry that one off. She shook hands with Alice, but looking at Hugh: 'But I thought ...'

Alice broke in: 'What else has he been telling you?'

Hugh interrupted: 'Well, you weren't exactly early, were you, my dear?'

'Not the one about his late wife?'

Chaite nodded.

Hugh looked contrite: '*Sigh no more, ladies, sigh no more, Men were deceivers ever* ... Let me get some more drinks ... my penitence'

He took orders, and departed. Chaite watched him go. The small man of indeterminate years with a ginger cat on his head had become a professor, a JP, and one of her sister's circle. She amused herself by trying to see him as she had at first, without the multiple accreditations.

The gins and tonics wrought their metabolic havoc, the evening became jollier and jollier; they set to work to set the world to rights through a thickening haze; the table supported bottle after bottle of wine. Chaite enjoyed scampi in the basket without remembering it much. The coloured lights in the trees indicated that it was closing time. They all rose and tottered round to Mercia's house for coffee and liqueurs.

As she undressed in the spare room, Chaite had a vague feeling of all being right with her world; that she'd had one of the most enjoyable evenings ever, holding her own in some seemingly high-powered company. And she noted with a pang that Mercia appeared to have taken Guthrie to her bed.

Some hours later, Chaite went downstairs and made a pot of tea; laid a tray; took it up to Mercia's bedroom. The door was ajar; Chaite knocked with the corner of the tray.
'Come on in'
Chaite pushed the door open. Guthrie appeared to have gone. The sight of Mercia lying in bed took her back to their childhood. Mercia saw Chaite standing with a tray bearing three cups, looking at the half-empty bed with the incredulity of a child watching a conjuror. Mercia laughed: 'It's quite safe – you can come in'
Chaite wondered at her little sister, going to bed with a man. It was not quite nice – like imagining one's parents preparing for one's arrival in nine months' time.
She put down the tray and sat on the bed:
'He's gone!'
'Yes, he's on earlies – he's a detective inspector'
Again, Chaite's perception flipped. She'd had no idea ... a policeman after all ... and policemen didn't spend the night with one's sister:
'He seemed to be knocking back the gins'
Mercia laughed again: 'Lemonades, actually. The company can make you high'
Chaite ingested that one. Then: 'Have you known him long?'
And so they fell to talking of Guthrie ... and Chaite, who needed to talk to someone so desperately, told Mercia more about Colley than she'd have believed possible – who he was, and how she'd met him, and what had (and hadn't) happened, and: 'I love him so very much – but I'd never dare tell him ... that's why I've got to move on. *I must be cruel only to be kind.* You see?'
Mercia saw.

So passed Chaite's week-end. She returned to Foxworth on Sunday evening, reassured that there was life beyond Colley.

Colley's new leaf stayed turned over too – he mowed the lawn, mended a chair, built a kite, took the children to the playfield to fly it, was a model husband and father. As his constructive week-end drew to a close, a great feeling of peace enveloped him.

On Sunday evening, he and Genista watched television – *The Secret of Stonehenge*. It touched a chord – a whole arpeggio – in Genista: 'I thought that was fascinating'

'I'm so glad – I did too, and I was terribly afraid you wouldn't'

'No, I love Stonehenge; it makes me feel ... at one with the past'

'We must go and see it again – though I'm not sure if you can get near to it what with hippies and barbed wire'

'I don't think it's like that all the time ...' doubtful Genista.

'Mind you ... [said Colley] ... I do get worried about it'

'How do you mean?'

'Well, whatever it was constructed for, I suppose we can take it that it's some sort of celestial record?'

'So?'

'So, to set it up, you'd need to make observations over a span of time longer than a single life'

'Unless you had someone who lived an abnormally long time'

'Yes, but you wouldn't know in advance that you were going to live an abnormally long time – anyway, the chances are that it would have to be calculated out over a long period'

'How would you record your observations?'

'That's the point. If you're advanced enough to be able to make and record your observations – to pass them on to your descendants – why do you need to build a great structure like Stonehenge?'

'What else is there? Clay tablets?'

'Wooden posts in the ground?'

'Perhaps that explains the remains of the wooden posts'

'It could indeed. But why then go to all the trouble of carting those socking great monoliths all that way; a wooden structure would – could – be just as elegant. And more accurate, if you're worried about sky sightings. And if it'd last a few hundred years, that'd be enough. *A post of yew will outlast a post of iron*'

'Yes, but Stonehenge is more impressive than Woodhenge. And Woodhenge has long since gone'

'But if Stonehenge weren't durable, it wouldn't be there, and we wouldn't be worrying about it now – if you see what I mean'

'Perhaps durability is the key. If it was built for some purpose of worship it would need to be impressive. Not just because the priests need to impress the ordinary people, but because the effort propitiates the gods'

'Who said anything about priests and worship?'

'What else is it for? If you can predict what's going to happen – albeit in the sky – you've got power. That's what priesthood is all about – power. So they needed an impressive structure to create an awesome atmosphere. It's the same today – throughout recorded history. An awesome building must be quite a large part of the paraphernalia of an ordinary mortal acting the part of priest. Think how long it took to build the great cathedrals'

'Part of it was to the Glory of God ... but I bet it was in the interests of the architects and master masons – or were the architects and the master masons one and the same? ... well – it was in their interests to keep the building going. Masons were as powerful then as they are now'

This was a side of Genista that Colley hadn't experienced for some time – or, if he had, he'd ignored it; failed to foster it. Of course she could be – was – every bit as good as – better than – Chaite. He felt stimulated. But he'd nearly lost the thread: 'What? Masons?'

'Yes, as powerful now as they were then'

'But in a different way. It's all Inspector Knacker and Arthur Daley now, isn't it? Making secret signs at the judge when it's too late'

'I don't know. Chief Superintendent Knacker, perhaps. But my grandfather was a Mason. We've still got the regalia at home. It all makes me feel a bit sick, actually'

'Why's that? Perhaps they just like playing Secret Societies'

'Perhaps. But I didn't find out till after he was dead. And then it put him in quite a different light for me'

'Yes. Anyway, the point is that I think the masons and the priests must have been pulling at opposite ends of the same string – a sort of mutual blackmail. They were both on to a good thing with their building to the Glory of God, and they needed to keep their financiers sweet. That way, they'd got everybody from the king downwards at their mercy'

'Some people must have questioned the system – hence the Inquisition, heretics, witches'

'I think that's a bit catch-all. But I agree that the Church – as we must now call what we're talking about – had a vested interest in its self-preservation'

'And it took a king to shake it – Henry VIII. And of course even he saw the necessity of keeping it going'

'Why *even* he? He was no fool. He transferred power from Rome to himself'

'Did he want the power for himself, or was it just to get the women he wanted? He could hardly have done a David – I honestly believe the old male chauvinist's motives weren't quite the same as you'd like to believe'

'Well, I suppose it's difficult enough to understand the ins and outs of it, let alone trying to imagine the problems of being king – and in the sixteenth century, at that'

'Certainly the king is both warder and prisoner. But we were talking about priests and masons being in putative cahoots'

'Yes we were. I submit that the contribution the masons made was more tangible. Everybody could see the results of their skill. Not quite the same as promising everlasting life – or alternatively hell fire and damnation. How could the priests know that what they said was true?'

'Well they didn't, of course, any more than they do now. But as long as people believed them, it didn't matter – except morally – perhaps'

'Ah ... but who's to say that the good they did in keeping things in order didn't outweigh the immorality? – If indeed it was immoral?'

'Hold on – you're making the assumption that they didn't believe. Was it so immoral if they were genuine believers? – as I think they were'

'And I think they still are ... must be'

'Maybe. But what worries me is that when it comes down to it, you – we – just don't – can't – have any proof of the existence of God. The study of theology doesn't mean you know anything about God:

> *I saw an eminent divine*
> > *A-shuffling through the library*
> *And suddenly I realised*
> > *He knew no more of God than I'*

'And if you were unknown to one another:

> *And suddenly I realised*
> > *He knew no more of God than me*

The accusative rhymes better, and could be equally true'

'Hmmm. I see what you mean. Perhaps our idea of God is mistaken. But I guess that the Robinsons and Cupitts of this world have explored that pretty thoroughly'

'Not to mention the Jenkinses. But leaving them aside, if God is omnipresent, then God must be everything, not just everywhere. So we must be part of God, whether we like it or not'

'*Oh God – if there be a God, Save my soul – if I have a soul'*

'What was that?'

'Said to be a prayer uttered by one of Cromwell's soldiers'

'Was he hedging his bets, or being intellectually honest?'

'Er ... both. However – let me put it another way – if we are but parts of God, surely we can't have the mechanism to comprehend him? Like – if

40

you're a 2-D being you could live on a 3-D surface not only without realising it but – even if you did realise it – you still couldn't comprehend it'

'The *Flatland* analogy. But look – if you live in 3-D (which is doubtless a concept you accept and agree to) and our fourth dimension is time, then our 3-D space could be a 5-D surface. Or else it's a 4-D surface and time is the fifth dimension'

'That makes it easier. But not much'

'That's all very well, but it doesn't help with a proof of God'

'I'm not trying to prove God; I'm musing on the dimensions. Anyway, don't you see, we can't prove God because if we can't comprehend we wouldn't know when we had a proof'

'Suppose we look at it this way. God gives us free will ...'

'I'm not sure that I accept that, but I'll take it as a hypothesis. What then?'

'Well, just take it that either we have, or we think we have, free will. So we have the choice of knowing (or not knowing) God. The choice *for* is what we call faith. But if we have faith, there's no question of having to make the choice. It's a vicious circle'

'So you're saying that for things we can't comprehend faith's the analogue of proof?'

'I didn't think of it like that, but it seems quite neat. Like miracles being the result of technology we don't understand'

'Oh, not that old flying-saucers-in-the-Bible stuff?'

'It's not that old. After all, we've only had flying saucers – as such – since 1948. But, yes, I think if you look at biblical mysteries, or miracles, in the light of modern technology, you might see my point proved. Well, food for thought, anyway. What do you think about free will?'

'I think that whatever happens at any given moment is determined by what happened the moment before'

'Uh-huh – *The ball no question makes of ayes and noes, But right or left as strikes the player goes* – this must be a universal property of matter. It was all determined at the moment of the Big Bang. We happen to be one embodiment of matter'

'You're presupposing that thought is matter?'

'Well, you surely wouldn't argue that thought doesn't reside in some tangible system; that memory has no physical mechanism?'

'No-o-o'

'So when you decide to do something – or not to do something – it's conditioned by what information – observed at the time or stored in your memory – you have'

'But surely, when I decide to do something, I make a choice; I have free will. Whether or not I take my umbrella; whether I walk or go by car; whether I buy cauliflower or broccoli. You can't say all these sorts of trivia, which go on all the time for all of us, are predetermined?'
'That's exactly what I *am* saying. But what I'm *not* saying is that you can predict what choice you're going to make'
'And do you think God can? It takes far longer to describe a trivial decision – let alone a weighty one – than it does to make the decision. You might say "Oh, sod it, I'll take my umbrella and walk." All the elements of your lifetime's experience which lead to that snap decision would take some unravelling'
'Of course, But you're thinking of it in our human terms again. And you know that if you tried to analyse the umbrella choice you couldn't anyway. But I think that God can understand it – if He wants to – because He is every*where* and hence every*thing*. And He doesn't necessarily work in the same time frame as we do. In fact, He embodies all time – past, present and future ...'

The telephone rang; some trivial query about manning stalls at the school fete. Genista attended to it. Colley felt a strange exhilaration at the conversation they'd just had. If the atmosphere was right ... but for now, the moment had passed. It was time for bed – again.
'Who was that?'
'A Person from Porlock' replied Genista.

As the week progressed, Colley saw Chaite from time to time in corridor and canteen. She seemed to be avoiding him. He was reminded of her more often by the continual stream of memoranda she was circulating prior to her departure. On Monday, she introduced him to her successor, Carolyn Banks. In some peculiar way, Carolyn's presence seemed to sever the link between Colley and Chaite; Carolyn spelt finality.

Most of Colley was now glad that Chaite had left his obsession. The rest of him was angry in turns that this could have happened – and it was that part of him that tried to recapture the thrill of seeing her – with a complete lack of success – that bolstered the morale of the larger part.

At lunch time on Friday 4 July there was a presentation to Chaite in the canteen. Colley had made his apologies; he could not attend and make the presentation himself owing to a subsequent engagement. He had signed the card, and contributed generously to the collection.

That Friday evening, Colley and Chaite met on their way to the front door. Colley beamed at her with born-again self-righteousness, thinking she couldn't possibly know how he felt. Then he saw the look on her face, and realised the truth, for ever has it been that love knows not its own depth until the hour of separation.

Colley: *Let me confess that we two must be twain*
Chaite: *O, call me not to justify the wrong*
Colley: *O, never say that I was false of heart*
Chaite: Our parting, oh so swift, shall be so long
That was it. They could not know that they would never meet again.

Thinking about the parting afterwards, Colley reflected that in his heart of hearts he'd always known that the end must come, but he could never have predicted that it would be like that. It seemed an age since he had been to see Leslie – in fact, it was just a month. He wondered if he should ring Leslie and tell him what had happened. He decided against it, but decided that he'd (try to) see Leslie more often.

8
Thursday 29 May – Thursday 5 June 1986

The inspiration to visit Leslie had come to Colley when he was sitting over a blank sheet of paper ostensibly composing a memorandum, but in practice thinking about Chaite. He was obsessed with her; what could – what should – he do? He was in despair when, suddenly, he had his brilliant idea. He would ring Leslie. It was so long since he had rung Leslie that he had to look up his number.
He found it; dialled it.
'The number you have just dialled has been changed ... [quoth the automaton] ... Please consult your new directory'
Damn. Colley consulted his new directory and found that the telephone area had been changed as well so that Frettleborough Polytechnic no longer fell within it. 192.
'Directory enquiries, which town?'
'Frettleborough'
'And the name of the people?'
'Frettleborough Polytechnic – it's a changed number'
'What was it?'
'Frettleborough 4174'

'The number is Frettleborough 274174'
'274174 ... thank you very much'
Colley tried again.
'Poly – *tech* – nic'
'315 please'
'We don't have a 315. Who do you want?'
'Um ... Leslie Benjamin'
'That's 2026, caller. Remember that. Number's ringing'
'2026 – Leslie Benjamin'
'Hello'
'Colley! ... Where are you?'
'In my office. But I'm coming over to Frettleborough'
'Good. When?'
'As soon as we've arranged it'
'Poor Colley. You've got a problem'
Leslie knew.
'Usually'
'Well ... can you come for lunch next Thursday ... or is that too soon?'
Colley knew his diary. Thursday would be fine.
'That'll be fine. About midday? Where?'
'Come to my office and we'll decide'
'I'll look forward to that'
Leslie hissed into the phone:
'Got to go. See you. Bye'

Now that he knew that he was going to do something – that he was
going to talk to Leslie – Colley felt more relaxed. He made a note in his
diary; then, without putting down his pen, he drew his notepad towards
him and wrote his memo fluently and flawlessly.

That night Colley slept well. He didn't wake at 3 o'clock thinking of
Chaite. He woke at 4.30 thinking of Leslie.

Wednesday was a day of interviews; electronic design engineers. A
presentation on WEL, a question-and-answer session, lunch, problem
solving, individual interviews. The day went like clockwork – but only
as a result of so much horological input from Chaite. She was so good at
her job – if only their relationship had never strayed beyond the
professional. It was all the fault of his rose-bush. But it was a good
group of engineers, and Colley even enjoyed the lunch, for in 24 hours'
time ...

44

That night Colley slept right through; it was 6.30 before he woke up mindful of a composite chimera; a Chaile; a Leste. He switched on Radio 3, predicted the key for the Philip Jones fanfare to introduce the Open University, got it wrong, and settled back to listen to a heavily-scripted impromptu discussion ['Well, John ...' 'Well, Rob ...'] between a heavily Scouse professor and an even heavilier Geordie doctor of philosophy – each proud of his mandatory regional accent's acceptability in the groves of Open Academe – on the Place of the Aristotelian Virtues in Benthamite Philosophy. 'And vice versa ... [thought Colley, who wasn't really listening] ... what's posterity ever done for me?' He wondered if Leslie was listening; he knew that his work had something to do with making such programmes.

And now Colley was in Frettleborough. It had changed. Not the buildings that closed over oppressively as he entered the inner city; they were still the same. It was the roads that had altered. A plethora of signs: No Entry, One Way Street, No Lorries Between 7am and 8pm Except on Sundays, Get In Lane, Keep In Lane, Cyclists Only, Traffic for Market Street Keep Right At Roundabout ... and yet you had to doff your cap to the city fathers: the traffic had been strangling Frettleborough, and now Frettleborough was strangling the traffic. *Who is the potter, pray, and who the pot?*

Colley found his way to a car park of concrete and red brick over a shopping centre and wound down his window as he stopped at the barrier. There was an oppressive smell, a miasma of modern Megapolis: overchoked cars mingled with concrete and a whiff of mikki. A ticket protruded rudely from a machine – he stuck his tongue out at it in retaliation and drew it forth. The barrier swang up like a railway signal; an incongruous ginger cat sockpoled purposefully past. *There's a whisper down the line where the year has shot her yield, and the ricks are ready to depart* intoned Colley, moving forwards.

Rows of radiators smiled as he spiralled, seeking a space. Here scurries a rep, samples and expectant order pad at the ready; here a woman sports a suit of a cut and shade betokening the pseudo-uniform, her billowing neckwear topped by a Tussaudian complexion; here a mother – tottering tot clasping a plastic bottle of Coke as big as itself – deftly compresses folding frame, Mothercare pushchair; here a man in a van, dirty white overalls, tea in thermos, savouring sandwich, scanning the *Sun* in the firm belief that it's a left-wing organ.

Suddenly the cars thinned, as though affected by the rarefied atmosphere. Colley selected his space and backed in, suddenly arrested with an embarrassing thud as his rear fender met the concrete solidity of the structure even as he was congratulating himself on his deft driving. He looked furtively around for witnesses, but there was none but a Great Dane constrained in the adjacent car, half raising its languid head; the Hound of the Baskervilles having a day off; he wouldn't tell.

Colley got out and put on his jacket, ritually checked his accustomed pockets, and locked the car. There was no apparent way out of the car park except by his route of entry – ridiculous. Then, in a distant corner, he espied a crude mural; a symbolic stick man striding purposefully up some ill-limned stairs. He made for the door which must surely be there. It was, but the handles were fastened together and: 'Please use other door' ordered a scrawl on a torn-off scrap of hardboard. Colley looked around in vain for the other door.

He peered over the parapet at the people going about their business at ground level, unaware that he was trapped high above them in an open prison. 'Me Tarzan ...' he looked for a liane on which to swing down; as his hopelessness grew he spotted that 'other door' ... close to where he had parked. He looked at his watch; what had been twenty minutes early would now be at least five minutes late. He scurried down the stairs as the door banged to hollowly behind him, blinking as he left the cool concrete darkness of the car park and emerged into a narrow alley-way struck by a shaft of sunlight, and a welcoming smell of fruit beckoning from the brightly-lit hypermarket. Experience showed that the shop could be a short cut to reality.

'Exit to car park only' said a sign. A uniformed octogenarian sought to stop him, holding up his skinny hand: 'Sorry, sir ... you can't ...'

Colley pointed vaguely into the shop: 'Iss my vife ... I help fetch ... microvave ... iss very heavy'

The Ancient Mariner became the Helpful Hermit, beaming understandingly, ushering him in the forbidden direction.

'Senk you ... iss kind' effused Colley, walking with what he hoped looked like a mittel-European gait. He passed down aisles high-piled with provisions, mountains of merchandise, 20p off this, 10% extra that, buy three and get one free.

He found an egress twixt the tills wondering if he might be apprehended for shop-lifting and so sue for wrongful arrest – what a shame they didn't stock grand pianos; the doors hissed, rolled apart automatically, and he debouched into the pedestrian precinct.

Whatever else, it was noticeably clean. All the sorts of people he had seen in the car park strolled slowly or paced purposefully to their appointed places, but there were many non-car-owners too, aliens among the automobiles, had they strayed from their circuit.

The barrel-shaped ladies, waddling with shopping trolleys, hats on immaculate wispy blue rinses and thick brown coats buttoned high against the sun; the old men, some shabby, shambling and unshaven, some in tweeds with a military manner; the young in pinks, greens and whites with much supererogatory pattern detail, or fringed leathers with random chains and complex insomniac hair.

So many sat on seats among the jigsaw of raised flower beds, the sun shone, and everyone looked so happy, that Colley found himself smiling as he sauntered, wondering why everywhere, every day, could not be as idyllic as this, bathed in beauty rather than in the more usual vague feeling of general despair – vandalism and violence, murder and mayhem, robbery and rape. Thus he arrived at Leslie's office benign and punctual after all.

Colley was shocked at the way Leslie had aged since last he saw him. 'And have I aged similarly?' he wondered, not believing it possible. They went to a 'little wine vault' Leslie knew.
'What'll you have?'
Colley had forgotten Leslie's infinite capacity for taking Pimm's.
'St Clement's ... if you don't mind'
Colley, who could fall over at the pull of a cork, knew they shouldn't start turning the screw. He gave an apologetic grimace, willing Leslie to understand that it was some old ulcer playing up, secure in the knowledge that Leslie would not ask about it, for to admit of Colley's possible infirmities would only lay open his own.

Leslie was clearly a regular here; how else would he have been served with a pint mug sporting a Carmen Miranda lookalike without even batting an eyelid? The St Clement's too, garnished with slices of oranges and lemons looked more eminently quaffable than the usual effete offerings.

Leslie led the way to a corner table whence, by some antiphasic miracle, the otherwise omnipervasive Muzak™ was excluded; a cone of silence. An impossible waitress materialised; Colley astounded that anyone could actually have got herself up to look so like The French Maid.
'Reading Greats ... [hissed Leslie] ... leading light of OUDS'
Colley wondered what he'd let himself in for; perhaps that explained something. The French Maid whisked out a pair of menus and presented them with a flourish: 'Good morning, gentlemen. What's it to be?'

Her voice was surprising: musical Mummerset. Practising, perhaps.
'Good morning, Lettice ... [said Leslie] ... mackerel salad, please.
Colley?'
'Er ... I'll have the same, please ... if that's all right'
He wondered why it shouldn't be all right.
'Of course, sir. Two mackerel salads. Will you have anything to start
with?'
Neither Colley nor Leslie had decided who was paying; neither
particularly wanted anything to start with, yet did not want to seem
inhospitable, should he turn out to be the host.
'I think the salad is all *I* want' said Colley, implying that if Leslie
wanted strips of tender young celeriac marinaded in Moët et Chandon,
boiled in a bleached linen bag at full moon until the cows came home,
deep frozen, passed through the microwave oven, lightly sprinkled
with fresh-ground cardamom and served on a bed of luscious iced
cucumber, who was he to stop him?
'Mackerel salad'll do me fine' said Leslie, snapping the menu shut and
handing it back over his shoulder to The French Maid with the half
patronising, half self-deprecatory, smile suited to such occasions.
'And would you like the wine list, gentlemen?'
Again Colley and Leslie exchanged glances.
Again Colley took the initiative, handing The French Maid his glass.
'I think I'd like another of these ...'
'And a Pimm's for me'
Leslie was glad to be let off the hook.
    Colley mused on the whole art of restaurant play – particularly the
subset food-speak – for all around people were assuming pabular roles;
as the food for their tables arrived, they would start slightly on the
buttocks, hold a finger at shoulder level, and pronounce: 'I'm the egg
mayonnaise' or 'I'm the rare steak' or 'I'm the cheeseboard'.
    Colley sat back and regarded Leslie, remembering times past when
they had shared rooms, had been as close as two men could be without
actually touching. He felt ashamed that he had not kept his friendship
in better repair. Yet it was that very depth of friendship which had
enabled him to make contact with Leslie after so long; the knowledge
that he *could* contact him if he ever wanted to. Sometimes he would
have a sudden intimation of immortality: a crushing fear that Leslie
might die without his seeing him again; then a dread that he might
have thought of Leslie because he had died, sending as he did so a great
pulse of energy around the world, resonating in all who knew him. And

then Colley had known that Leslie had not died, and the signals became subsumed in the noise again – until the next time.

Had Leslie changed? Was his once-so-valuable trait of putting his finger straight on one's troubles no more? The mackerel salads came, mountainous as the drinks.

'They do you very well here' said Leslie, tucking in. Colley was amazed to see him filling his mouth with wickedly curved fish-bones – then realised that it was probably stems of cress or pieces of thinly-sliced raw onion. Colley was amazed, too, at the thick showers of dandruff on Leslie's shoulders – how could it be that the myriad of available panaceas had passed him by?

Momentarily, Colley experienced a revulsion from someone whom he had held dear for longer than he cared to remember. Perhaps he had subconsciously felt this, and this was why he had allowed his friendship with Leslie to lapse. He had expected to bounce his problems off Leslie; now he felt that he couldn't. He felt angry, thwarted, frustrated. Once again, his selfcentredness came to the fore, as though Leslie existed solely to bolster him up whenever he deigned to ask, to be folded back into the box like a marionette when Colley had finished.

'I'm glad you've come ... [said Leslie] ... I've got a problem'

Colley started. What was the answer to that? What, indeed, was Leslie's problem – not dandruff, surely? To give Colley his due, he suddenly realised that he had been so intent on discussing his problems with Leslie that it had never crossed his mind that Leslie might have problems of his own. Could it always have been so? He experienced a cold flush; he had used Leslie as a sounding-board so often; now it was time to reciprocate, and he didn't relish the sudden, sharp realisation that as long as he could talk about himself he didn't much care about anyone else. He composed himself: 'What's the matter?'

Colley looked, he hoped, serious and receptive.

'Jaguar trouble'

Colley almost laughed: 'What's wrong?'

'Well, I've been running the Old Girl so much that all sorts of things are beginning to go wrong at once – king pins, gearbox, rear axle, brakes – and I don't know how I'm going to be able to afford to restore her. I really shouldn't've used her so much, but it's such fun and ... what's the good of a car if you don't use it? Mind you, when I *do* get it fixed, I'll be a jolly sight more careful, but I just don't see how I can at the moment'

Colley thought. Was it like promising God you'd be good if He'd get you out of your present predicament? If Leslie cared that much, he wouldn't

have run the Old Girl into the ground. It really was so easy to see what other people ought to do:
'Have you got another car?'
'Yes ... not such fun, of course'
'Of course not, but it's a start. Now, how much do you need to spend on the Jag?'
'More than I'd like to think'
'Oh, come ... Shouldn't you start by finding out? Unless you know, you can't begin to plan – and I certainly can't'
Yes, other people's problems were really so simple. Turn the problem back on itself; analyse it; help its owner to approach it logically; defining the problem was a long way towards finding the solution. Come to think of it, that's what Leslie had always done. Leslie had never given advice, just asked probing questions. Colley felt less selfish by the second.
'I'm sure that if you run your other car – that'll save you some money – and draw up a plan for getting the Jag refurbished over a period, you'll feel a lot better'
Colley knew how much the XK120 meant to Leslie; without it, he'd probably curl up and die. They went over the detail of what was needed.
'I feel a lot better already, Colley. You've really cheered me up ... [Colley hoped he looked modest, self-effacing, pleased] ... And why ... [continued Leslie] ... did you suddenly pop up again after all this time?'
Colley felt genuinely guilty. What could he say?
'Don't look so guilty ... [Leslie laughed] ... I really am pleased to see you, you know. I do think of you, often; the times we had together ... of course, we've moved on a bit since then, and it's better to remember the past with affection than try to force something that can never be. How's Genista?'
Colley started.
'Oh ... she's fine. She really enjoys looking after children, you know ... I think'
'You think?'
Leslie looked exaggeratedly surprised.
'Yes, I think ... I know. I don't know. Oh hell; we don't talk about that much'
'What *do* you talk about?'
'Nothing much. Oh, it does worry me; there's such a lot I'd like to say – want to say – but somehow it doesn't ever seem right – the right thing – the right time'

'So who *do* you talk to?'

Leslie putting his finger on it again. He knew that Colley always had to talk to someone, and for a long time it had been him. Now it was him again. He could see Colley's mind churning over and over.

Colley told him about Chaite, what fun she was to be with, how much they had to say to each other, what tender feelings he had towards her, how indispensable he thought she was to his wellbeing.

In fact, he was telling Leslie about his idealised Chaite; his mental Chaite. He did not tell Leslie about the physical Chaite, and the fact that her attitude towards him seemed to have changed – which was why he'd come to see Leslie in the first place – perhaps seeking some reassurance for which it was neither right nor realistic to hope.

'So what's the problem? ... [Leslie felt somewhat brutal] ... Are you going to bed with her?'

'No ... not really'

'How do you mean "not really"? Are you or aren't you?'

'Well ... it doesn't work ... for either of us'

'So you're asking me to tell you it's all right to worry Genista sick ... [Leslie held up his hand to stop Colley from speaking] ... worry Genista sick as long as you don't go to bed with Chaite. You see that as the boundary between adultery and innocence'

From Leslie, it didn't sound old fashioned.

'Genista doesn't know'

'Who're you kidding?'

Colley's mouth fell open. Once again, he felt that new realisation of selfishness flow over him – it was exactly like standing at the edge of the sea and being knocked flat by a tsunami.

'Look ... [said Leslie getting out pencil and paper] ... here's you ... [he wrote a C] ... and here's Genista ... [he wrote a G] ... You've known her even longer than you've known me; you lived next door to each other, you went to the same school ...'

'Yes ... I've known her since she was in her pram'

'You're thirty ... six?'

Colley nodded:

'As good as'

Leslie wrote 36 beside the C:

'And Genista's ...?'

'Thirty four'

Leslie wrote 34 beside the G: 'So! You've known each other virtually all your lives – all your conscious lives – getting on for 70 person years. You know each other so well that it's hardly surprising that you haven't much to say to one another sometimes – if you don't talk work, or current affairs, or any of the myriad new experiences you can share – nothing to do with your common past'

Colley looked sharply at Leslie. Was he joking?

'Now ... [continued Leslie (who wasn't)] ... you say that Chaite is twenty seven and you've known her about a year. You realise that you've got getting on for forty – let's say – years of independent adult experience to share between you. You and Genista can read one another like books. You and Chaite can't – not in the same way. There's chemistry there, and that makes it worth pursuing. It's a novel experience for you, it's a bit naughty, and you probably think you're in love'

Colley baulked: 'I didn't say that'

'No, but you do'

'But ...'

Once more Leslie raised a restraining hand as Colley started to speak: 'And I'll tell you something else'

Leslie telling, giving advice, not questioning? This was new. But making statements was a way of questioning. Colley had to say something: 'What's that?'

'You're attracted to Chaite because she's free and independent. You want her because you're jealous of her freedom and independence. But you can't magically transfer her admirable qualities to you by possessing her. Don't you see that (a) it's impossible to transfer those qualities, but (b) – much more important – if you did possess her that in itself would rob her of the very freedom and independence you think is so vital. It's sheer atavism: the ritual sacrifice of the divine king; cannibalism is about eating parts of the wise or the courageous in order to transfer their attributes to yourself. It doesn't work'

'Wow' was all Colley could think of to say. Leslie had really put his finger on something; why hadn't he seen all that? Why hadn't he seen a lot of things?

'So what should I do?'

'My dear chap ... I'm not here to tell you what to do ... even if I knew. I'm just trying to make you think ... [you're doing that] ... to put a different point of view. You have to decide what to do. But I'll tell you this: your independent Chaite is liable to leave you as suddenly as she came. *I come like water, and like wind I go*. No malice, nothing unnatural about it. Just a manifestation of the quality you find so fascinating; part of the way she is. So I should go on enjoying it while

you can, never forgetting that her freedom is an essential part of her, and that – paradoxically – if you want to go on enjoying her you must never let on that you want to keep her. End of sermon'
There was a long silence. Wave after wave knocked Colley over; he kept standing up again like the Chinese Mandarin. He felt like a punch bag; a shadow boxer on whom the shades had turned the tables; he reeled round the ring; the bell rang:
'Last orders, please, ladies and gentlemen ...'
Colley went to the bar for a last order, paid the lunch bill in gratitude, returned drink laden to the musing Leslie.
"Cheers" they said in unison.
'Thanks ... [said Colley, adding emotionally] ... old friend'
He was sure that from now on everything would be crystal clear.

9
Monday 26 May 1986

Colley was lying in bed looking at the clock, a blurred circle which seemed to be saying either twenty-five to five or twenty past seven. It didn't matter. The mountain that was Genista spoke: 'Are you awake?'
'No. Anything I can get you, madam?'
'A cup of tea. Strong. At once'
'Certainly, madam. Will madam be requiring anything else?'
'No thank you, James. That will be all'
Colley rolled out of bed, donned dressing gown and slippers, and padded to the kitchen, not waking the existing children. The kitchen clock was larger, more informative: it must have been twenty past seven after all – not a bad time for waking up; a good time to enjoy the tea. When he returned with it, Genista was, of course, asleep again. Colley waited for the tea to draw – 'as long as it takes to sing the Miserere slowly' ; he had no idea how the Miserere went – let alone how long it took to sing it; whenever he thought of it, he meant to find out, but then was never the time for research. He poured out the tea after a decent interval:
'Room service for basking sharks!'
Genista rose up, and they greeted one another as they had every morning for some twelve years.
'It feels as though something might happen to-day'
'Time something did. Hairnt got a lot on at the offas' There was a scuffle and a knock at the door.
"Come in, they chorused" they chorused.

Nikki and Giles tumbled into the room.
'Don't bounce the bed ... !'
Nikki stood on one leg.
'Um ... if we get some cups ... can we have some tea?'
'Yes ... but then you must get dressed'
Nikki departed for the kitchen at top speed: there was a loud crash.
'It's all right' she shouted.
"GOOD!"
She returned with the cups: 'Mummy, if I'd broken that little milk jug
you don't like, would you be cross? ... [Genista opened her mouth to say
something] ... because I haven't'
Colley poured the tea, and the room became relatively quiet.

Colley left before the usual morning rush of mislaid combs, books,
ribbons, plimsols; Mrs Drewitt came to pick up the children and the
house was suddenly empty. Genista washed up and tidied round. She
knew it was going to come today. She had just put the kettle on for a cup
of coffee when the twinges began.

No sooner had Colley put down the phone than it rang again; it was
Jinny the switchbird: 'Genista rang while you were on the phone. She
said to tell you that the midwife's been, and her bag's packed, and her
mother's on the way, and all she needs is you'
'I'm on my way'
Once again, Colley reflected that parents are the very worst people to
have children; he ought to have a better idea of what it was all about
third time round, but he was by no means sure. Would it be a boy or a
girl? Did he care as long as it was all there? It was a bit of a cliché;
people kept saying it when they knew Genista was pregnant: 'Do you
want a boy or a girl?'
And then they would answer the question themselves: 'I don't spose you
mind, as long as it's healthy'

Colley arrived home: Genista was lying in an armchair.
'You look like a bloated plutocrat'
'I feel like one ... two. Come on – the case is in the hall'
She heaved herself up and waddled to the door; she sang: 'Quand deux
poules vont au champ ... [together] ... 'La première marche devant"
Colley picked up the suitcase and followed her out, locking the door
behind him, yet contriving to arrive at the car first so that he could
help her in.

The journey to the hospital was uneventful. Every time there was the slightest hold up, one of them said something like: 'Company director delivers baby in traffic jam'.

In no time at all, it seemed, Genista was in bed, Colley sitting beside her holding her hand and feeling important as he timed the contractions. Efficient blue ladies with aluminium trumpets came and went. Colley and Genista got the giggles, Genista's stopping short with a sharp intake of breath and a grimace. A doctor came in, looking even younger than a policeman, and broddled about: 'Have you been timing her?'

'Yes – it seems to be about eight minutes'

'Ah ... I don't think anything's going to happen just yet Mrs ... Er'

He squinted at the label, and turned back to Colley: 'And you're Mr ... Er?'

Colley nodded, sorely tempted to say that he was a passing purloiner of placentas, but even *he* thought this was in questionable taste. The doctor continued: 'I should go and get some lunch if I were you. I very much doubt if anything will happen before this afternoon'

He glid out, developing his professional walk.

'Go and get some lunch ... [commanded Genista] ... It'll be a very long afternoon'

'Do you think I should? You've been very quick before'

'Then you should go and have very a quick lunch. You can try that new place over the road. Then I'll know where you've bin'

'Good bye, dear Octopus'

She squeezed his hand as he kissed her lying helpless in the bed. He glid out, developing the professional walk. A passing blue lady eyed him through curious spectacles.

'Just a touch of rigor mortis' he murmured.

She glared at him.

He turned to wave to Genista, but there was no line of sight.

Colley walked out into the bright sunlight, with birds twittering in the bushes in the hospital grounds; he ignored his car, as though the imminent event gave him divine right of parking – the miracle of life, he thought.

He crossed the road to a little goldmine recently opened by a young man with a striped shirt, an ear of gold studs, dark glasses, a hairy medallioned chest, and a strong sense of purpose. He looked at the menu in the window and didn't feel hungry.

'But I must have something' he fussed at himself, a surrogate Genista.

He went in, noting that the ashtrays on the smoking tables were suitably large – and, he was glad to see, clean.

A take-it-or-leave-it-looking waitress in tee-shirt and jeans sidled up and gave him a languorous menu, somehow contriving to caress his cheek with her long blonde hair. He looked up at her and smiled; she smiled back, bosoming his left ear. 'How does she do it?' wondered Colley. 'Is there an evening class in it? "Your turn to be the diner" "But I was the diner last week" "You'll be the diner every week until your hair grows – sit down"'

'Have you come from "over there"?' she asked in inverted commas.

Colley wondered if the evening course provided conversational algorithms. He thought of a useful book: *Conversational Algorithms for Servile People*. Would it work?

'Yes'

'Is y'wife having a baby is she?'

'How did you guess?'

'They don't usually come here lunchtimes *after* it's been born'

It all seemed to make sense, but he was hungry:

'I'd like a prawn omelette with trimmings'

She wrote it down busily: 'Would you like anything to drink at all? We've just got our licence' Proudly.

'Sweet sherry ...' said Colley, wondering if that were what he wanted.

'A large one' she assumed, taking an extraordinary amount of time to write down what need hardly have been more than five characters – L Sw Sh.

' ... and then a draught Guinness'

His faith in human nature was such that he believed she'd tell him if they didn't have draught Guinness. However, they didn't, and she didn't.

At last everything was inscribed, and she went away. Colley looked round. There was a lot of pine and dimness and not many people – 'but then,' he reflected virtuously, 'most babies come at less convenient times'.

There were two copy waitresses at the quilted plastic bar, discussing techniques of spiking hair. On shelves and brackets there were bygones desecrated by some mind whose bizarre creativity beggared belief – two mincing machines with ferns growing from them; a knife-polishing machine converted into a lamp; a stuffed eagle on the log with a cheap clock movement mounted in its belly; an Alba horn gramophone with a tinny little speaker forced down its throat from which issued a lackbass sound even more unpleasant than its spoliation.

He suddenly realised that he was not worrying about Genista; then wondered if the horrors of the décor had been deliberately perpetrated with that in mind – like the tank of fish in the dentist's waiting room. He knew that Genista would be all right, and that everything would wait until he returned.

The sherry came; the omelette and trimmings were satisfying; even the 'draught' Guinness was passable. Colley found that he was hungry after all; he ordered apple pie and cream and finished with an Irish coffee.

Alcoholically speaking, it was all stronger than he'd bargained for; having paid the bill, he returned to the 'bedside vigil' (as he now thought of it) in a floating saunter. But somehow, he got lost in the works of the hospital.

Usually bustling with life, it was now double siesta time. He came to a blank wall. Turning round, he seemed to be enveloped in the corridor.

There was a door; he tapped on it, and waited. Nothing happened. He opened it slowly, put his head round it, and looked in. It was a bare room, with a bare wooden floor and an archaic gas-stove in the corner fireplace. The walls were painted gloss green and brown. Colley wondered if he had been teleported to the waiting room of a rural station circa 1923.

He withdrew his head, and shut the door reverently. Now he saw another door: 'When one door shuts, another door opens' he murmured, tapping discreetly.

'Come!' shouted an imperious female voice.

Colley opened the door, to be confronted by the blue rigor mortis lady glaring over her curious glasses. Colley wondered if these were the 'obscene spectacles' that the law forbade.

'Yes?'

'I'm, er, looking for my wife'

'She's in the delivery room'

'You must have second sight ... [Colley combined her instant recognition of him with her fearsome eyewear] ... Can you tell me the way? Please?'

'Certainly ... [was that a kindly smile?] ... out of here, turn left and left again. Delivery Room 2. It's on the door. Good luck'

'Thank you'

Colley wondered whether the luck was for the parturition or his journey into the unknown. As it was, there was no difficulty in finding Delivery

Room 2; Genista grinned, then grimaced; something was going to happen very soon now. The window was wide open, looking out on to a courtyard of surprisingly noninstitutional aspect: trees laden with blossom; a lawn; flower-beds. A hidden thrush warbled in the branches. Colley looked round the room: it was less clinical-looking than the ward; he couldn't quite make out how this had been achieved. There was something infantile about the décor: gambolling lambs amid daisy freshness ('perhaps they're kipling' he thought), designed to put mothers – parents – in the mood ... it could hardly be for the new arrivals.

He sat on a comfortable chair by Genista's bed (noting appreciatively that, comfortable as it was, it was not too low) and squeezed her hand. Genista was heaving and grunting, and the thrush was singing its heart out. And now: 'Push! Push!' the midwife was exhorting, aluminium trumpet at the the ready. Colley could feel a strange sympathetic stirring in his loins; he was excited and breathless with the effort, wondering whether it would be a girl or a boy.

Everything was unexpectedly quiet – except for the thrush singing, the midwife moving about, Doctor ... Er coming in and mumbling at her in subdued technicalities.

Time stood still, marked only by the warbling of the thrush and the obtrusive ticking of Colley's watch as (from habit) he noted the intervals between events – not that that had much relevance now.

Then things started to happen. Colley moved a bit to get a better view without obstructing the professionals – savouring their quiet professionalism. A head appeared: 'Good, it's got hair, lots of hair' Anterior shoulder.
Intramuscular syntometrine.
'Push! ... Push!'
Posterior shoulder ... body ...
'Wow! A quart in a pint pot'
An expectant wait for the moment of truth. Heave!
'Darling ... it's another boy!'

And so William was born, mucus cleared, clamps, scissors, injections, measurements, bathing ...
'All neatly wrapped in swaddling clothes' thought Colley as he studied Genista holding their new son for the first time. And waves of love washed over him. And then he was allowed to hold William, before he was laid in his cot, and a wonderful, wonderful tray of tea and biscuits

materialised. And time stood still for all alike as they enjoyed a post-natal cup and 'three cheers for the National Health' thought Colley.

Happy and relaxed, Genista was now wanting to get some sleep. William himself was asleep, the doctor had gone, the midwife had gone. Colley sat and Genista lay, appreciating one another.

'Darling?'

'Yes?'

'Thank you for a lovely birthday present'

'He could have waited another day'

'Don't be so literal'

'Well, a closer birthday present than Nikki was a Christmas present'

At last, he kissed her; went out into the fresh summer evening thinking how clever everybody was, and: 'It's a boy! It's a boy!' pounding through his whole being.

From wanting to tell everybody in the world, he remembered that there were certain people he *must* tell – his parents, Genista's mother patiently waiting at home ... and Nikki and Giles would want to know too. A telephone box stepped out remindingly; prepared Colley pulled out a handful of change.

He would have to phone his parents and his mother-in-law; then he would be free. It's a boy! It's a boy! He dialled his parents' number. The telephone rang and rang and rang. He waited until honour was more than satisfied; then hung up and dialled his home number.

'Yes? Hello?' It was his mother-in-law.

'Hello, it's a boy'

'Is that you, Colley?'

Colley looked at his reflection in the glass and cast his eyes upwards in sympathy with himself: 'Yes, it's a boy, and he weighs seven pounds eight ounces, or three point four kilograms as they say nowadays, and Genista is well, and sends everybody her love, and hopes the children are being good'

'Give her my love and tell her she's got to get plenty of rest'

'Yes, I expect she'll do that'

'When will you be home?'

'Are the children in bed?'

'Yes, they're reading – they're looking forward to seeing you'

'Give them my love, and tell them I'll see them in the morning, and they'll be able to see Mummy tomorrow probably'

'All right. Are you going to see Genista again?'

'I expect so ... I've been too busy to look at the times ... [not strictly true, but he must keep the upper hand] ... so expect me when you see me. Don't wait up'

'You'll be late then?'

'Might be. I'll get myself something to eat ...'

'I'll leave something out for you ...'

'No, don't worry. Good bye – and thanks for everything'

'Good bye ...'

Colley hung up, leaving his mother-in-law staring into the mouthpiece. Nikki and Giles had gone to bed; once he'd gone home he wouldn't decently be able to go out again – neither would he want to.

He thought the opportunity of not going home too good to miss; he owed his mother-in-law some company, but tonight he didn't relish the way she would cosset him, cook him some huge, plain meal he didn't want, and keep up a non-stop barrage of comment and criticism at a volume level even higher than that of the television which would form the focus of her attacks, turned up so that she could hear it from the kitchen. But, dammit, he was hungry, he realised; in that same moment he saw, smelt and tasted a Great Indian meal; the salivary pain was excruciating.

He found his car patiently waiting, drove to Chilton Crescent, and parked out of sight of his house. He was now intent on celebrating, even if he had to celebrate alone. He walked back to the Market Square, going the long way round to avoid passing Chaite's flat. Half of him would dearly have loved to have seen Chaite; the other half was all too well aware that an out-of-office meeting must surely be incompatible with his new office of fatherhood. He went into the Great India Restaurant, greeted with familiar smiles and deferent movements by the staff – but he hardly noticed, for there in the far corner, studying the menu, sat Chaite. Had Providence come to his rescue; made up his mind for him, as so often She did? Should he go to a different table and pretend not to notice her?

'Don't want to upset Providence' he said to himself ... just as Chaite looked up and smiled beckoningly at him. He went over to her table.

'Congratulations – come and join me. I've only just sat down'

'Thanks. How did you know?'

'It's all round the office ... well, not in so many words, but everybody knows where you went, and I don't suppose you'd be here if it weren't congratulations. I'm going to get you a drink – what'll it be?'

Chaite exercised her will on a waiter – she had restaurant presence – and gestured towards Colley. The waiter flourished a menu and a wine list in elaborately-tooled maroon carapaces before him:
'Yes, Sir? Something to drink?'
'A pint of draught Guinness – NO – let's have some bubbly'
Chaite didn't restrain him as he chose a modestly priced candidate.
'Are you ready to order Sir? Madam?'
'Oh ... four poppadoms and a sumbol tray – please ... and a sweet sherry and ... [to Chaite] ... have you a drink coming?'
'Yes, I've ordered a G&T'
'Gin and tonic, Madam? Very good'
The waiter melted before he could be reprogrammed. They waited. Then three waiters bore down on their table with four poppadoms, a sumbol tray, two gins and tonics, a sweet sherry and a pint of draught Guinness. A fourth arrived with the cooler and bubbly. Chaite and Colley laughed quietly, relaxed with one another in the oneness of the moment.
'Well?'
'Well what?'
'What is it?'
'Oh, I can hardly believe it. Two boys and a girl'
'TRIPLETS???'
'No – another boy – two ... [he saw she was teasing] ... you know what I mean ... [He felt he ought to keep things going] ... He weighs just over seven and a half pounds. Three point four kilograms to be precise'
'And Genista?'
'I can't remember what she weighs ... [Colley wished he hadn't said that] *And* he's got all his ... um. Do you know, it's Genista's birthday tomorrow? Isn't that strange? What are you going to eat? This is on me, of course'

The choosing was uneasily punctuated by that ambiguous noise which is either the cook scraping rice in a pan or the proprietor clearing the saveloys out of his throat.

Chaite was hungry – she had been working hard all day and had missed lunch. Colley had been working hard, albeit vicariously; he too was ravenous, in spite of his lunch. Their meal lasted a long time, from chicken tikka via king prawn mossolla to kulfi. They got through two celebration bottles. A succession of waiters with satyrical smiles enquired as to their enjoyment of the meal.

Their conversation was pleasant, but less animated than it might have been of yore. Colley thought that it lacked sparkle because they were both tired; Chaite knew that it was because her liaison with

Colley was nearing its end. She liked Genista very much, and refused to be the instrument of any unhappiness. Colley just needed saving from himself; strange that such a man of business should be so ignorant of reality. He would get over her departure quite rapidly; she hoped – expected – that he would become absorbed in his newly-extended family. The time for her to leave had come.

'Coffee, Madam? Coffee, Sir?'

They looked at one another.

"No thank you"

Before Colley could ask for the bill, the waiter dematerialised again. After some age, Colley was able to catch an eye and make the scribbling-on-the-palm-of-the-hand sign that universally achieves instant results. Chaite rose to pay a visit to the loo. The bill arrived on a plate.

'Do they wash them before recycling them?' Colley wondered as he surreptitiously slid his Access card on to the plate. The waiter bore the arcana away for his rituals; the chit arrived with its total box empty.

'I thought service was included' said Colley, not unkindly.

The waiter peered at the chit as though he had never seen it before: 'Sorry, Sir, you are right, service *is* included'

Unhurriedly, he performed gradus secundus: scrutiny of signatures, checking of carbons, parting of perforations, return of regalia.

Chaite reappeared, having realised that Primrose Cottage lay between the Great India and Chilton Crescent.

'Well timed'

The waiter vanished; rematerialised at the door, holding it open: 'Thank you, Sir. Madam. Good night'

"Thank *you*" they said, stepping out into the warm May evening.

'Where's your car?'

'I left it at home so I could celebrate ... I'm on foot' he added unnecessarily.

They strolled along. He tried to take her hand, but she avoided his approach. Yet, this was not the night to deflate him completely, so she sought out his and grasped it. And still Colley got the feeling that she was beginning to elude him. He stopped; sat down on a low wall.

'What's the matter?'

'I feel slightly ... it'll pass ... the food's excellent, but I just don't like their coffee'

'You didn't have any of their coffee ... [Chaite came straight to the point] ... do you want me to invite you in for coffee?'

'Er – oh – YES – thank you' Clumsy Colley.

They reached Primrose Cottage; Chaite got out her key. Colley
followed her up the steps; they went in. Miss Primrose, ears like those
of a hawk, called up stairs: 'Can you come down a minute, Chaite? I've
got something I must tell you'
'Can't it wait? I'm very tired ... [Even as she spoke, Chaite feared that
Miss Primrose would come up and find Colley and get the wrong idea] ...
all right – I'm coming. But I'm nearly asleep ... [she would be huffing
alcohol and curry all over her landlady – explain in advance] ... I've
been celebrating'
'With your friend?'
Chaite had reached Miss Primrose's sitting room; she deliberately
stayed standing, by the door: 'Yes?'
'I had The World, Judgement Reversed, Knight of Coins, Six of Swords,
and Six of Batons'
Chaite knew that whatever it meant it would touch her condition
somewhere: 'Were you Consulting for me?'
'Yes. You're going to bring something to a successful conclusion; it's the
end of one of your cycles of destiny. At the same time, you'll feel some
sense of loss, some guilt, perhaps that you're being punished for some,
failure. However, don't worry – you're following a code of honour based
on the highest moral principles and values of mankind. You'll have to
work hard to do this; you may even have to move away from the
problem – or danger – I'm not sure what it is. But your victory over
adversity will be complete, and you will emerge pure and shining.
That's all'
'All? It sounds as if – whatever it is – I'm in for a change'
'I should think so, dear. Good night. You'll sleep well, I know'
Chaite made her way upstairs. She could tell by the lights that Colley
was in the kitchen; now she could hear him making coffee.
'What was that? What did Madame Sosotris want? Oh ... you look
done in'
'Oh, Colley'
Chaite sat down, and burst into tears. She laid her head on the table.
Unsure what to do, Colley sat down beside her and tried unsuccessfully –
for it was topologically impossible – to put an arm of comfort round her.
'Come on, drink your nice coffee and go to bed'
He had some far-fetched and fleeting notion of accompanying her, but
knew that it would be inadmissible. Chaite recovered, reached for the
kitchen roll, blew her nose, wiped her eyes. How much should she tell
Colley? Not that there was anything in the Tarot, of course, but what
Miss Primrose had said was in no way at variance with her own

deliberations and conclusions. Yet if she told Colley, he would be bound to think that she was letting the cards influence her.

'I had a few things on my mind ...'

'Don't I know it?'

'... and I'd sort of decided what to do and, funnily enough, everything Primmy said sort of confirmed it'

'And what *are* you going to do?'

'I'm going on holiday in July, and I was wondering where to go'

'Are you? Yes, I remember. Where are you going? You don't need cards to tell you that, surely? ... [He put on a conventional ghostly voice] ... You're go-ho-hing on a jou-hour-ney ...'

'I think I'll go and see my sister. But right now I'm go-ho-ing to turn you out because I'm go-ho-hing to be-hed'

She joked to show that, though she was serious, she was not unkind. Colley went like a lamb. It was a lovely night. He was home and into bed in no time. Nobody heard the coming of him. In the morning he couldn't even remember trying to go to sleep.

10
Wednesday 7 – Sunday 11 May 1986

Chaite sometimes saw her mind as a safe deposit vault – a series of discrete discreet lockable boxes into which thoughts and memories were sealed, never to be retrieved if that were the way it was to be. Thus it was that details of her accident were locked in a box within a box; in the outer box was the 'official' story; it was to this that she had access when needed.

Other locked boxes in her vault related to her intercourse with Colley. If anything had happened between them of which she should be ashamed, it would be locked in a box. And since no 'official' story would ever be needed, that box, if indeed it existed, would be unmarked.

Chaite had found tremendous pleasure in the company of Colley. They had fallen easily into conversation on what seemed, at the time at least, profound topics, and she knew that he had enjoyed it as much as she had. But Colley was ten years older than she, and they were still at an age when that made a difference – ten years was more than a third of her life and, yes, that made one hell of a difference. But what was more important was that Colley was a husband and father and, enjoyable as the liaison was, Chaite had no desire to prevent his performing his roles unencumbered.

He worked all hours anyway; that he should prolong his absences by dallying with her was untenable. Had she been able to see into the future she would never have let the alliance begin; now at least four factors intervened to deter her from stopping it.

1 She couldn't deny that she enjoyed it.
2 Colley certainly enjoyed it.
3 Colley was the boss and she felt uncertain enough of the big world to want to stay at WEL – anyway, she liked it there.
4 Just as a soldier can shoot to kill in times of war, his finger would rest less easily on the trigger were he to know his adversary personally, for that would make him a murderer.

In this sense, Chaite was a soldier, not a murderer, for she did not know Colley's wife and family; she had never met them nor, as far as she knew, had she ever seen them. Colley seldom talked about them – certainly in no way which made either him or Chaite feel uncomfortable. Thus it was that Chaite stayed at WEL and she and Colley continued to meet very socially.

On Wednesday, it being that sort of day, Libby had invited Chaite out to lunch. They had gone to the Cold Collation at the Four Anvils and it was by chance that Elinor, a friend of Libby's, had joined them. Elinor was a partner in a firm of estate agents based at Addercote; having worked with James Sellis, Chaite and she had immediately hit it off. As a result, Chaite and Libby had taken an even longer and more enjoyable lunch break than they'd intended, and Chaite had been invited to a party at Elinor's that Saturday night. Elinor's cottage was in the middle of nowhere so Libby, by some spurious reasoning, suggested that Chaite should travel with her 'because she knew the way'.

The cottage was indeed in the middle of nowhere and Chaite was glad that she had neither to drive, nor to follow directions from Libby the scatterbrained – who got lost a couple of times anyway. Furthermore, she thought, not having to drive she would be able to drink.

When at last they arrived the party was going quite loudly, the majority of people congregated around the drinks table in the kitchen. Elinor greeted Chaite like a long-lost sister, throwing her arms round her and kissing her ... not that this was anything but par for the course, for Libby got the same treatment – as did everyone else Chaite saw arrive.

There were one or two other people from WEL that Chaite knew, but she found herself introduced into a small group talking about children's education. She didn't feel she could contribute much to that, so she drifted away to refill her glass and found herself in another group running down the NHS.

She was about to throw an hefty spanner into their works when the appreciation of the possible consequences of arguing with unknown people (she could imagine them all turning on her in some HM Bateman-like situation – 'The Girl Who ...') overwhelmed her and she drifted away to refill her glass.

It was at that moment that food was announced; thoughtful Elinor came up to Chaite and gave her a plastic picnic tray with compartments and a grip like that of an artist's palette:
'Here, you ought to be able to cope with this'
Chaite could – it was one of the best party tricks she had ever seen. She loaded it with buffet and moved away to refill her glass; then began to enjoy her food.

A young man sidled up to her with a paper plate and a glass: 'My, you seem to be doing all right, where did you get that tray from? I always say you need three hands at this sort of do'
He didn't seem to notice how Chaite was holding the tray, and she saw no point in confusing him.
'My name's Arden – I'm a graphic designer'
'How do you do? My name's Chaite – I'm a people person – that's to say I'm in personnel'
'That must be very interesting – meeting new people all the time. Where do you work?'
'WEL'
'Where?'
'WEL – Wilkinson Electronics Limited. You mean you've never heard of it? How refreshing. Where do you design?'
'Oh, I've got a studio in Little Bygrave ... [he noticed Chaite start] ... do you know it?'
'Yes, my sister Mercia lives there. In Rock Lane'
'Not Rock Lane? What an amazing coincidence. We're on the corner of Rock Lane. Where does your sister live?'
'In the white house at the end of the lane – behind the pub'
'Is she quite tall? With long ... come to think of it, she looks extraordinarily like you, doesn't she?'
'So they do say. Do you know her?'
'We wave at one another as she walks – trots – past'
'That's Mercia ... excuse me'

There was a slight commotion as Libby, who had been standing nearby, seemed to crumple on to the floor like the yogurt-pot puppet as seen on Blue Peter. Chaite put down the tray, to Arden's astonishment, and went over to Libby. Elinor had arrived, and her husband and brother. They decided to carry Libby up to the spare room. There was nothing Chaite could do – 'Bang goes my lift home' she thought. She went back to refill her glass, feeling decidedly otherworldly. Talking to Arden about Little Bygrave would be an easy option, but ordinary people who say 'excuse me' at parties are seldom able to start again where they leave off. She refilled her glass yet again, thinking that she might as well be hanged for a sheep as for a lamb.

Elinor saw Chaite standing uncertainly and pushed through the crowd to Genista: 'Genista, you *must* come and meet Chaite'
Genista, who was being more than adequately flattered by an inebriated architect, once more wondered at the musts of meetings. Elinor steered her towards Chaite, shouting a potted history in her ear:
'Lives near you ... works at WEL ... mysterious accident ... must know Colley ... Chaite ... this is Genista ...'
Elinor melted, leaving them wondering what to say after they'd said hello.
'Hello ... can I fill your glass?'
'Thank you – it's here. Have you tried all these marvellous cheeses?'
'I'm just about to – the trouble is, you need three hands ... oh!'
Chaite laughed: 'People are always saying things like that to me – don't worry'
Genista changed the subject: 'I hear you're at WEL?'
'Yes ... most people are, don't you find?'
'Sooner or later. I expect you know my husband'
'Do I?'
'Colley ... hey ...'
Chaite felt as she looked, distinctly green. She had picked up her glass; swayed and reached out to put it on the table so that she could find something to hold on to. She missed, caught a pile of paper plates; a Leaning Tower of Pizza, layer upon layer, interspersed with chicken bones and handle-heavy knives; the whole structure cascaded to the floor; wine spilt; discarded spherical morsels – baby beets, pickled onions, stuffed olives – a boiled egg, even – rolled about among the feet of the assembly. Chaite swayed. Genista quickly deposited her own handsful on the table, put her arm round Chaite, and stumbled her to a miraculously empty sofa.

'Are you all right?'

A banal question. Genista produced a tissue from her reticule; she thought it might help. Chaite blew her nose rhythmically; an 0–6–0 tank engine. Genista had heard of her ... heard what? But, what was far worse, Genista was clearly very pregnant.

'Quite all right now ... you've heard about me?'

'Elinor gave me a potted biography before she introduced us ... are you sure you're OK?'

Chaite was lying back on the sofa, shaking.

'I need a drink'

'Are you sure? Hold on'

'Red ... please'

Genista pushed herself up, found a couple of likely glasses, gave a confirming Last-day-in-the-old-home through-squint at the light, and waddled off through the crowd to the kitchen. The inebriated architect still held sway, swaying. Now, he took no notice of Genista, who could hear him saying exactly the same things to someone else ... ['... so I said to Rod, I said: "you want to take a leaf out of Owen's book" ...'] ... as he had said to her. She shrugged to herself, searched for a bottle of red wine that wasn't empty, filled her own glass with a grape simulacrum. Back to the sofa.

'Here you are'

'Thanks. What have you got there?'

'Grape juice. I'm driving ... anyway ... [she patted her tummy] ... Mmmm. Now are you sure you're all right? What was it that Elinor was telling me about you?'

'Oh ... I'm the people person ... [suddenly something dawned on her] ... what did you say your name was?'

'I didn't – Elinor did. It's Genista'

'Oh ... I thought she said you were her sister'

Suddenly, Chaite became daring. She indicated Genista's shape – 'Is that your first?'

'No, we've two already – Nikki's nine and Giles is just seven'

'And where's your husband?'

'Colley? He had to go away this weekend of all weekends and set up some ponky semiconductor deal in Glasgow. Why it couldn't wait, heaven alone knows. He always seems to be away these days'

Chaite winced inwardly.

'Is *your* husband here?' asked Genista.

Chaite winced outwardly: 'No fear ... er, that is, I'm not married ... er, well ... he left me'

Genista had another tissue at the ready. She was all set to explore Chaite's marriage, but at that moment Elinor materialised looking conspirational: 'Will you be able to take her home?'
She explained about Libby.
'Well ... I was about ready to go ... [Genista patted the old excuse once more] ... if you don't – she doesn't – think it too early for her'
'Would you like some coffee? I think there's some on ...'
Genista knew it wasn't anything like coffee time at an Elinor party; her ears filled with uncomfortably swelling chatter. She looked at Chaite's glazed gaze and was certain that it was time to go.
'I'll just get my coat; did you have one?'
Chaite wobbled to her feet ... ['No, I didn't bring one'] ... and made apologetic thanking noises at Elinor.
'Genista's going to take you home' said Elinor in a does-he-take-sugar sort of voice, seemingly having forgotten that that was why Chaite had risen.
Chaite was in a turmoil, but it was too late now not to go home with Genista.
'All right then!'
That was too sharp; she smiled at Elinor:
'That's very kind of her; very kind of you, too'
She made her way into the hall so as to create minimum disturbance, pushing her way through the crowd, nodding '''Good-night'''s, acknowledging '''Going already?'''s, '''Nice to see you again'''s, '''We must meet up sometime'''s – conventions, some from people she'd never met, a remark in your direction, then turn back to the business in hand. The guest who leaves a party is as useless and forgotten as a solved crossword clue.
    Genista was at the foot of the stairs, having sorted out her coat. Final pleasantries and kisses were exchanged. Off with the old and on with the new – the door shut just a little too quickly behind them as they debouched into the chilly, starry night, and the party went on without them.
'Where did I park? ... [Genista fumbled for her keys] ... Where's my quaint old half-timbered car?'
'Here's one ... ' Chaite was elaborately inscient.
'The key seems to fit; this must be it' rhymed Genista.
She unlocked the doors and they got in.
Chaite couldn't close the door. She got out unsteadily.
'What's the matter?'

'Silly me. The door's stuck open – resting on something. I must be putting on weight. All right now'

She ungraunched the door and got in again. Stay silent; you'll give yourself away. But *does* Genista know about me? She could be acting. Wasn't she into amateur theatricals?

'Have you ever done any acting?'

'Yes ... why do you ask? Have you seen me in something? I was Dorinda in *The Beaux' Stratagem* last month. The lump made it even funnier'

'I *did* see it. "So – she's breeding already" Was that you? You were magnificent'

Chaite was relieved, and looked sideways at Genista with warm admiration.

'Thanks. I think it was good. Everybody said so – except *The Telegraph*'

'Rushton? He doesn't count. Bet he never even saw it'

She became daring again: 'Where do you live?'

'Chilton Crescent. Number 5'

Chaite knew perfectly well. The rose that must be tied up because it fell on people. The gate that needed mending. The lawn that wanted cutting. Must, need, want.

'Colley loves it ... he says ... [That wasn't Chaite's Colley] ... but he never does much to show it'

That *was* Chaite's Colley. Why was Genista telling her this?

5 Chilton Crescent. Genista swang into the drive and pulled up with practiced quiet. She got out, shut the door, and went round to release Chaite. Chaite looked closely at the looming shape of the house street-lit. Genista opened the front door; ushered Chaite into the sitting room where lights flickered as guns blazed over the stirring music of sun-baked plains. She snapped on a standard lamp, and snapped off the television. Silence reigned.

'Do sit down'

Chaite sat down. Was this Colley's favourite chair? Genista was bending over the sofa. An incredibly willowy figure in tight T-shirt and jeans slept *en escargot*, much to Chaite's surprise. She uncoiled.

'This is Fiona. She's been baby-sitting. This is Chaite'

'Hi'

'Hi'

'All quiet?'

'Not a sound. I've been asleep'

'Coffee?'

Fiona rose:

70

'No thanks. Better be getting back. Do you want me next week? I've got second-year exams'
She picked up her books. To Chaite: 'Night'
'Night – Fiona'
'Night – Chaite'
Fiona moved into the hall with Genista, discussing details of diaries. Money changed hands. Footsteps and doors. Genista returning.
'Now, about that coffee. How do you like it?'
'Black, please ... no sugar ... can I help you?'
'No, it'll only take a minute'
Kettle filling, cups rattling, some old washing up. Chaite looked hazily round the room. There were some pieces she would have been proud to own had she lived in that sort of house. Others she would have been ashamed to have bought from – or even to have given to – a jumble sale. Chaite and Genista went to different sorts of jumble sales. She was amazed at the precarious piles of intermingled LPs and colour supplements in the alcove. She was astonished at the tangled mass of clothing in a basket on the piano, arms and legs hanging from an amorphous centre, an enormous knot of knitted netsuke. But most of all, Chaite noticed the pictures, hung with expediency rather than taste, wherever there happened to be a space. Had she been less well brought up; had she felt less tired, had she not divined Genista's imminent return – Genista's domestic immanence, even – she might have risen and peered at the pictures. She didn't. Genista returned with the tray: 'Here you are then ... [She put it down] ... Can I help?'
'No, thanks, I can manage'
Now Genista was flustered: 'I'm sorry ... I didn't mean ...'
Chaite laughed: 'Please don't worry. I'm used to it'
'How ... ?'
'It was a car accident. I was pushed off the road into a ditch late one night ... I was trapped, and by the time they found me, it was too late to save it'
She rather liked that one.
'Did they ever find ... ?'
'No'
'So what happened?'
'Nothing much. I learned to live right handed ... 'cos I was left-handed. So now I'm at WEL'
'That's clever of you. Don't you find it ... ?'
'Sometimes. But I don't spend much of my time at the keyboard ... for example. And anyway, the miracles of word processing ...'

'Can you do that? I don't understand it myself, though Colley tries to tell me. He says it's easy, but ... "Come, my dear, we'll talk of something else ... I'm sorry, madam, that it is not more in our power to divert you; I could wish, indeed, that our entertainments were a little more polite ..."'
Genista broke off, confused.
'Go on, Dorinda. What's happened?'
'It's rude – to you – "... our entertainments were a little more polite, or your taste a little more refined" Sorry'
Chaite laughed: 'Don't mind me, I love the voice'
Genista thought again: '"My lord has told me that I have more wit and beauty than any of my sex"'
Chaite winced and tried not to look sullen; to herself she thought: '"But I'll lay you a guinea that I had finer things said to me than you had"'
Genista must have known this, but the significance of the line was lost. Chaite hoped.
They fell to talking of the play. Chaite asked: 'Did you know that Farquhar's original title was *The Broken Beaux*? And that at the time it was advertised simply as *The Stratagem*?'
'No ... but perhaps it changed to *The Beaux' Stratagem* because it helps to sustain the archery theme ... I've always wondered about that apostrophe'
'Ah, yes ... Bows, Beaux', Archer, Aimwell ...'
'And Aimwell calls me – Dorinda – "the sharpest arrow in his quiver" – and did you realise that none other than Colley Cibber took the part of Gibbet the Highwayman when the play opened in 1707 – and the second night was his benefit night?'
'No – how odd! Was your Colley named after him?'
'I think there's some sort of connection, but I'm not sure what. I don't think he is, either'
They fell to talking of the parallels between *The Beaux' Stratagem* and *The Beggar's Opera*.

Colley paid off the taxi at the end of the Crescent to avoid waking his immediate neighbours – not to mention Genista. If she was back from Elinor's party. But it was after one o'clock in the morning ... and Genista was heavily pregnant. She must have returned. Or perhaps Fiona was staying the night. Or perhaps ...
 He stood putting change away, checking his pockets for things he knew were there, but whose absence would throw him into a flat spin ... Almost as though he were seeking excuses for not going into the house. He picked up his overnight bag and his briefcase and consciously plodded

wearily his homeward way. He heard some unidentifiable ornithological sound. 'I thought I heard an owl mope' he said to himself; then laughed uncontrollably at the image of himself and Genista in bed, the Thurberian seal replaced by an owl.

There was the quaint old half-timbered car. And the downstairs light on. So Genista was back, but not in bed. She had returned from the party with a man. They were having a night-cap. Fear overcame hope overcame fear. He would storm in, discover them, storm out again, and go straight round to see Chaite. But suppose Chaite were out? Or unwilling to receive him? The sequence lasted but a few microseconds; he couldn't countenance that ... could he?

He put down his cases, and crept up to the sitting-room window. But the curtains, which normally refused to meet in the middle, seemed to have cured themselves. He thought he could hear Genista talking. He thought he could hear the rumbling of a man's voice.
'Good evening, sir!'
He swang round, to see a caped policeman who had arrived, silent as the bat he resembled, on his bicycle.
'Good evening ... officer. It's all right – this is my house. I've just got back from Scotland, and I wanted to see if my wife was up so that I wouldn't disturb her unnecessarily'
He got out his keys, went to the front door, and unlocked it. He picked up his bags and faced the policeman: 'I hope that's all right?'
'Very good, sir. Good night, sir'
'Good night. Nice to feel we're protected. Good night'
What a relief; no point now in even thinking of going round to see Chaite. He went indoors with his cases, and stood in the hall uncertainly. He could hear Genista standing by the door, talking on as she did with her hand resting on the door knob. Who was this Captain Macheath she was talking about? The door opened. Genista emerged.
'Ooooh! Darling ...'
'Here I am, darling. Surprise, surprise'
'Colley ... Why the hell didn't you ...?'
'Didn't know I'd be back. Thought you'd be out'
'What, at *this* time of the morning? ... [she remembered Chaite] ... anyway, I've brought someone back from the party'
Colley went into the sitting room: 'Chai ... Kind of cold out ...'
'Chaite, this is my husband, Colley'
'Yes, we've met ... at WEL'
'Of course you have'
'Don't get up'

73

"How d'you do" they laughed at one another.
'Sit down Colley, and I'll get some more coffee. We've just been talking about you'
Genista went.
'Was it a good party?' Act natural.
'Very good, thank you. How was Glasgow?'
'Fine – was it a good party?' Bis; flustered Colley.
'Very good ... [she decided not to tell Colley that Libby had become incapable] ... Your wife, Genista ...'
'That's her name'
'... was kind enough to bring me home for coffee when I was overcome'
'Overcome with what?'
'Oh, I don't know ... just ... overcome'
Genista returned: 'It's just making – why don't you sit down?'
'Er ... yes'
Colley was still hovering about; Chaite sensed that she was sitting in his chair; she got up and moved to the sofa.
'Don't ... thanks'
Colley sat down in his chair. Subconsciously he heard the electric kettle click off. Genista went out to the kitchen; Colley leapt up again, excused himself and followed her.
'I think she's sweet ... [Genista, not telling on Libby] ... and she wasn't feeling well so she's going to stay the night'
Colley didn't realise that this was Genista's private idea; that it had not yet been put to – let alone approved by – Chaite.
'Fine!'
He returned to the sitting-room: 'I hear you're staying the night'
Chaite was about to deny this, when Genista came in:
'I haven't told her yet, but she is ... [she said] ... there's everything she needs in the spare room'
For some reason, Chaite felt unable to argue. And she's rather looking forward to seeing that spare room again.

After coffee, which none of them really wanted, Genista took Chaite upstairs, and there it was – the spare bedroom with its green washbasin, matching flannel, towel and soap all in place; a nightie – long sleeves; thank you, Genista – and a dressing gown laid on the bed; the sheet turned down. Chaite was charmed: '"It's very pleasant when you have found your little den ..." It's beautiful ... what are these colours, by the way?'
'Oh, I can't remember ... they have such peculiar marketing names ...

Colley ... [she called downstairs] ... what are the colours in here?'
He came upstairs: 'What?'
'Chaite wants to know what these colours are – they look quite different in daylight – you know, their special names'
'Oh ... [Colley looked Chaite straight in the eye] ... *Morning sun* and *Forget-me-not*'
There was a silence. Genista broke it: '"Well, my dear, I'll leave you to your rest"'
'I'm sure I'll sleep like a log. What happens in the morning, by the way?'
'Nothing much ... good heavens, it's nearly three o'clock. Let's wait and see'

Chaite did sleep like a log, until she became dimly aware of rustlings and children's voices outside the door.
'Go on, *you* knock'
'No, *you*'
'No, *you*'
This could go on for ever; she called: 'Come in'
The door opened; Nikki carrying a tray: 'We've brought you some breakfast'
Chaite sat up, keeping her left arm under the bedclothes. She felt like nothing on earth: 'Thank you very much'
'No, Giles, put that chair there'
Giles obediently put the chair by the bed; Nikki put the tray on it.
'Thank you very much' said Chaite again.
She stretched out her hand:
'How do you do ... you're Nikki ... you're Giles ... I'm Chaite'
The children shook hands with the gravity of polite children.
'I know ... [said Nikki] ... Last time I saw you, you only had one hand'
'Is that why you're hiding it under the bed-clothes?' asked Giles.
There was no fooling children; Chaite uncovered her arm:
'When did you see me last time?'
'You were walking along with my Daddy'
Chaite, who had begun to feel better, felt sick again. Should she pursue this? She must know more: 'Where were *you*?'
'Going along in a coach on a school trip to the Zoo at Shalthorpe. And we went to the ruined castle at Marby on the way back. Where that big oak tree is'
The subject had changed – should she concentrate on the Zoo and the castle, or pursue the sub-serendipitous sighting?

'I work with your Daddy – we do walk along together sometimes'
'Why was he holding your hand?'
Chaite's mind was in overdrive: 'I expect he was helping me across the road'
'Yes, he takes us by the hand when we're crossing the road ... [said Giles] ... grown-ups ought to do that'
'Yes ... [said Chaite] ... Have you been to the Zoo as well?'
'We all went last summer. I liked the fish best. I want to have a quarium, but Mummy says I'll have to wait'
'My friend Sarah's got an aquarium ... [Nikki getting it deliberately right] ... Would you like me to pour your tea for you?'
'Yes please'
Giles considered: 'Which of these little packets of cereal would you like? ...   There's All Bran, and Coco Pops, and Special K, and ...'
'I'll have the Special K. Would you like to open it for me?'
'Yes. I don't expect you can manage very well' Serious Giles.
'Silly – she has to manage at home' Brisk Nikki.
'It's nice to be waited on for a change'
'Where do you live?'
'Primrose Cottage, opposite the church, overlooking the Market Square'
'That's not very far away – why are you staying in our house?'
'I went to a party with your Mummy ... [that seemed like a stroke of genius in the circumstances] ... and she brought me home afterwards and invited me to stay'
Giles had opened the packet and managed to empty most of the contents into the bowl. He poured on the milk, and then offered the bowl to Chaite: 'I'll hold the bowl for you and then you can eat your cereal'
'Thank you very much' said Chaite yet again.
She pushed herself up and started to eat.
Genista put her head round the door: 'I hope they're not worrying you. Perhaps you'd better leave Chaite in peace'
'She couldn't eat her breakfast without me' said Giles importantly.
Chaite saw no need for a discussion centring on her: 'They're being very sweet. I like children – my sister's got four – two of each. A bit younger than Giles and Nikki. They live in Shalthorpe – where the Zoo is. So it's nice to have these to talk to'
'As long as they're not worrying you. Anyway, I expect Chaite will want to get up soon, so then you must leave her alone'
'Of course we will, Mummy' Nikki, half disdainful.
'Don't you want us to help you dress?' Giles doubtful.
'I think I can manage' Chaite laughed; children were refreshing.

'Well ...' Genista withdrew, looking like a doubtful mother.
'We're going to have a little brother or sister ... [said Giles] ... Did you
see our Mummy's tummy?'
'Yes. When will that be?'
Nikki took over: 'About the end of May, Mummy says. I'd like it to be a
girl'
'I've got one sister ... [said Giles] ... I think I'd like a brother now. Why
can't Daddies choose when they plant the seed?'
'Perhaps Mummies could choose ... [mused Nikki] ... I'll choose a girl
when I'm a Mummy'
Chaite felt a bit out of things: 'Perhaps it's better to have a surprise. I
think I'd like to get up soon'
Nikki took charge: 'Come on, Giles. She – Chaite – wants to get up now.
Put those things on the tray, and let me carry it'
A grave little procession left the room.
'Good bye ... [called Chaite] ... and thank you'

Washed, dressed and armed, Chaite went down to find the sitting room a
hive of silent activity. Colley and Genista were working on the prize
crossword in the *Observer*; Nikki was sewing something for school; Giles
was constructing something complex from his birthday Lego.

Seeing the domestic scene made Chaite realise with a jolt just what
an outsider she was. Colley at work was one thing; Colley with her was
another. Now here was a third Colley – perhaps the real one – the one
upon which the other two encroached. Colley needed to be at work to use
his technical and managerial abilities. At home, he had his family.
With her, he was in a no-man's-land; he ought to be able to do well
enough without it. Thus did Chaite for the first time see her
relationship in its true perspective – and she didn't like the look of it at
all.

Thank God Genista didn't know. Or did she? From now on, her
relationship with Colley must be strictly professional. Could she
maintain this stance? She resolved:

I must be cruel only to be kind;
Thus bad begins, and worse remains behind.

Colley smiled:
'How did you sleep – on a log scale one to ten?'
'Oh, nine ... no, ten'
'Good'

Somehow, without stirring, the family welcomed her into its bosom. But their very kindness made her feel even more of an intruder.
Genista stood up: 'Now Chaite's here, I'll get us something to eat'
'Oh ... you haven't been waiting for me? That's good of you – let me help'
She followed Genista into the kitchen:
'You must think me an awful nuisance'
'Not at all. Colley's been telling me all about you ... [all about me?] ... you seem to have done a great deal for WEL'
'I'm glad he thinks so. I've certainly enjoyed my time there. It's only eight months or so, but I seem to have been there for ever'
'Eight months? I wonder why I've never heard of you before?'
'Perhaps I've only just started to make an impact'
Genista was scraping potatoes. Chaite surveyed the scene: 'What can I do?'
Genista looked at her quizzically: 'I'll tell you what I need, and then you can ... Five plates from that cupboard there; we can either put things on them or let people serve themselves'
'It's a bit like last night ... God, was it only last night?'
Chaite felt half queasy. Genista came to the rescue: 'Perhaps we'll let people serve themselves'
Chaite got out some dishes and prepared cucumber, shredded carrot, radishes and spring onions. Genista conversed relaxedly and easily. She was getting to like Chaite, and was looking forward to developing their friendship.

Chaite sat at one end of the table between Nikki and Giles. Colley faced her at the other end of the table; Genista was on his right, next to Giles. Genista presided over the food; the children talked gravely to Chaite; Colley in the main kept silent, marvelling at the eutrapely. Giles sat watching Chaite surreptitiously, and practising eating with one hand.
Suddenly: 'What happened to your hand?'
'Giles! ...'
Chaite looked teasingly at her right hand: 'Nothing. Why?'
'No, the other one'
'GILES!! ...'
'An shark got me ... [a pause] ... no; it was a motorcycle accident'
Colley knows, not necessarily that this isn't true, but that it's a new story. Genista is surprised, but keeps silent.
'What happened?'
'I got tangled up with a lorry'
'Did it hurt?'

'Of course it did ... but it got better'
If you could call it getting better.
Nikki felt a need to help: 'There was a girl at my school who broke her
collar-bone, and she had her arm tied up for ... for ages and she soon
learnt to manage'
'Yes ... [Chaite serene] ... one does'

Any awkwardness there might have been was past, as Giles tried to
imagine what it was like getting tangled up with a lorry.
Chaite thought rapidly: 'What are you going to call your baby?'
'It depends what his name is ... I expect we'll know when he's born ...
certainly not before'
'I'm named after my Auntie Nikki'
'I think Giles is a horrid name – why did you have to call me Giles?'
'Because Daddy and I liked it – it's a very nice name'
How can Chaite help?
'I've got a second cousin called Giles – I think he's a very nice person.
Stick with it; you'll be OK'
'Anyway, whatever the baby's name is, he – I always think of him as he
–'s all set to arrive on my birthday?'
'Oh? When's that?'
'May the twenty-seventh'
'That'd be a coincidence'
Colley's not sure about coincidences: 'Do you know how many people you
have to ask when their birthday is before you're more likely than not to
get two the same?'
'Three hundred and sixty-five'
'One hundred and sixty-nine'
'That's pancakes'
'A hundred'
'Two hundred and twenty-two'
'No, how many?'
'Twenty-three'
'Really? How's that?'
'Well ... suppose in a random selection of n days out of 365 – it's only the
month and the day, by the way; the year doesn't matter – anyway,
suppose in a random selection of n days out of 365 no day is counted more
than once. The total number of possible selections is 365 to the n. Yes?'
'Ye-es'
'And the number of selections in which no day is counted more than once
... [Colley reached for a piece of paper and pulled out his pen; he wrote:

365 x 364 ... (365 − n + 1)] ... is that; the probability is ... [he wrote again: 365 x 364 ... (365 − n + 1)/365^n] ... that. Now, if this expression equals a half, it's as likely as not ... yes? ...'

'... Yes ...'

'... as likely as not that two of the chosen days are the same. So if we write [he wrote: $(1 − 1/365)(1 − 2/365) ... (1 − (n + 1))/365^n = 1/2$] ... that, we can work out − take my word for it − that n into n minus one is five-0-six ... [he wrote: $n(n − 1) = 506$] ... from which you can see that n is twenty-three ... [n = 23, he wrote with a flourish] ... See?'

'We don't do sums like that at school'

'I'd like to be able to do sums like that'

'I'll take your word for it'

'I never was any good at maths'

'Look, it's quite easy ...'

'Yes, yes ...'

'Well, let's take some birthdays ...'

They listed birthdays of people they could think of until they got to Genista's grandmother: 'My grandmother was born on November the fourteenth'

'That's the same as Prince Charles'

'He's not on the list'

'No, but my sister's husband Rupert was born on November the fourteenth. And in nineteen forty-eight, too'

'That's it then'

'How many have we got on the list?'

'Let's see ... [Colley counts] ... nineteen. That proves it ... for this case, anyway'

Thus the meal returned to its magic.

When they finally rose from the table, Chaite was refused access to the kitchen; there was nothing for it but to doze in an armchair with a section of heavy newspaper. Now all the boxes in her brain − save that of the moment − were tight shut.

When she had been gently roused and enjoyed a cup of tea, she knew that it was time to go. Unhurriedly, she expressed her thanks. There was a lot of parting, and hopes that she'd come again. She stepped out into the evening feeling immensely sad that she'd just had the privilege of a glimpse inside a domestic scene which she might have continued to share, had it not been for the roses now bowing sarcastically at her from the fence.

When she got back to Primrose Cottage, she managed to avoid Mrs Primrose; she went to her sitting room, put on Beethoven's Ninth, and poured herself a gin and tonic – not because she wanted it, but because she truly felt like drowning her sorrows.

If she hadn't gone out with Libby, she wouldn't've met Elinor; if she hadn't gone to Elinor's party, she wouldn't've met Genista; if she hadn't met Genista ... and Nikki ... and Giles ... she wouldn't now be resigned to resigning.

And yet, it must all be Meant, she mused. That was why the Tarot 'worked' – everything was interlinked, and right from the very moment in which the universe had begun everything that would ever happen was laid down; the emergence and life of each particle was determined; the course of her life was there, the preparation and consultation of Mrs Primrose's Tarot pack – well, everything. There was no free will. There couldn't be. Could there?

'But ... [she thought] ... suppose I *hadn't* met Genista when I did. What might have happened then?'

Her mind boggled.

Sheltering in inevitability, Chaite felt a great burden lifted from her. And so it was that her relationship with Colley became strictly professional.

And so it was that Colley, knowing that something had changed between them since his trip to Glasgow, finally perceived that he couldn't serve both Genista *and* Chaite, and that Chaite knew which of them had to go.

11
Friday 30 August 1985 *et seq*

Colley and family arrived home on Friday after five days in the Lakes. They found cat Hervey decidedly off colour.

'Daddy, Hervey's not well'

'No, he's got a lump on his face – come and see'

There was Hervey lying listlessly in his basket. Genista appeared:

'There's a note from Mrs Drewitt; he's got some sort of abscess – I'll ring
the vet; we can have him neutered at the same time'
'Oh, that's really cruel'
'What's neutered?'
She went through to telephone; could be heard setting up Hervey's fate.
She returned to apprise Colley of the arrangements:
'You can take him in tomorrow between nine and ten and I'll pick him up
on Monday. There should be a cat box in the shed – if Carole brought it
back'
'What, they work on Saturdays?'
'Why not? It's animals'
Colley went to look in the shed; Carole had brought the basket back.
Thank goodness.

The next morning, Colley was up early, mowing the lawn, feeling
virtuous. After breakfast, he gathered the library books; then put
Hervey in the box and set off for the vet. All the way, Hervey kept up a
constant barrage of miaowling which Colley turned into a dialogue – or
was it a catalogue? – by interspersing the word 'Yes' in as many
different inflections as he could.
    As he walked through busy Saturday Foxworth, he amused himself
by imagining the scene in the vet's waiting room: 'There'll be an
assortment of high-backed dining chairs round the walls; in the centre
of the floor, an oak drawleaf table of the thirties laden with genteelly-
tattered copies of *Country Life*, *The Field* and *The Lady*. There'll be
people sitting all round, some with boxes; some with loose animals,
talking with a camaraderie you'd never find in a doctor's waiting room'
    He arrived at the premises and pushed open the door; laughed out
loud, since the scene was just as he'd imagined it – apart from the
people.
    He was the only one there – rapid transit. The door of the inner
sanctum opened, and a girl in a white coat ushered out a large, stooping
countryman with mottled skin, brown suit, and flat cap, leading a fat
old dog indeterminate on a plaited leather lead, acknowledging canine
instructions with flapping false teeth: 'Right you are ... thank you,
Miss'
'GOOD BYE, MR HATTON'
She forgot to stop shouting: 'WHO'S NEXT?'
Colley looked around elaborately: 'Not much choice. Where's
everybody?'

The girl laughed: 'It's one of those days. You should've seen it last Saturday. Come through, will you?'
Colley followed her through the door, which huffed shut in a seedy, veterinary sort of way. The girl examined Hervey.
'Right, I'll give him a shot of penicillin now – there shouldn't be any problem with that abscess'
It was dawning on Colley that this girl was the vet; though he had no need to feel embarrassment (for she could not have known that he'd mistaken her for a junior helper); he nevertheless felt himself reddening. First policemen, then doctors, now vets. Whatever next? He must be ageing rapidly. He tried to think of something to say: 'I believe my wife arranged for him to be neutered?'
'Yes; we'll do that this afternoon – your wife's picking him up on Monday'
'Right – what time?'
'There'll be someone here between five and seven o'clock'
She pulled out a card from a filing drawer: 'What's his name?'
'Harvey – with an E'
'Where?'
'Second – H–E–R–V–E–Y – pronounced Harvey. It's Johnsonian. We love him – only he's a cat. And a very fine cat indeed'
'Oh'
She took down Hervey's – and Colley's – particulars. While she did so, Colley reflected how much more difficult it must be to be a vet than a doctor, having to deal with dozens of different sorts of animals, none of which can tell you what's wrong anyway ... not that the majority of humans is much more articulate. How much larger than life vets seem, putting on old clothes and wellies, and administering pills the size of footballs, and wielding syringes as big as Saturn rockets, and climbing inside ungulates to help them give birth. Why do vets seem to make doctors seem so over-cautious – like mothers who keep their children on reins beyond school-leaving age?

Reflecting thus, he emerged into the sunlit High Street – and bumped into Chaite.
'Well, well ... [Colley felt incredibly original] ... we meet again. Hey ... you seem to have two arms ... [Should he have said that?] ... not like last time'
'Have I? Oh yes ... when we last met I was armless, wasn't I?'

83

Chaite was not usually so open with comparative strangers. And yet, though she had met Colley but once, she felt that she knew him intimately ... which, in a sense, was true.

'You? Harmless? Don't tell me ... how about coffee?'

'Ye-e-s. All right. Where?'

'The Olde Peacock Inn – over there' He gestured.

They picked their way through the shoppers, and found themselves at The Olde Peacock Inn where time was standing still even before Good King Edward popularised appendectomy.

They went in, made their way to the grandly-named Ballroom, and sat down. Chaite looked round, appreciating the architecture:

'I suppose this is the covered-in yard of an old coaching inn'

'Yes – it dates back to the fifteenth century ... [Colley taking a proprietorial pride in his knowledge of local history, sparse as it was] ... those brackets ...'

'The ones like cornucopias?'

'Yes ... they were cast in the last century by the Butterley Ironworks'

'Why do they use silken ropes to tie the walls together?'

Colley looked, then laughed uproariously: 'Oh-ho-ho – they're steel tie-rods – ha-ha – invested with fluff and cobwebs'

Chaite laughed: 'An investment truss?'

This was fun. An incredibly seedy waiter shattered the scene: 'Morning coffee for two? Sir? Madam?'

'Yes. Please'

The waiter withdrew. As if this were a signal, a trio – piano, violin and 'cello – struck up behind Colley. Startled, he turned; then subsided: 'I expected to see them on that musicians' gallery'

Chaite considered the cracks in the ceiling; the tastefully peeling paint: 'I don't think that would do – it'd all come crashing down'

'A heap of wood, plaster and strings – and imagine the noise'

'Prince Charles would visit it, and say "something must be done"'

'The musicians would be ordered to strike up something jolly, rather than *Abide with me*'

They fell silent, absorbed in the set; in spite of appearances, the musicians were euphonious and versatile. At last they finished; amid enthusiastic applause, the ageing trio shuffled out as only an ageing trio can.

'Perhaps they're suffering from enuresis diurna'

'Or diuresis eterna. I wonder if they were ever young?'

Coffee arrived, accompanied by a plate of genteel egg sandwiches, crust off, cress garnished; iced cakes which would have been more fattening had they been larger. Colley and Chaite looked at one another.
'Well, here goes'
The offering was surprisingly welcome; the coffee surprisingly good.
'I must remember this place' said Chaite.
'How could you forget it?' asked Colley.
They munched.
The trio shuffled back, licking their lips. The violinist exhaled cigarette smoke.
'Did you see that?'
'Yes – perhaps he's just come in from the cold'
'Perhaps he's in league with the devil'
'Paganini reincarnate?'
'Whatever it is, he won't last long'
'He seems to have lasted quite a long time already'
The 'cellist now took up his position behind a drum kit; on the bass drum was a circular placard announcing : 'Algy Hyde and the Key-tones'.
'What a name – hello, here's another'
Enter a tall, silver-haired man carrying an armful of saxophones to polite applause.
'One of your local folk heroes?'
'Yes. He's good ...'
The trio, now become a quartet, began to produce a sound reminiscent of Victor Sylvester – which appealed to that audience.
'Would you like to dance? '
'No thanks – it's a bit old fashioned ... anyway ...'
'Yes'
They sat back and enjoyed watching the dancing; some of those on the floor, they speculated, must have been shuffling round every Saturday for over fifty years.
Chaite asked Colley about his holiday. He told her at length. She didn't mind – and she didn't mind that he didn't ask her how her week had been.

At last the audience started to thin; Colley wanted to get to the library, and Chaite hadn't managed to do any of her shopping. They emerged into the High Street. Colley saw Chaite in a new light – a verbal sparring partner: 'We must do this again'
'Yes; I'd enjoy that very much'

He kissed her, furtively and lightly. She enjoyed that too ... and wondered how he would react when he found she was his people person.

Colley's weekend passed in agony. He would have to meet Chaite again – soon. But where – how – to find her? He could have saved himself the worry; when he arrived at WEL on Monday, he found a note from Chaite on his desk. When he'd got over the shock, he called her in: 'What on earth are you doing here? Why the hell didn't you tell me?'
'That's a difficult one ... I didn't know how you'd take it. Anyway ... I had an interview with Ted Crowe while you were away the first time, and it seemed to go all right, and I was able to start quickly ... so here I am'
'Well, I must say it's good to have you in the company ... [In spite of himself, Colley had switched into general welcoming mode] ... and I hope you'll enjoy it here. We have our little ways of doing things; I'm sure you'll soon get used to us'
'Yes – I hope you'll soon get used to me too'
Chaite's eyes twinkled. Then she clanged her social compartment shut, and went over the things she had to discuss with her research director. Colley was shaken, but not stirred. When they seemed to have finished, he ventured: 'I ... wonder if we could ... continue our conversation?'
'Probably not ... [his heart sank] ... but we could start another. I'd like to go to the Peacock again'
'We've got a few things to discuss ... in more relaxed surroundings. How about Friday?'
'My diary's yours – so to speak'

So it was that they met for lunch that Friday. The intervening hours were hell on earth for Colley. Everything he did seemed to be done by someone else. At home, he felt jumpy and snappy; he therefore said little for fear of revealing himself, so that Genista sensed there was something wrong anyway. He slept fitfully, thinking of Chaite. She was there as he dropped off, and she was there when he woke. It was a long time since he'd felt that way, and he comforted and excused himself by thanking God that he *could* still feel that way.

Friday came. Colley and Chaite went separately to the Peacock. There was no reason why they shouldn't have gone together for an official business lunch: the research director discussing manpower requirements with his personnel manager. For some reason, each thought that the other preferred the clandestine mode of arrival.

Chaite felt neutral about it. Colley, on the other hand, felt as though everyone was looking at him. The Ballroom was closed on weekdays; lunches were served in the Lounge Bar. Chaite was already there, seated at a discreet table with a half of shandy. Colley veered past: 'Anything else you'd like?'

'To drink? No thanks – but can you find a menu?'

Colley got himself a St Clements, and asked for a menu. The barmaid pointed: 'It's up on the wall'

'Yes, but we're sitting over there – we can't see it properly'

'I'm afraid you'll have to come closer then. We don't have portable menus'

Colley reported back: 'You should've brought your opera glasses'

'You should've brought your Polaroid'

They moved across to a place of visibility, chose and ordered.

Leaning forward at the end of the counter, Colley could see that the Public Bar was jammed with people, whereas the Lounge Bar was just comfortably crowded to the point of anonymity. Someone recognised him across the great divide: 'Hello, Colley – coming round this side?'

'Er – business meeting ... see you later'

The acquaintance returned to his loud cronies, Colley forgotten.

He sat down; knives and forks arrived, wrapped in paper serviettes; surprisingly well-groomed bottles and jars of sauces and mustards. Chilli con carnes on rice, in ubiquitous earthenware dishes, with chunks of brown bread and too much butter.

'It's the same the 'ole world over ... Where do they get all this British Standard food from? Is there a secret factory churning it out and distributing it to pubs everywhere?'

'I don't know ... but the menus seem remarkably the same these days – and not just in pubs. Take the sweet trolley for instance ... [Chaite simulated a waitressy voice] ... "There's sherry trifle, and figs in syrup, and oranges in grand marnier, and profiteroles, and Black Forest gâteau, and strawberry cheesecake ..."'

'Perhaps it's something to do with training courses?'

'No, I think there's a definite sweet trolley conspiracy – a foreign power setting out to sabotage British business by overfeeding the British businessman'

'And that's why the countermeasures bureau has come up with the keep-fit-and-healthy-diet movement...'

And so their lunches continued. Sometimes they went to The Olde Peacock Inn; sometimes further afield. Evening meetings had to be further afield. Sometimes they would talk seriously, sometimes frivolously. Wherever and whatever, Colley found it immensely stimulating; found (he explained to himself) some new joy in life; in living. He told himself that he had never met anyone like Chaite. Just to catch a fleeting glimpse of her in the corridor, or crossing the car park, gave him a frisson – as did seeing anyone who bore some vague resemblance to her in the distance. He really wasn't sleeping at all well; he would wake in the small hours and lie thinking of Chaite, recalling what he thought of as her words of wisdom – how she made him think again; live again.

He recalled every new facet of exploration.
'What do you think of Millais?'
'Ooh ... the painter. "From today, painting is dead"'
'Ha, d'you think so? From what I know of the way they carried on, it took them longer to compose a photograph than to paint a picture'
'Surely not? Think of Lizzie Siddall lying in the bath in Gower Street in December, and Millais reporting at the beginning of March that he'd finished the head. Think of the detail of the flowers – *Ranunculus penicillatus* var *calcarius* (R W Butcher) C D K Cook. You can't get much more esoteric than that'
'Yes, and what about Holman Hunt painting *The Light of the World*, having "an imitation door with adjuncts" built in his studio, and painting by real moonlight until four in the morning "until it no longer suited"'
'It's not just the PRB, is it? What about Marcel Duchamp and all his elaborate preparations of randomness – for the *Large Glass*, for instance'
'*The bride stripped bare by her bachelors, even*. And the ninety-four documents of the *Green Box*'
'Turn to box ninety-four. It's very odd that what started out as a sort of joke has turned itself into as much a revered work as the *Mona Lisa*'
'Has it?'
'Well ... one sort of feels that there's art there, even if the original intention was ... Take the *Three Standard Stoppages* for example'
'Yes?'
'Duchamp visited Herne Bay in 1913 – I'm not sure what that has to do with it – but when he got back he took three long canvases, painted them Prussian blue, and dropped on to each of them a thread one metre long from a height of one metre. As they fell, the threads "twisted at will" ... and he glued them down on the canvas with varnish, just as they fell'

'And?'

'And then he cut the pieces of canvas and glued them on to strips of board, and the three were reverently housed in a wooden box – later to be used to derive some of the shapes for the *Large Glass*'

'This certainly seems to be a more painstaking way of creating a work of art – if it *is* a work of art – than dubbing a comb or a urinal a "Ready-made"'

'Are you suggesting that the longer it takes, the more artistic it is?'

'No ... but I suppose you could say that what is constructed without effort is examined without enjoyment'

'Or you don't get out more than someone else has put in ... no, that doesn't make sense, either'

'It's ironic, isn't it, that Marcel Duchamp scribbled a moustache on the *Mona Lisa* ...'

'... L H O O Q ...'

'... yes ... *because* he thought that revering artists and placing enormous values on their works was ludicrous ... and now that defaced reproduction is itself priceless ... well, fairly priceless'

'I think that in the end he just sighed and lay back and enjoyed the joke ... if people wanted to revere his tomfoolery ...'

'"The picture's value is the painter's name" ...'

'Exactly. If you can't beat 'em, join 'em'

Colley revelled in it. He just wanted to talk. The doxy rationale – bore another man, lose another friend. But he'd never met anyone else who could match Chaite's knowledge – by which he meant, could he have but seen it, anyone else who had a field of knowledge sufficiently similar to his to provide the frisson. Why doxy? Heterodoxy is another man's doxy. δοκοσ – a shaft; δοχη – a receptacle. Strange, that.

How one's point of view can change from second to second – shimmering like a squid. Modified from without; continual monitoring. Do I think that I think in my head because I know my brain is in there, or because I can feel the thoughts there? My brain sits like a spider in a web – a super-arachnid – stretching out to the rest of the world; the whole of space. And the rest of space is stretching out to me, the web of life – everyone has a line on the surface of the globe starting where he was born and finishing where he is disposed of. The world's littered with thought-trails from those who've gone before.

And what happens when two thought trails run parallel in space and time – as do mine and Chaite's? I must discuss this with her. Colley tried, but it didn't gel. It was a big disappointment; why *couldn't* she see what he was driving at? What *was* he driving at? Had he got a message there that she couldn't see, or was there really no message? That one kept him awake for some nights, while he tried desperately to try to think what it was he was trying to think about. Eventually, he came to believe that there was nothing there to discuss, and forgot it. After all, there were plenty of other topics to explore.

They were talking about urban myths, a genre which had existed from time immemorial, but which suddenly seemed to have been recognised and categorised. Colley had told Chaite of a filler paragraph in the paper, which stated that some workmen, having been instructed to build a protective wall round an old ruin, had used material from the ruin itself to build the wall.
'"Thereby producing a wall built round a vacant space?"'
'How did you know? That's what it says here – have you seen it already?'
'No, but the story isn't new – I've read it in Harry Furniss's *Confessions of a Caricaturist*'
And so they had pursued the scale of Chaite's interest in and knowledge of the popular (and generally forgotten) writers and artists of the previous century, and Colley had marvelled at (the breadth rather than the content of) her knowledge. He could always see what other people *ought* to do; he remembered particularly an evening which had developed in Chaite's flat: 'You know so much about these people; you ought to write it down. Before it's too late'
'Sooner or later I will – I must. But at the moment, it's all jumbled up. It's ... pieces of fibre, before they're spun to make the yarn to be dyed and woven into the tapestry – and it's only the finished tapestry which is the useful outcome of the work – as far as anyone else is concerned'
'But not quite like that – you're not only the collector of the fibres; you're the spinner, dyer and weaver as well. "The umpire, the pavilion cat, the roller, pitch, and stumps, and all." You're not only the block of stone inside which the finished sculpture resides; you're also the sculptor herself'
'And the mallet, and the chisel, and the scaffolding ...'
'Oh, it's a big sculpture, is it?'
'Enormous. A veritable Ozymandias'
'Hold it. You've moved into a different ballpark. Something that big would be made out of separate blocks'
'So ... my work will be in several volumes'

'That's another difference: each volume will just be a book until it's opened; People will have to read it to find out what's inside. As far as the statue is concerned, it's only the external appearance of the assemblage of blocks which means anything'

'But each block contains an infinity of sculptures ... oh, all right. Anyway, I haven't got as far as the trunkless legs yet, let alone the trunk ... and the visage. All I've done up to now is a bit of blasting in a particular quarry of knowledge, and picked over a few loosened chippings'

'A Newton, "playing on the sea-shore and now and then finding a smoother pebble or a prettier shell than ordinary, whilst the great ocean of truth lies all undiscovered" before you'

'Mmmm ... Newton's truth was different from mine. He was surely concerned with mathematics and mysticism, masonry and mastery of the mint. Anyway, how could he equate the pebbles – my chippings – with the ocean? His analogy is pretty, but won't stand scrutiny'

'Very few analogies will if you try to carry them too far. Ours doesn't. But it's a framework on which to hang the development of thought. On one level, we use the analogy to explain something by equating elements of each. On another level, it's not the strengths but the weaknesses of the chosen analogy which help us to see the detail of the original'

'We always return to the Procrustean bed. The mistake people make is to think that there's something wrong with the original something if it doesn't have elements each of which exactly equates with those of the analogy'

'Well, in this particular case, we might ask if the loose chippings in your quarry could be ground up and cast into tablets of stone in cuneiform moulds – it's like printing books. How many books are concealed in a tree?'

'If you think there's a sculpture inside every block of stone ...'

'Not just one; an infinity. But once the sculptor has decided which one she's going to chip out, the stone takes on a different complexion'

'She probably never Frinks of the other possibilities; just the one she's homing in on. What I want to ask you now is whether you think that all piano music resides in a piano'

'Ouch. It would be a great deal more interesting to set up computer-controlled machine to play all the piano pieces which could ever be composed than to set up a typing engine to replace the monkeys who write Shakespeare'

'I've always worried about those monkeys. I mean, Shakespeare himself has already done Shakespeare, and you'd be bound to come across a lot of other writers on the way – past and future. And just think: the monkeys get through the whole of Hamlet, almost to the end, and then you find "thy rent its solace", or "braxinofalch" ... it spoils the whole thing. The problem is, you – someone – would have to read it all to evaluate it. And it might be in any language expressible in the set of characters your print-out machine will produce. Language is so flexible, and there are so many languages'

'My goodness ... if you used a dot-matrix printer ... I can't stand it'

'Well, this is worse: a television screen which will run through every picture you could ever have on a television screen. It would thus be able to show you anything – and everything – that had ever happened, or ever could happen. Not that there would be enough time ...'

'With music, it's universal – well, it transcends the boundaries imposed by language. You could *listen* to it rather than have to read it. And you could allow yourself a little programming artifice to limit the potential cacophony, and work up to the more esoteric possibilities slowly'

And it was here that they had picked up God's omniscience and explored the possibility of time running at different rates, if only to give the people in heaven a chance to keep up.

Colley returned home to Genista. He told himself that it was early – only 10 o'clock – and that he was making a great sacrifice by leaving such an interesting discussion early. It was a wonderful gesture, he thought, tearing himself away from the knife-edge intellectual excitement of Chaite and returning to the cozy calm of Genista.

As he approached his house, he could see that all the lights were out. So Genista was either watching television or in bed. Damn, damn, damn – if Genista had gone to bed, why had he bothered to come home early?

He thought of going back to Chaite; then realised that there was no way of recapturing the conversation; that it was futile to expect that it could just be picked up again from the point at which it had left off, as if nothing had happened. To avoid making a noise, he switched off the engine so that he could coast into the drive silently. Hervey the cat (usually lovable; now clubbable) appeared from nowhere, and Colley had to brake, losing his impulsion and getting the car stuck across the pavement. Damn some more.

He started the engine – which of course refused to fire immediately – and pulled into the drive, having made more noise than if he'd never cut it in the first place. Somewhere a dog barked. An owl hooted. 'We ought to get some geese' he thought; 'do it country style'

There was no end to Colley's trouble – Hervey weaving in and out of his legs, the pirouetting milk bottles, the falling keys, the squeaking door, the Benares brass tray striking in the hall – resistentialism was rife. He stood for a moment; 'Hellish dark, and smells of cheese' he thought. There were flickering reflections on the ceiling of the sitting room. He pushed the door open quietly. There was the firm but genially abrasive question master, on his right the smoothie (he must be the MP) and the man in the dark shirt with hairy tie and corduroy jacket (he must be the educationalist); on his left the bishop (no mistaking his weeds) and a well-built floral black lady (she must be statutory – statuesque – a thin girl trying to get out – and what would you do with the residue?)

Genista lay on the sofa, snoring.
'Oh come, that was not what I said' ... 'You can hardly accuse me of being militant' ... 'It's essential to look at this from a moral standpoint' ... 'You only gorra looka the kids on the stree'corner near where I come from' ...
No wonder Genista snored again. Colley turned the sound right down but retained the picture, anxious not to miss it if – when – they came to blows. He knelt by the sofa and kissed Genista gently. She looked at him, not crossly, he thought.
'Oh Gosh ... [she held her head] ... How did it end?'
'The Sardinians gatecrashed the wedding and ate all the sandwiches'
'Cucumber?'
'And tuna, and prawn, and smoked salmon'
'Very fishy. What's the time?'
Colley massaged it: 'Just after ten'
'It's nearly eleven'
'It was just after ten when I came home'
'Where have you been?'
'Oh ... I worked a bit late, and then fell to philosophising. Have you ever thought how many books are potentially concealed in a tree?'
Colley's challenge.
'No, why should I? It's as stupid as angels dancing on the head of a pin Anyway, what's that got to do with anything?'
'It's a direct analogy with the sculpture inside the block of stone'
Half of Colley wants Genista to understand; the other half doesn't.
'Or the thin man trying to get out of the fat man?'
'Or the clown wanting to play Hamlet?'
'A cigar-shaped clown?'

Yes, the Genista frisson could be as strong as ever; undimmed by Chaite's contribution. That was a good thing. And yet Colley still thought he needed Chaite to develop his 'serious intellectual themes'. He thought Genista couldn't see his need to; he couldn't understand that Genista was somewhat wearied of his wonderful themes – she'd heard them time and time again. He'd invested her mind with an aura of black and white, believing that everything to her was either obvious or pointless.

Completely overlooking the fact that this was a figment of his fertile imagination working against him, Colley told himself that he wasn't in the least worried about it; he took heart from Chaite's dictum: 'You couldn't possibly expect to get everything you need from one person'

Chaite had thrown the remark away; Colley the self-centred had picked it up and polished it; had seen it as referring specifically to *him*; had used it to console himself; as an excuse to derive intellectual stimulus from Chaite. In this mode, he felt himself to be the centre of the universe. He got 'things he needed' from a number of people – not least Genista and Chaite – to each of them he exhibited (he thought) a specially-tuned facet of his personality. But he never thought that each of *them* might be saving a matching facet for *him* – he thought he owned them totally. Then he saw himself as a soap-bubble among soap-bubbles; as a cell in a plant, parenchymatous, touching his circle of cell friends ... until – as usual – the analogy burst asunder like the soap films themselves.

He didn't have to look far to appreciate that, in Genista, he had something beyond price; Genista, whom he had singled out to marry – and who, equally, had singled him out – Genista, who transcended Chaite – Chaite who had appeared by some divine Providence to complement Genista and give him, and receive from him, her share of things needed.

Self-centred Colley saw himself reclining on couch, laurel wreath on head, bevies of stylised Genistas and Chaites stroking his brow, feeding him grapes pendulous, nectar and ambrosia ... blessed office of the epicene.

Self-centred Colley never thought of Chaite's pronouncement as it might have referred to *her*. He somehow believed that it was *he* who supplied all her needs; that when he was not there, she went into some state of suspended animation – he could not bear to think of its being otherwise.

Stupid, arrogant Colley; dog-in-a-manger Colley; dangerous, jealous Colley. In no way did he own Chaite (she made quite sure of that), and yet he was wont to think as though he did. During the period of his obsession, he resented her having any life apart from the one they shared. He didn't mind being Chaite's slave ... as long as he was her master.

12
Monday 26 & Tuesday 27 August 1985

Monday morning; the events of the previous Saturday were locked in a safe-deposit box; there would be no need to refer to them ever again. It was Chaite's dream to be able to walk to work ... and here she was, living it on her first morning with a new job, making a new start. The walk took twenty minutes. As she entered the vestibule at WEL, she had a severe attack of the déjà vus, as though she had arrived there every morning since time immemorial. But this was a friendly feeling; it was not as if she was in a rut – she belonged here.

Jinny gave her a receptionists' smile.
'Is Ted Crowe in yet?'
'No, he's not in today ... [Chaite wondered if this were usual] ... but he's left you a long message in your office'
'Ah, yes ... my office. I've got an office?'
The feeling of belonging strengthened.
'Yes, and what's more, you've got plenty of work waiting for you'
'Well, that's what I'm here for. I only hope I'll be able to find out what to do'
'The only thing you'll have difficulty with is who's who, and that's where I can help you. Here's a telephone list, and here's a map of the offices. Now I'll give Dawn a ring and get her to show you where to go. She's Colley's secretary'
'Colley? Who's Colley?'
'The research director. He's very nice. You'll have a lot to do with him'
'Oohh ... I'll look forward to that ... [Chaite's heart beat erratically] ... is he in yet?'
'No; he's on holiday for another week. I'm sure he'll want to see you when he gets back'
'I'm sure he will'
So ... Colley was the research director. Dawn was his secretary. Ted was company secretary. Jinny was the switchbird. She was the people person. She knew five people already.

Dawn arrived; there were introductions. Chaite followed her up the main corridor. The light through the high windows was joyous at that time of the morning. Chaite wanted to ask how the light changed in the corridor as the days and seasons progressed, but decided it was too difficult to frame the question. Dawn was pointing out the loo, and explaining about coffee machines, lunch breaks and so on.

At last they came to Chaite's office – next door to Ted's, with a connecting door.

'Here's your office'

'I'd never have found it myself'

Chaite reflected that it wouldn't be long before she could find her way around the whole of WEL all by herself. She hoped.

Chaite sat at the desk – her desk – feeling even more that she belonged, and opened the drawers. They were not empty or untidy; they seemed to contain everything she might need. With mock importance, she said to Dawn: 'Take a seat, please'

Dawn laughed; explained time sheets and stores requisitions to her; then: 'But I'll confuse you if I go on much longer ... [Chaite thought to herself that she'd have to start putting a book of house rules together] ... And here's Ted's note, and here are the files he wants you to deal with. If there's anything at all you want to ask, just call me. I'm on the telephone list – here ... [Dawn pointed] ... You'd better deal with this one first: she's a wiring girl, coming for an interview at eleven o'clock – talk to Grace about her: that's the head girl; I'll take you to see her'

Colley, Dawn, Ted, Jinny, Grace ... I went on my holidays, and I took a toothbrush, and a comb, and a clock ... Talk about being thrown in at the deep end.

'Talk about being thrown in at the deep end' said Grace.

Dawn withdrew.

'We can only do our best ... [Chaite involving Grace with the Foxworth "we"] ... What do you normally do about interviewing wiring girls?'

'Well, normally, we give them a test. We've got some standard test circuit boards; for this particular job they've got to be able to pick the right components, get the diodes the right way round and so on. I know Ethel. She used to work for me at my last place. Before she had a family. I'd like to have her here'

'We ought to give her the standard test. From what you say, she should pass with flying colours, and if she can't we ought to find that out too. We must start the way we mean to go on'

Chaite wondered if she were teaching her grandmother to suck eggs.

'I agree. I wouldn't like anyone to think Ethel'd got the job because she knows me. And if she's lost her touch ... If you come through to the shop, I'll show you the things. I've got a bench ready for interview tests. Or I could bring them in here'

'I'll come through ... [Chaite stood up] ... and I can get a cup of coffee as well'

'It's not too foul this morning; the machine's just been done. Normally, I don't drink that stuff'

'Surely it's just as easy to make good coffee as bad coffee if the basic ingredients are OK?'

'You'd think so, wouldn't you?'

'Perhaps that's one thing I could get sorted out' said Chaite, feeling very important. She referred to a file Ted had left her; she discussed Ethel's rates of pay and conditions of employment with Grace.

She got back to her desk at about quarter-past ten, confident about Ethel's interview. Last week the interviewee; this week, the interviewer. She read Ethel's application form, which didn't tell her a lot except that she was 39 and couldn't spell much. A late starter, Ethel had left work eight years before to have a family – triplets, Grace had said – and her mother would look after them now. Chaite tried to think of a few questions which would advance her task of assessment, and to which she professionally wanted to know the answers, and scribbled them down in the margin of the form.

Prepared for the interview, she now turned her attention to the detail of the desk drawers. She opened them carefully in turn, noting the contents; then rearranged them with the things she thought she'd need most in the right-hand drawers. She arranged her telephone, and slipped an elastic band on to her desk diary – 'never been used, and the year two-thirds gone', she observed to herself.

She turned to the file containing her defeated competitors. Ted had left a list of the names in the front of the file; beside her own was YES!!! written in red. She knew he'd written it since her interview. She started to draft what would become her first standard letter, but the telephone interrupted.

'Double two double two'

It was an internal call; Bill Martin from the machine shop: 'Can I come and see you for a minute?'

'Of course – come now'

The telephone clicked; she had a reel of visions until there was a knock at the door and Bill Martin entered – nothing like she'd imagined, but as soon as she saw him, she remembered – a short, florid man with greying hair, wearing a white coat, his hands surprisingly clean and delicate.

'Sit down, Bill'

'Thanks – I can call you Chaite, can I?'

'Of course'

'I've come to tell you we need another toolmaker'

Chaite put aside her draft letter, and started to make a note. The telephone rang again.

'Double two double two'

It was Jinny: 'I've got a Mr Lee on the line. He's just moved to the area, and he wonders if we have any vacancies for toolmakers'

Chaite couldn't believe it.

'I'll talk to him ... [Chaite made a signal at Bill which he couldn't interpret] ... Mr Lee?'

'Hello ... it's Mr Lee here. I've just moved to the area, and I wonder if you have any vacancies for toolmakers'

'You're a toolmaker? ... [she spoke elaborately, to give Bill the message; Bill's face broke into a wide grin] ... May I have your address please? ... [Bill was indicating that he'd like Mr Lee to come in that afternoon] ... Can you come in this afternoon? About two thirty? ... [Bill was nodding frantically] ... I'll leave an application form in reception; get here about two, and fill it in for me, will you? ... Yes ... Good bye, and thank you for calling'

Hearing herself saying it, she almost added: 'Have a nice day'

Bill was looking at her admiringly. What a stroke of luck. It had been nothing but pure coincidence (hadn't it?) but she knew that the story would get round; perhaps from now on people would view her as some sort of miracle worker, disregarding every occurrence that didn't fit that view and attaching disproportionate importance and reinforcement to those that did. She looked at Bill:

'Do you want me to advertise as well?'

'A day or two won't make much difference – let's see this bloke, and decide after that'

The telephone rang again. Ethel had arrived.

Chaite's first interview went well, with Grace in attendance to supervise the wiring test; an offer made – and accepted; more gratitude.

So the day went on. Incredibly busy, Chaite wondered whether it always had been – and always would be – like this, or whether everything was happening because it was her first day. She managed to finish drafting her letter; she gave it to Dawn with the list of names and addresses; Dawn arranged for it to be printed out; Chaite signed them; they caught the post; Chaite felt tremendously virtuous. She started to sort out the other files and began to find out how little she really knew about this job.

In came Dawn: 'It's nearly quarter to six. Coming a-Woning? – that's to say, coming for a drink?'
Even as she said it, Dawn wondered if Chaite would get the impression that they were always going to the pub.
'Just over the road? OK. It'll help me to wind down'
'Are you wound up?'
'Not really, but I've got through an awful lot, considering how little I know, and it really does feel like the end of a day'
They went across to the Woning; Dawn showed her the Dutch woodcut ('Rembrandt's Woning') from which the Golden Lion took its WEL name.

There were a few people in the bar, mostly from WEL. Dawn introduced Chaite; no one minded talking shop (for it assuaged their consciences) and she pursued several trains relating to her new job. She also learned that there was an open-all-hours supermarket on her way home. The WEL party seemed inclined to disperse at about quarter to seven, so she set out to buy herself something special to round off her first day at work.

She finally chose a ready-cooked chicken and a selection of salad vegetables which would last her a few days, and a bottle of 'that delicious pink stuff we had at Margaret's' as the Queen was reported to have described it.

She got home in time to listen to a prom as she prepared and ate her meal. It was not until she had cleared everything up and settled back in the most amazingly easy chair that the excitement of the day gave way to consideration of the totally unreal events of ... when was it?

After the experience of her first day, Chaite looked forward to her second even more. Ted was back in the office today – anyone else would have been looking forward to impressing him with all the things she'd done, but Chaite expected to be efficient; one of her faults was expecting everyone else to be as efficient as she was.

Ted was in before her; he'd left a message with Jinny and another on her desk – in case he was away from his office when she arrived. Making assurance doubly sure. Chaite went into his office with an easy familiarity: 'Morning, Ted'

'Morning Chaite. How'd it go yesterday?'

'Swimmingly ... I interviewed a wiring girl – Ethel Craxton – and took her on – with Grace's help; found a possible toolmaker for Bill Martin ...'

'Ah! You want to watch out for Bill – he's always complaining that he needs another pair of hands ... [Chaite smiled as Ted flustered] ... and I'm not surprised he tried to take advantage of you – being new. You'll really have to check with Colley on that one. When he comes back. How have you left it?'

Chaite explained how the appointment came to be made and: 'Bill's seen him – I've got his notes here with the form'

'Right ... so if he seems suitable, you can tell him it was a preliminary interview, and you'll be reporting to the research director when he returns next Monday. And if he's not suitable, there's nothing to worry about. But I should have a word with Bill Martin ... and hold that advert till Colley comes back. What else?'

'I got off the letters to my rivals ... my erstwhile rivals ... with Dawn's help. And organised my desk. And looked through those files you left for me. Anything special you'd like me to do today?'

'We've got a group of engineers coming in for interview next Wednesday – a week tomorrow. Colley's back on Monday – as you know ...'

Ted went to his filing cabinet and pulled out a file; took it to his desk and sat turning over the papers ruminatively.

Chaite waited: 'Yes?'

'Oh ... memories. This is the group interviewing programme we've rather sunk into ... [he passed her a sheet of paper] ... They arrive about eleven o'clock; you give them coffee and get them to make their expenses claims – this gives a bit of time for stragglers to catch up. Then you go into a spiel about the company – it's a good thing to talk to people in groups ...'

'... because you don't have to keep saying the same thing to everyone separately ...'

'Precisely. And they can spark one another off asking questions. Then one of the engineers takes them on a tour before lunch'

'And do you learn much at lunch time?'

'Yes ... how they can hold their own with strangers ... we're not particularly concerned with how they hold their eating irons ... [What a quaint idea, thought Chaite, as Ted flustered again] ... but if they join us, they'll have to meet clients and prospective clients – people they've not met before – so it's important they know how to make a good impression ...'

'Isn't it rather an artificial situation? After all, they don't know one another ... yes, I see ... Who comes to lunch?'

'Probably the engineer who shows them round, you, Colley, perhaps another engineer ... that's all. Usually. You're there to make sure it all goes smoothly – to anticipate anything that might go wrong if you didn't'

'It all seems a bit daunting before I've tried it ... but I expect it'll all fall into place'

'Oh yes. Always remember – they don't know what *ought* to be happening (except within the broad limits of the programme) so they don't know if something's going wrong, somebody's away ... it's up to you to improvise as necessary. I know you can do it – I wouldn't've taken you on otherwise'

'Thanks for your faith. Is there anything in particular you want me to do now?'

'Yes ... I'd like you to think about this programme as a complete outsider and see if we're necessarily doing the best thing. Colley and I keep meaning to discuss it ...'

Chaite thought for a little. She had a few ideas, but decided to keep them to herself until she'd thought them through – it'd look more impressive if she waited and developed her own thoughts into a report than if she discussed them off the top of her head and risked their getting lost – or appropriated by someone else ... unwittingly, of course. Ted handed her the file: 'You'll find some background in here – you can either read it first, or approach the problem with a completely open mind ...'

Chaite took the file: 'Thanks. I'll go and do this, then. See you later'

She went back to her desk. She decided not to look at the file just yet. She pulled out the programme Ted had been discussing and went through it carefully. Then she lifted the phone and called Jinny:

'Have we got an engineer who's been here a couple of months or so?'

As she said it, she realised the need to get together some personnel records – people papers – so that she could answer questions like that.

'Yes – well, about ten weeks – no, twelve – that's three months isn't it? – cos he came when I was on holiday and it took me ages to remember his name'

'Go on – what *is* his name?'

'Seb Thornhill. 2494. Er ... you want to watch him'

'Oh ... why's that?'

'Nothing ... just watch'

'Oh ... thanks'

Chaite keyed 2494.

'Seb Thornhill'

'Hi, I'm Chaite, your new people person. I wonder if you could come and
see me for a few minutes?'

'Sure – Chaite people person – where are you?'

'In the office next to Ted Crowe's'

'Yeah ... I know it. I'll be right there'

In no time at all, Seb Thornhill filled the doorway, stooped over
Chaite, shook hands. He sat down: 'Chaite. That's an unusual name. Do
you eat ethnic food?'

'Ye-es ... why?'

'Well, I'm going to an ethnic food party to-night, and you'd like to come'

Chaite was breathtaken. Not 'you might like to come' or even 'I
wondered if you might like to come' – more of a command performance ...
no wonder Jinny had warned her.

Chaite sat watching and thinking: 'Of course I would ... [what *would*
Seb think of her?] ... where and when?'

'Where do you live?'

'In Foxworth. Market Square – Primrose Cottage – opposite the church'

'Right. I'll pick you up about seven thirty. Now, why did you want to
see me?'

Chaite slammed her social compartment shut: 'As you know, I'm new
here, so I'm having a look at WEL practices. You came here for
interview quite recently, so I wondered if we could go through the day's
programme and see if you've got any comments – ways of improving it.
Not that I want to meddle with it if it's all right ...'

She passed the fast worker a copy of the programme. He looked at it:
'I've not seen this before'

'No?'

'No ... I think it might be a good idea if interviewees were sent a copy of
it beforehand'

Chaite was writing notes: 'Mmm?'

'I didn't think much of the map you sent'

Chaite felt unecessarily defensive: '*I* didn't send it ... [she wished she
hadn't said that] ... Good. And ...?'

'The expenses claim forms are pretty crap for a go-ahead firm ... Apart
from that ... let's think. Jinny's very welcoming'

'Did you ask her out?'

Chaite's tongue running away again – she's unnerved.

'She was wearing a wedding ring. You're not wearing any rings'

Chaite can't tell whether or not he's twigged.

'No. *And* I'm coming out with you. So ... anything else?'

'The welcome was good ... the chat was good ... I've been to quite a lot of interviews where either they don't tell you anything or they lecture you about how wonderful it all is. WEL tells it like it is, and wants you to make up your own mind'

'Who told you about WEL?'

'I saw an advert in the *Guardian*'

'No – I mean when you were here – who told you about the company?'

'Colley, mainly. Ted joined us at lunch time. That's another thing – it's a good lunch'

Chaite, who had experienced but two lunches, agreed. As is the way with such interviews, now that it seemed to be over, Seb opened up:

'It'd've been a good thing if we'd been given name cards – you know, to stand in front of us, so we knew who we all were. And the same for the WEL people – perhaps potted CVs so we'd known what specialties people were. I did feel that the technical interviews were a bit sausage machiney. Perhaps you can't do much about that'

'Perhaps not. If you've got four or five people to be seen by two or three people for half an hour or so each, it's got to be a bit of a conveyor belt – otherwise it gets a bit out of hand ... [As she speaks, Chaite can hear herself taking a somewhat defensive managerial viewpoint] ... But we ... [have I caught the Foxworth "we"?] ... can certainly try to tone down the sausage machine aspect'

'The thing I must say about it is that it was hard. And fair'

'You're comparing it with other interviews?'

'Yes ... but it's incomparable, really. I'd advise anyone to apply here. If they get in, they'll know they're somebody'

Chaite had got in. She felt like somebody: 'So you feel like somebody?'

'I certainly do'

'Right. Thank you very much, Seb ... [Chaite could hear officialdom in her voice] ... you've been most helpful'

Seb could hear it too: 'Thanks, Ma'am. I'm pleased to have been of assistance ... [he grinned] ... see you tonight. Primrose Cottage. Half-past seven'

He left the room.

Now Chaite opened the file and started to go through the papers; it read like a history, the development of the WEL engineering interview programme. Now she was going to develop it some more.

Time for a walk; out of the office, and down to Jinny: 'I thought I'd come and see how the workers are doing. And whether they'd like a coffee'
'Thanks – Rule One – no coffee at the board. But don't worry – Pat's coming on in a minute so I can have my break. Then I have my coffee, and do the post round and various other things until lunch time, and then go back on the board till Pat relieves me for the afternoon break'
'I see. And what does Pat do for the rest of the time?'
'Oh ... running out Mailmerge letters – she did yours yesterday, didn't you know? – and photocopying, and telexing ... very technical, is our Pat. Ah, there you are. I was just telling Chaite how technical you are'
'Mmmm – all the latest machines. I'm the only person who knows where to kick them when they go wrong'
'Do they often go wrong?'
'No ... my sandals are too flimsy'
Jinny passed on some work in progress to Pat, and slipped out of her chair: 'Come on, Chaite, let's go for a coffee'
They walked up the corridor. Chaite remembered her pledge:
'I promised Grace that I'd see if I could improve the coffee'
'Really? How could you do that?'
'Well ... first, look into the cleaning schedule – I haven't caught up with who does it yet, by the way'
'Oh – Maria in the kitchen looks after it – one of her girls – she's very defensive about it'
'I'll bet'
They reached the machine and conmanded it to produce two cups of white without.
'There's another machine in the workshop ... [said Jinny] ... Have you explored yet?'
'There's still masses I don't know. But it's only my second day, after all. Grace gave me one from the workshop machine – she said it'd just been cleaned so it was better'
'That's it. I often use it on some pretext or other. How d'you get on with Seb, by the way?'
'Get on with him? Fine – he got off with me'
'He's a right Noggin the Bonce. I told you he needed watching'
'You have to watch carefully – he goes so fast you could miss it. Anyway, I'm going out with him tonight. Ethnic food. I didn't ask what'
'He likes his ethnic food, does Seb. If you like yours, you'll be all right. Other things being equal. I must go and do my post now – see you at lunch'

104

Jinny vanished.

Chaite walked towards the kitchens for an exploration with Maria.

Maria the irrepressible: 'Hello Chaite. This is where it all happens. Come to see how it's done?'

'Yes. At the moment, I'm interested in coffee machines'

Maria's hackles rose: 'Oh, what about my coffee machines? Spotless, they are. My girls keep them spotless'

'Of course they do. Only it says on my list of things that coffee machines come under welfare, and I look after welfare – among other things – so I thought I'd find out how it's done'

Maria relaxed slightly: 'We clean them every other day – Monday, Wednesday and Friday – first thing in the morning. Lou usually does it. Mind you, we do have a spot of trouble with the mixers, sometimes'

Chaite became sympathetic: 'Oh? Can you show me?'

Maria picked up a great bunch of keys and they went to the coffee machine. She opened the door and showed Chaite how the powder was released into the mixer funnel: 'You see – sometimes a bit of powder gets stuck there, and gets washed down next time. It's all right if the next drink is the same as the last one. If it isn't, they complain that the coffee tastes like tea, or whatever it is'

'Have you contacted the makers?'

'They keep sending a man when I complain, but the difference never seems to last'

'Ah. When did they last come?'

'Oh ... about a couple of weeks ago'

Chaite was studying the mechanism intently; elaborately polite, she asked: 'May I touch it?'

'Go ahead'

'Look – this bit here's out of alignment. It needs screwing round so that the lip here comes under the nozzle'

She turned it. Maria was secretly pleased: 'Oh yes. Those two marks ought to line up. Let's try it again'

They did so. Every bit of powder was washed out.

'You see? ... [Chaite turned on the charm] ... You've solved it'

'It's that Lou – I'll ave er guts for garters. Thanks for sorting it out'

'Oh, me? I'm just a catalyst. What's for lunch?'

'Chicken pieces today, in mushroom sauce'

'Great! I'm looking forward to that'

Chaite went back to her office. As she settled into her chair, the phone rang.

'Double two double two'

It was Pat: 'I've got a Cindy Best on the line wanting a secretarial job'
'Oh ... do we happen to need any secretaries, I wonder? Let me have a word with Dawn'
She got through to Dawn: 'Do we need any secretaries? I've got one on the line'
'It's always worth taking their details. I like to keep a pool of possibles'
Chaite got back to Pat: 'Can I speak to Cindy now?'
'Putting you through'
Chaite arranged for Cindy to complete an application form and come in for a chat; then rang Dawn: 'Could you get together a sample swatch of WEL forms for me please? One of each'
Sure, I'll get Lou Two to bring them asap'
'Who?'
'Lou Two. Lou One's in the kitchen – you've met her – we call her just Lou cos she was here first. Lou Two looks after stationery – among other things'
'Thanks'
Chaite started to sketch out her report. It suddenly occurred to her that it might be a good idea if she had a word processor at her disposal.
Judging from the absence of noise, Ted was either out or asleep. She knocked on the dividing door: 'Come in, Chaite'
She went in, taking the bull by the horns: 'I wonder if I might have a word processor in my room? It could save an awful lot of time, and if I had a database program as well I could get all the personnel records on to it, and it would all help to make me – WEL – more efficient'
Ted was quite taken aback:
'Yes ... I should think so ... Are you sure ...?'
'Well, I'd like to try – I had one at my last job ... it can be easier than handwriting'
Ted raised the phone and called Dawn: 'What happened to the IBM PC David Paul used to have? ... Mmmm ... So it's spare? ... Well, could you get someone to bring it along to Chaite's room? ... Oh, as soon as you like ... Thanks ... [he put down the phone] ... There, that's fixed'
Chaite was impressed: 'Thank you, kind sir. What it is to have friends in high places'
'Don't mention it'
Chaite was no sooner at her desk again than Jinny popped her head round the door: 'Time for lunch ... if you want any'
'Do I? Chicken and mushroom'

'Oh, good. By the way ... if it's not a silly question ... why are you wearing a plastic glove?'
She doesn't realise.
'You haven't noticed? ... It's an artificial arm'
'What? Good heavens ... is it? But you're wearing all those bangles'
'Why shouldn't I?'
'Well ... How ...?'
'It doesn't matter ... I like compliments ... I'll tell you sometime'
They went to the dining room; Jinny surreptitiouly helped Chaite to collect the various things they needed and take them to their table; at last they were settled. Chaite sighed before taking up her fork:
'The morning seems to have flown by'
'Don't tell me – it's been crawling for me – every time I look at the clock it seems to have gone backwards. It must be because I'm on hol next week'
'How does the clock know that?'
'Silly – it's me, not the clock'
'Sorry'
Chaite looked serious.
After the chicken, fruit salad or chocolate pudding; Chaite had no objection to sitting while Jinny fetched for her.
'It's really good here, isn't it?'
'Mmmm. Yes. At my last place, everybody used to complain – I used to take sarnies and a flask. And before that, we all used to go out to the pub. It used to make lunch hours awfully long – when it was crowded, I mean. Everybody getting there early to beat the rush, you know, and then staying on. Still, there wasn't much to do there, so it didn't matter too much. Not like here'
'Where were you before?'
'Oh, I used to work up the Furniture – I was the Girl Friday. Used to have a job a bit like yours – interviewing young hopefuls every day – and not so young. We used to get lots of applicants, but never enough good ones. That was why we had to interview them all'
'What did they have to do?'
'Trimming. You need strong wrists and a straight eye. I could usually tell before giving them a trial. Like – you've got a straight eye, and ... ummm'
'I get about four a day ... [said Chaite] ... Don't worry'
'Sorry – I still can't believe it ...'
Lunch drew to a pleasant close.
'Coming out for a wander?'

They sauntered out into the warm September air, and into the arboretum. Chaite looked up and around:

'These really are magnificent trees. Do you know what they all are?'

'No idea ... Wish I did. I love trees'

'I've got a tree book at home – I'll bring it in. However ... that's a Stone Pine ... and that's a Black Poplar – quite rare, I think ... Where did they all come from?'

'Lord Someone-or-Other, who used to live here. I've got a little notice in reception, but it's fallen down, so I keep it in my cupboard'

Chaite resolved to make more of the history of the house and grounds. Never mind that WEL was a high-tech company; high tech didn't spring out of somebody's head with its arms full – it was based on what had gone before, and Lord Someone-or-Other's house and grounds had gone before WEL – well before.

It was time to go back. As Chaite went into her room, she was delighted to see that there was an IBM PC on her side table, with the cursor blinking on the screen, all ready for her to process words, should she so wish.

She did wish. She had a look at the book of words, and then thought she'd short-circuit the learning process by getting a few tips from Dawn; after that she was away, and her report on the engineers' interview days began to take shape.

So the afternoon passed until once more there was a tap on the door.

'Came the Dawn' thought Chaite, but it was Jinny: 'Got time to come a-Woning before going out with Mr Universe?'

'Why not?'

She saved her work, switched off, tidied her desk and was ready.

There was quite a crowd in the Woning that evening. Chaite looked around: 'Are we celebrating something?'

'No, I don't think so. Not unless it's Charlie's four cycles'

'*What?*'

'Charlie Ford. In the stores. He's got this idea that he ought to be able to win a seaside talent contest by juggling a bowler hat, an umbrella and a briefcase'

They were joined by Pat and an engineer called Nick Wells. There were introductions.

Chaite wanted to know more:

'Sounds original. About Charlie Ford. Do you think he'll be able to?'

'He's been trying for three years to my knowledge ... in between bouts of morphology'
'Morphology?'
'The study of form'
'Oh ... Ha'
'If he can do four cycles after three years, he should be able to do eight after ... six years'
'Possibly enough to work into an act'
'Does it work like that? It could be a square law'
'Sixteen cycles after six years?'
'Something like that. Or there may be a breakthrough point where if you can do it for n you can do it for ever'
'The theory of juggling. I wonder if anyone's done a thesis on it?'
'Wouldn't be surprised'
Nick turned to Chaite: 'Can you juggle?'
Chaite flipped up a beer mat and caught it: 'That's about it'
Pat kicked Nick under the table; he suddenly realised and became confused: 'Oh ... sorry ...'
Chaite twinkled at him: 'I take it as a compliment really. What else is Charlie going to put in his act?'
'I'm not sure if he's thought of that'
'He couldn't go far on the City Gent theme. The borderline between ineptness and monotony is very unclear. Indeed – they may even overlap'
'Probably at the wenge point'
'Can he sing?'
'Never heard him ... do you think he should have a song in the act?'
'Why not? He could do the juggling, then sing the song, then juggle and sing together as a finale. He'd get first prize, and then he could finance a monocycle for the next time'
'I'd forgotten the monocycle'
'What about it?'
'Charlie gave it up when he thought of the juggling act. Thought it would be too monotonous'

Chaite thinks that the whole thing is in danger of becoming monotonous – there'll be plenty of time to explore WEL characters; she ought to go and get ready for her outing. She excuses herself and makes her way home.
As seven-thirty draws near, she is less certain that she wants to go out with Seb. But ... Why not?

She's told herself she wants to develop a social life, and this is as good a start as any. She is taking some trouble with her appearance – a blossoming blouse, a swirling skirt, shining matching shoes. She applies a light touch of make-up. She eschews earrings, partly because they're a bit difficult, and partly because her coppery hair, sphinx-like, covers her ears anyway. She looks out of the window, and sees Seb arriving, driving slowly round the Market Square with the air of one seeking an uncertain destination.

She dons a jacket straight from the dry cleaner's packet, slings her bag over her right shoulder and pushes her left arm into the deep pocket – as much to support its weight as to hide it. She checks her keys, and appears on the pavement just as Seb decides where to stop: 'Hi'

'Hi'

'Put your things on the back seat'

Chaite unwinds herself again – it's a warm evening.

'Take your coat off too, if you like. Best to do it before we start'

Chaite decides to have no inhibitions; she takes off her jacket again, and lays it on the back seat. She gets in and belts up: 'Are we going far?'

'It's on this side of Frettleborough. About forty minutes – but worth it'

'And what is it?'

'It's sort of ethnic ... Eats at the Eagle, they call it'

'Oh ... alliterative'

'What? Yes. Last month, it was Polynesian; the month before it was Korean'

'And this month?'

'Chinese – hope that's OK'

'Yes. And the Eagle's a pub?'

'Yes. They've got a large room at the back they set aside on the first Tuesday of the month for ethnic eats. They hire in an appropriate cook'

They'd hardly hire in an inappropriate one, thinks Chaite.

'And do you go there often?'

'Every month I possibly can. And I cook a lot at home. You must come and try it'

'You *are* a fast worker'

'Do you think so? Just showing a new girl the sights ... [he sees the double meaning] ... new to WEL, that is'

'And new to you. Don't you have a girl friend?'

'Er ... I'm trying to give them up'

'Well, you're not making a very good job of it, are you?'

They travel on in silence. Seb has a vague feeling that he hasn't quite got the upper hand. Chaite feels reasonably relaxed, her hands in her lap, right over left. Seb is hoping that the evening will be a success; he and Yvonne have just split; Chaite (who does not know this) bears some slight resemblance to Yvonne (so slight that only Seb can see it) and seems to be available. And she's new to the area, so he can show her the ropes without getting involved. Unless he wants to.

Seb's got to know something: 'What happened to your hand?'

Chaite runs through her stock of answers ... should she tell everyone at WEL the same tale, or spread a lot of different ones to keep them guessing?

'It was a coach crash in Spain. As a matter of fact, I was lucky to get out alive ... several of the party ... I'd rather ... [her voice quavers] ... not talk about it'

'Doesn't it give you nightmares?'

Chaite could very easily work herself into a state: 'Yes ... yes ... even after two years ... more than two years'

That's answered *that* question.

'Only two years? You seem to manage very well'

'Yes, thank you. I can manage very well'

Another silence falls.

'We'll be there soon'

'Good. I'm ravenous – I had a good lunch, but I've worked jolly hard too'

'Me too. How are you enjoying it at WEL?'

'It's a bit early to say, but judging by first impressions, I'd say it's ... fabulous. Very exciting. A challenge. Lots to do. Never a dull moment'

They see a string of coloured lights down in a dip as they come over the brow of a hill.

'That's it'

'Wonderful'

The thought of eating ethnic food – any food – off paper plates has been appalling Chaite. But as soon as they enter the welcoming room she feels her perception of the event flip – china plates, proper cutlery, tables at which to sit. It's obviously well organised; Chaite is glad she's come.

Lettice comes bouncing up: 'Hi, Seb, have you got a ticket? They're four fifty – each. Is this your new friend?'

'Chaite – meet Lettice. She's a very old friend of mine – up at Oxford. You'll usually find her waiting at her father's wine bar in Frettleborough – in the vacations. This is Chaite'

Chaite wonders at this manifestation of The French Maid; Lettice
wonders what's happened to Yvonne. Lettice keeps her mouth shut. Seb
gives her a tenner: 'Cheap at half the price'
Lettice gives him one pound change and two pieces of purple pasteboard.
'Slick tickets'
'Glad you like them; designed them myself. Now, plates are there, food
all along there, sauces and chopsticks and napkins at the other end – or
forks if you prefer – wine's there too'
Seb picks up a tray; Chaite places two plates on it. They slowly move
along, loading their plates, exchanging banter with girls on the serving
side of the table, all of whom seem to know Seb, all of whom eye Chaite
curiously.
'Bed of rice ... sweet and sour prawns ... pork ... chicken ... water
chestnuts .... egg noodles ... spring rolls ... prawn crackers ...'
The plates fill; at last Chaite gathers the napkins and cutlery and
follows Seb over to an empty table: 'It gets quite full, doesn't it?'
'Yes. Very gratifying for the old man'
'Which old man?'
'Lettice's old man. He owns this pub as well'
'Ah'
And Seb goes to get some wine, and Chaite sets out the table, and settles
warmly into a comfortable chair preparing for an interesting evening.

After the meal, and seconds, and banana fritters, and coffee, and Seb
introducing Chaite to some of his friends who continue to talk among
themselves, they drive back in silence – but a reasonably comfortable
silence; Chaite dozes most of the way. She awakes as they reach
Foxworth: 'Oh, sorry. Not very good company, I'm afraid'
'Don't worry ... it's good to assist the sleep of the innocent'
What does that mean?
'Would you like to come in for a coffee?'
She feels quite warm towards Seb, and wants him to see her luxurious
flat.
'Yes. Yes please. I'd like that'
They draw up and get out; Chaite runs up the steps and opens the door;
ushers Seb in and up to her sitting room. She goes into the kitchen to put
on the kettle; Seb stands in the middle of the floor taking it all in.
Chaite returns. Seb indicates a jungle scene somewhat reminiscent of Le
Douanier: 'That's a very striking picture. Who's XS?'
'Me – that's a Greek Chi for Chaite ... as in Christmas'
'What, X-mas?'

'No, Chi-mas.

'When did you do that?'

'About three years ago. As a matter of fact, I haven't done one since'

'Have you tried?'

'No ... I was left handed. But I keep telling myself ... the freedom of oils
...'

'What else don't you do ... now?'

'Play the guitar ... the piano. I was quite a good guitarist ... used to take
part in college recitals'

'You could take up the trumpet'

The kettle turns itself off. Chaite goes to make the coffee, rattled. She
returns with the tray: 'Just because you can play one instrument doesn't
mean you can play any instrument'

'I didn't think it did'

'Why did you suggest the trumpet, then?'

'Because ... How about the electronic organ then? You can get automatic
rhythm, and it fills in the chords ...'

Chaite is becoming angry: 'Why not just put on a record and have done
with it? I don't need to be reminded of my ... shortcomings ... Seb. I have
to live with it – for ever more. Think about it'

But Seb is incredibly insensitive: 'You really ought to try these things –
not let yourself be beaten ...'

'Beaten? BEATEN? What the hell do you think I've been doing for the
last two years ... [she goes over to the door, and holds it open] ... OUT!'

'What? Chaite, let me ...'

'OUT!'

Seb still can't grasp what's happened: 'If that's what you want ...'

'That – is – what – I – want'

'Well, thank you very much for coming out with me. I'll ... see you
around'

Seb slinks out.

Chaite hears him leave the house.

She stands, weeping.

She removes her arm and, with the care demanded by symbolism – as it
were flinging a Military Cross into the foam – she casts it on to her sea
of troubles and, by opposing, ends them.

She throws the coffees, untouched, away.

She pours herself a very stiff whisky, swigs most of it, coughs, refills
the glass and totters up to bed ... floating on the memory of the previous
Saturday.

13
Saturday 24 August 1985

Chaite's first morning in Foxworth; early morning – before even the sun's
perpendicular rays properly illumine the mist presaging the heat of the
day to come; Chaite wakes to the dawn chorus. A solitary leader, a
reply, and off they go. What is it all about? Do they wake and feel
constrained to exchange dreams? Are they promulgating information
about marauding cats, and birds of prey? Is it a daily thanksgiving? Or
an exchange of diaries? Whatever it is, we all ought to have a dawn
chorus.

Chaite has been giving the Forty Eight in what she knows in a dreamly
way is the Dummer Bummer Hall; she has just finished; the audience
has risen to its feet in acclaim. It takes her some time to return to reality
– an enantiomorphic Paul Wittgenstein – and recall that playing the
piano is not now her forte. It is at times like this that she thinks her
brain must be trying to get its own back on itself.

She gets out of bed and looks out of the window; recognises the day
for what it will be.

She goes through to the bathroom, splashes her face, dries herself,
returns to the bedroom and slips into some old clothes – a pair of
knickers, an old pair of slacks with elasticated waist, a bright red
pullover several sizes too large for her which someone forgotten has
never claimed.

The sleeves hang right down; she looks in the long mirror and feels
almost whole. She hangs a front-door key round her neck on a string and
tucks it down inside – it's cold! – slips on some sandals and saunters out
into the market square with the virtuous air of one who has got up
really early.

She sniffs the morning smells, exchanges purrs with a fat
tortoiseshell cat, and pleasantries with the milkman: 'You're up early'
'Yes – lovely, isn't it?'
'That's going to be a hot day'
'Certainly is – time we had some summer'
'This is it'
'You're right – we're having it now'
Not wishing to prolong the banality, Chaite strolls on and round the
corner. Why doesn't she get up this early every day? You can do so much

at this time of the morning – a day's work before you get to the office – explore the area in which you live.

She turns another corner and finds herself walking along Chilton Crescent – a boundary fence on the right; bijouised dwellings on the left. It is here that an overpowering smell of roses arrests her; a trellis atop a fence covered in magnificent blooms. She reaches up to pull down a cluster, the better to inhale its fragrance ... and with a creak and a crack the whole structure topples forwards – swoosh – and envelops her in a thorny bower, holding her fast.

Her first reaction is to try to flail her way out, but she quickly realises that her captor is very powerful indeed, and has really got its prickles into her pullover. She stands stock still and takes stock. She tries to back away slowly, but the bower moves with her, yielding yet remorseless. She pulls at her left sleeve with her right hand, and makes some progress, but can't see how to go on from there. She wishes she was wearing her arm. She wonders if she could free herself if she slipped out of the pullover. But people are beginning to stir and a topless girl emerging from a rosebush and streaking home might cause more problems than it solved. She hears the milk-float whirring and clicking away into the distance; no help there. A feeling of impotent rage sweeps over her – the whole episode unreasonably reminds her of Roy – when she hears a voice: 'You seem to have got into a right old predicament' It is the proverbial tall dark stranger – this one wearing a silk paisley dressing-gown and sheepskin slippers. Were he thinking about it, he might conclude that he looked bronzed and manly, the old James Bond image; in fact he looks more pale and haggard, a stoned Holmes. 'Yes ... you'd think it'd be easy to get away, but I'm completely stuck – bushed, in fact' 'I'm sorry about this ... oh! It's my rose, you see. It shouldn't really go falling down on people' 'Well, it's all my fault. It smelt so good ... I reached up to smell it better ... [will he think I was trying to steal his roses?] ... and it all came down on top of me. It's me who should be sorry' Sherlock Bond starts by freeing Chaite's hair, gently, caressingly, making her spine tingle. Then he eases her pullover and the rosebush apart. At the same moment as Chaite realises that he will discover that she's asymmetric, he discovers it. He is freeing the left sleeve; suddenly freezes: 'Ooh ... did the rosebush get your hand?' 'No, it happened when I was on a pirate boat in the South China Seas' 'Seriously?' 'Very serious ... it was an accident'

115

An accident. It could hardly have happened on purpose.

'There'

'Thanks'

Chaite steps back, free at last: 'That's better. Well ...'

Before she can suddenly take to her heels like a shy animal released from a snare, he grasps the dangling sleeve and makes to lead her into his house: 'You can't go just like that – come and have some breakfast'

Chaite's mind races; she can find no reason not to have breakfast: 'I couldn't possibly ...'

The aroma of coffee drags her into the hall; now she's sitting in his bijouised pine kitchen. He's bustling round, getting out bowls, plates and spoons, packets of cereals, cutting bread: 'Do you live round here? My name's Colley, by the way'

'Colley ... like the poet laureate?'

'Exactly ... [the poet laureate – O, rara avis] ... Tea or coffee?'

'Coffee. I'm Chaite'

'Chaite? Unusual, that'

'Yes – it's Greek – means "long, flowing hair" or "a horse's mane"'

'Forget the horse. How did your parents know your hair would grow like that?'

'They couldn't've done ... it just growed – and it seems right. But it's like having a lawyer called Justice – if he weren't a lawyer, he'd still be called Justice'

'And then it would be like calling your first child Septimus'

'Not a bit ... but I see what you mean'

'I suppose your parents were classically inclined. Mine were obviously into the Restoration – and there's some connection with the Cibbers, though I'm not sure what it is. ... And where have you come from today?'

'I've got a flat in a house over overlooking the Market Square ... [Chaite waves vaguely in the general direction] ... Primrose Cottage'

'Oh yes. Chaite ... pretty. Why haven't I seen you before?'

'Because I haven't lived here for very long – in fact, my sister Mercia helped me to move in yesterday'

Colley is taken with this damsel in distress, rescued from the dragon rose, who knows of Colley Cibber. Everything about her seems mysterious, especially at this time of the morning.

He looks at her again, goes over to her unasked, and gently rolls up her right sleeve: 'Now you can eat'

'Thank you, kind sir'

'How ... ?'

'It was a motor accident. I don't like talking about it'

116

This is true; she doesn't like talking about it, because it can reveal flaws in her account.

'I'm sorry ... I mean, I'm sorry I asked'

'It's perfectly natural to want to know ... perhaps, one day ...'

Chaite's standard put-off. Will there be a one day?

'Can I ask ... were you alone in the car?'

'Please ... Not twenty questions'

There is a silence. Colley pours coffee: 'How long ago?'

'Oh ... over two years. *And* I was left handed'

'How long did it take you to become right handed?'

'As soon as I lost my left hand, of course. I got used to it quite quickly; it's marvellous what you can do when you have to ... [Chaite the matter of fact] ... Now tell me about you. Do you live alone?'

Chaite the excited: 'At the moment ... [Colley hesitates; Chaite's heart leaps] ... my wife's visiting her mother ... with the children'

Chaite's perception flips, as so often it does: 'Ooh ... how many children?'

'Two: one of each. Giles is six and Nikki (after her aunt)'s nine'

It's far too early to mention the possibility of another on the way.

'That's neat'

'When Genista comes back, we're off for another week in a caravan in the Lakes. Back to work on Monday week'

Why is he telling her all this? Chaite feels it oppressing her. How to escape?

'What do you do?'

'Me? I'm an engineer – at WEL ... [it wasn't untrue] ... Do you have a job?'

For some unaccountable reason, Chaite doesn't want to tell him that she's just got a job at WEL.

'Looking after an auction room'

'Single handed?'

As he says it, Colley colours; Chaite laughs: 'It's not the first time it's been said. And it won't be the last. There're quite a lot of hand phrases when you think about it. I have to be used to them all'

Colley contemplates Chaite. Time stands still. He thinks – with no basis for such a thought – that he has some inalienable proprietary right over her. He has rescued her from his rosebush and she is now his – for a minute; an hour; however long it might be. He feels like The Collector; he possesses her, wanting no more (at that moment) than the possession. Because she is there (and therefore nowhere else), and no one knows she is where she is, she is his. He wonders how long it can last;

thinks hard of a way of framing a question: 'Is anyone waiting for you back at the buildings?'

'No, I live alone. It's a good job I trust you, isn't it?'

Chaite too is enjoying the thrill of the moment, and wants to put Colley out of his misery: 'I used to be married ... to a football fanatic'

'And then?'

'Well ... I'm *not* a football fanatic. So I stopped being married to him'

'How long ago was that?'

'Oh ... over two years ...'

Chaite suddenly realises that Colley might put two and two together, and make six of one and half a dozen of the other.

'I see ... [he doesn't] ... so what happened?'

'He walked out on me. I wasn't there to stop him'

'Would you have been able to stop him if you had been there? Would you have wanted to? Where were you?'

'Probably not. No. Away for a change of scenery ... Can I use your loo?'

'Of course. There's one there ... [he waves vaguely hallwards] ... and one at the top of the stairs'

'I'll go upstairs'

She goes. Colley waits. Then he rises silently, goes upstairs, and stands in the spare room looking out of the window. Chaite emerges. Colley calls: 'I'm in here'

She joins him: 'What are you doing?'

'Looking at the garden. I must cut the grass before ... before I go away ... And I ought to fix the rose ...'

Chaite comes up behind him, clasps him round the middle as best she can, nuzzles his shoulder with her chin.

Colley quickens: 'It's all very well for you to trust me ... but can I trust you?'

'Not unless you want to'

Colley doesn't want to. He feels many things, mostly submerged in a sudden, burning desire to have Chaite – because she's there. Forgetting what happened just six days before, he tells himself that life with Genista has become tame of late – and what does he know of Genista, who only Genista knows? Trustworthy Colley suddenly rationalises what is about to happen; it will be a therapeutic session: no harm will come of it – in fact, it will do good.

Chaite bends forward and flings up her arms: the old red sweater flies away on to a chair. She quickly steps out of her sandals and her trousers and her knickers. She stands naked, one-and-a-half arms outstretched. For the first (and last) time, Colley sees her complete incompleteness.

Chaite's hurry to throw off her clothes is not because she wants to get to it, but because she wants to get through it. She has always felt uneasy at her attitude towards her body and what it might be for. The ethos in which she has been brought up and educated; the literature – and non-literature – she has read; her friends; all imply that a girl's best friend is her body, and that there is to be a sacred relationship between man and woman.

Her stormy and short-lived married life with Roy did nothing but confirm her fears that practical sex was like the emperor's new clothes – such a build-up to its being the very pinnacle of human relationship and then, with Roy, less fulfillment than boredom.

Is that what it's all about? Who's kidding whom?

So her fears that everyone was living a lie were confirmed, and her dislike of her body turned to an impotent hatred. Colley, of course, can know none of this. His own high expectations of the physical part of his relationship with Genista were fulfilled but gradually ... and they'd produced children ... and that was what it was *really* for – wasn't it? – they'd done their bit in Mother Bionature's scheme of things.

Chaite falls back on the bed, one-and-a-half arms still outstretched. Colley has already kicked off his slippers; now he throws off his dressing gown and, mentally leaping on to the bed, crawls on to Chaite, Bond subjugated by Holmes. Out of the corner of his eye, he notes that the bedside clock says it's twenty to seven.

* * * * * * * *

The bedside clock still says it's twenty to seven. Surely it wasn't that quick? Then he realises that the clock has stopped. But it *was* quick. His hopes that he might have learned something to justify his momentary unfaithfulness are unfulfilled.

Chaite's suspicion of her body is reaffirmed, save that she now knows that her lack does not bar her to men – and that is the greatest comfort of all; one of her most secret fears dispelled.

Each feels profound sorrow that the opportunity – such a golden opportunity – seems to have failed them.

The telephone rings – who on earth can it be?

'Who on earth can that be?'

Colley struggles to his feet and goes to the bedside telephone in the next room: '371849'

'Darling. Did I wake you?'

All the furniture glowers at him menacingly, sharing his secret.

'No, I've been up for some time. Pottering about ... you know ... [Genista will be satisfied. Sometimes, Colley is infuriated by her lack of curiosity; now he is thankful for it] ... What can I do for you? It's lovely to hear from you' He remembers to say it.
'I just rang to say we'll be leaving after breakfast, so perhaps you can get home at lunch time ...'
'But it's Saturday! I'll be here, waiting. I'll cook you an omelette before we set off'
'And naughty chips?'
'Yes, and naughty mooshy peas'
'Darling ...'
'Yes?'
'I'm so looking forward to getting back ... and us all going to the Lakes'
'I'm looking forward to it too. Have you had a good time?'
'Yes, but I'll tell you about it later. You know how they fret about the telephone'
'Yeah. Give them my love. Drive safely'
'Umm ... oh, Giles's got his vest stuck in his zip ... must go ... byeee'
Colley goes back into the spare room. Chaite is dressed again; looking out of the window. Naked, Colley feels ashamed. Elaborately casual, he picks up his dressing gown and puts it on.
'Genista's coming back at lunch time'
Chaite turns round, smiling genuinely: 'Nice for you. I must go now. I expect we shall meet again. Soon'
How odd it all sounds.
'Yes, I'm sure we will. Thank you for dropping in'
'Not at all; thank you'
How formal can they get? Chaite is at the head of the stairs; at the foot of the stairs; in the hall. Colley follows her down. She turns and gives Colley a sisterly peck on the cheek. Anticipating that she's going to have trouble opening the door, he lets her out. She is gone.

Colley clears up the kitchen and checks round the spare room. He takes a long, contemplative shower. He lies on the bed; sleeps deeply for an hour or so until the milkman rings, wanting money.

What happened earlier has now become a dream; two other people must have been the protagonists.
Good – let it stay that way.
He dresses, fixes the roses, mows the lawn, mends the gate. Virtuously, he prepares the table for Genista's return.

14
Wednesday 21 & Thursday 22 August 1985

'Here it is! This is the one'
For four weeks, Chaite has been staying with Mercia, searching diligently for a suitable job. Now the *Foxworth Evening Telegraph* has yielded an attractive possibility. Mercia comes and looks over her shoulder.

Wilkinson Electronics Ltd
needs a
PEOPLE PERSON
to oil the wheels for recruitment and selection of staff by helping heads of departments with the banausic parts of the task. Must be good at people, good humoured, good at organising and improvising, unflappable *etc*. Freedom from technofear and an ability to process words an advantage.

Apply to Ted Crowe, Company Secretary
WEL, Foxworth Manor, Foxworth.
Telephone 494494

Such agonising there had been at WEL about that advertisement, first drafted by Bob Wilkinson himself. Should they use the unheard-of title People Person? Should they use the words banausic and technofear?
'I want the sort of person who either knows what banausic means, or will look it up. I don't think we need a technical person, but they shouldn't be put off by the fact that we're a technical company'

Bob had got his way, and, by some stroke of Providence, that particular edition of the *Foxworth Evening Telegraph* had been seen by the one applicant WEL needed – Chaite.
'It looks weird'
'Have you got a dictionary? What's banausic?'
Mercia was looking:
'"Proper for a mechanic" Eh?'

'I see. Well, I can process words ... and I don't know what technofear is –
I mean, I don't suffer from it. Do you think I'm good at people, good
humoured, good at organising ...?'
'Didn't you have to be – weren't you – all these things before?'
'I suppose so. Doesn't everybody have to be like that?'
'To a certain extent, maybe. No – I don't think so. I think this job looks
very like you'
'So?'
'So I should go for it'
'How far's Foxworth?'
'About forty miles from here. The road's pretty rotten as well.
Especially when people are travelling to and from work'
Chaite mused on a sudden vision: 'I ought to be able to get a flat there'
She saw herself independent again. She had come a long way since her
accident, but she had always lived with one of her sisters – first Mercia,
then Cepha (admittedly self-containedly), now Mercia again. A new
job, a new flat, a new Chaite.
She rang the number at the foot of the advertisement – Foxworth 494494.
'W–E–L – can I help you?'
'Oh, hello. Ted Crowe, please. I'm enquiring about the advertisement in
the *Telegraph* for a People Person'
'Putting you through'
'Ted Crowe'
'Ah – I'm enquiring about the advertisement in the *Telegraph*. For a
People Person'
'Yes. What can I tell you?'
'When can I come for an interview?'
'Oh ... well ... Can I take your name and address, and we'll send you a
form and some information about the job'
'Fine – then what happens?'
'You send the form back – after you've filled it up of course – and we let
you know if we want to interview you'
'Oh. Well, I wondered if it might be possible to come over and fill in the
form and then you could interview me after that'
Chaite the pushy – or perhaps it was Chaite the decisive. She hoped
that she sounded organised enough to get her way.
'May I have your name and address first, please?'
Chaite revealed the details, concluding:
'What I'd really like to do would be to call in when I come to Foxworth
tomorrow to collect the form, and arrange a time for the interview on
Thursday'

Ted is under her spell: 'Right ... I'll leave a form in an envelope in
reception, and we'll pencil in ... ten o'clock on Thursday. Bring the form
in before that. But I can't promise to see you ...'
'I quite understand that, Mr Crowe. Thank you ... And good bye'
Chaite terminated the call on her own terms. Had she impressed them,
or antagonised them? Time alone would tell.
Ted felt quite exhilarated. He rang Bob: 'I've just had the reply to the
People Person'
'And ...?'
'I said it was *the* reply. She's just right'
'Good. What does she do now?'
'I ... ah ... didn't ask her'
Bob laughed: 'She must have made an impression'
'Yes, it was her ... her ability to improvise'
'Ah. So what's happening next?'
'She's picking up a form tomorrow and provisionally coming for
interview on Thursday. If she's any good on paper'
'She will be, won't she?'
'I rather think so'

Chaite rang Foxworth 494494 again.
'WEL – can I help you?'
'Yes. I'm coming to WEL tomorrow, and I'd like to know how to find you'
'Oh, you're the People Person who rang Ted Crowe just now'
'Yes, I didn't like to waste ... take up his time asking him for directions'
'Oh, he wouldn't mind. How are you coming, by the way?'
'By road, I should think. From Little Bygrave'
'Ooohhh ... there's no problem, then. You come towards Foxworth along
the Bygrave Road, and you'll see a sign pointing to the right saying
"By-road to Addercote" – before you get to Foxworth itself. We're about
a quarter of a mile down there on the right – there's a sign pointing to
Foxworth Manor, and you'll see our sign at the gates ... [Chaite waited
for it ...] ... you can't miss it'
How Chaite dreaded those words. The speaker could see the whole
route so clearly in the mind's eye – to that eye there was no way of
missing it. The listener, without that visual advantage, might as well
be blind.
'Just one thing'
'Yes?'
'If you were coming from the Dunsthorpe direction, you can't go straight
through; that's when you're going back. You've got to go round the right-

hand side of the market on Church Road, and then turn left back on to the Stanfield Road when you see a large red-brick building on the corner'

'Thanks ... [reeled Chaite] ... I'm sure I won't be able to miss it. I'll see you tomorrow afternoon?'

'Yes, I'll be here. Goodbye – and thanks for calling – again'

Mercia was in the kitchen. Chaite went through: 'I think I've fixed it'

Mercia wiped her hands on her apron and flung her arms round her elder sister: 'Well done! What happens now?'

'I'm coming over to Foxworth tomorrow, to pick up an application form at WEL. I'll stay the night to be ready for Thursday morning, and suss the place out ... and then I'll look for digs if I get it. Which I think somehow I will'

'I don't think you ought to tempt Providence like that'

'It's Providence that's tempting me'

So the next day, Chaite was up early. She had decided not only that she wanted this job very much, but that she was going to get it. She would drive over to Foxworth in good time, to give herself time to have a look at the place and find a B&B.

Nothing untoward happened; she arrived at about half-past ten, to find it was market day. Providence had saved her a miraculous parking place in Church Lane. She walked across the green churchyard to the Market Square.

The first thing she wanted to do was to buy a map. She looked around the Market Square, and saw Twiney Family Newsagent next to the church. What was a Family Newsagent? What was a Family Butcher, for that matter? What was a High Class Family Butcher, apart from some aristocratic chainsaw massacrist, despatching his kin as seemed to appear more and more frequently in the annals?

What about a Family Off Licence? Claret for boys, port for men, brandy for aspiring heroes.

What *did* a Family Butcher supply? Beefburgers for boys, white meat for women ... but he who aspires to be an hero should eat ... stallion??

Perhaps a Family Newsagent offered photography, soft porn and motoring on the top shelf; cookery, knitting and homes beautiful in the middle; *Bunty*, *Whizzer & Chips*, the *Beano etc* at floor level.

Chaite ventured in to Twiney Newsagent. The bell jangled mercilessly. Imagine having to live with that.

'Good morning'

'Good morning, dear, what can we do for you?'

The Royal we? Or some grandiose notion that she spoke on behalf of the management of the emporium?

'I'd like to buy a map. Of Foxworth'

'Certainly' said the old lady, as if they boasted an extensive map department. She shuffled down to the end of the shop, and tugged at a drawer: 'I think they're in here'

The handle came off.

'I'll have to go and get Mr Feste'

'Mr WHO?'

But Twiney was gone. Chaite expected Mr Feste to enter in cap and bells. How had he got a name like that? She waited, wondering whether it was worth all the trouble – for her, or for Twiney.

Should she run away? It would be a bad start to what she expected would be a continuing liaison with Foxworth and its denizens. She turned over a hobby magazine, and looked to see if WEL was advertising. It was ... and here was an article about the company. *Bon chance* – she would be on the ball.

'Here we are'

Twiney returned; judging by his garb, Mr Feste was the butcher – High Class Family, Chaite didn't doubt. He was carrying a small jemmy: 'Where is it?'

'That one. Mind you, there's no call for maps today, everybody going by car and all'

Chaite was anxious not to be forgotten: 'I'm calling for one'

Mr Feste was examining the drawer with interest: 'No wonder th'andle come orf – see – you got the worm, missus'

'Don't tell me about the worm, just open the drawer. This young lady ain't got all day'

'Festina lente ... [said Feste] ... you know what that means'

'Yeh, sLatin fer pull yer finger out' cackled Twiney.

There was a crash; the front came off the drawer, and maps cascaded on to the floor.

'First prise ... [exclaimed Feste] ... You wanna throw this out, missus, fore th'ole lot goes'

'Get along with you. My husband built that, before the war'

'In the Crimea, wazzy? Ere, I gorra go; carn stan roun gosspin'l day'

Chaite, who now realised that she should never have asked for a map in the first place, thanked him profusely.

'How much is it, dear?'

'It says three and six – and the magazine – here's a pound. That'll be all right'

'Very well, dear. If you say so. See you again, I expect'

'Yes – I hope so'

Chaite emerged into the brightness of reality, and sat down on a bench to look at the map. There was Foxworth Manor ... and there was the scale. Yes – she measured roughly with her fingers – she ought to be able to walk it in less than half an hour.

She refolded the map – thank God for a still day – and looked around. She spotted a sandwich bar, and felt hungry. She'd have a snack, then find her B&B, then walk to WEL. Or perhaps she'd find one on the way. You never know. The sandwich bar was clean and inviting; the choice endless. Chaite settled for egg, anchovy and gherkin – testing herself, for it was not very easy to eat – and a diet Coke off the rocks, sat at a non-smoking table and watched the people of Foxworth going about their daily doings.

At length, she walked back across the churchyard to check on her car as though it were some powerful talisman ... and it was, for she found that she'd parked opposite a sign saying 'Ruskin House, B&B, Vacancies'.

She looked the place up and down; decided it was Meant; up to the door; press the bell. A somewhat willowy-green lady answered: 'Yes?'

'Er – I wondered if you could put me up for the night. Perhaps two'

'I'll have to know'

'I'll be able to tell you tomorrow. I'm going for a job, you see, and if I get it I might want to stay another night. While I find some permanent accommodation'

'Well, if you book provisionally, it'll only cost your deposit'

'How much is the deposit?'

'A pound. That'll be two pounds, please – tonight and tomorrow'

'Well ... er ... could I see the room ...?'

Would this unleash a fury? No: 'Of course. I'm Mrs Taylor, by the way. Come in'

'Thanks. My name's Chaite Slatterthwaite'

'Oh. Ah. There's the TV lounge; the dining room's through there ... [Upstairs] ... There's the bathroom ... [then Mrs Taylor threw ope a door as it were a royal chamber] ... THERE!'

Chaite's sight was assailed by a multiplicity of sensations – curtains, wallpaper, carpet and bedspread – oh, and sheets and pillowcases – all garish in their own individual ways and all shouting at one another. Mrs Taylor missed Chaite clapping her hand to her forehead and reeling slightly. She regained her composure – she could always wait until it was dark and go to bed with the lights out. She was pleased to see a washbasin, with soap and towels. She felt in her pocket and sorted out two pounds; handed them to Mrs Taylor:

'It's WONderful. Thank you very much'

'Right you are. Thank you. Now, it's eight pounds for the bed and breakfast – per night – only it's high season, so I charge eight pounds fifty'

'Fine'

'And tea's at seven o'clock sharp – three seventy-five if you want it'

Chaite looked meaninglessly at her watch: 'What's on the menu?'

'Tomato soup or fruit juice; shepherd's pie with beans and broccoli, pineapple chunks with ice cream additionally, *or* cheese and biscuits, *or* cheese and biscuits additionally. And coffee or tea. Additionally'

Chaite carried out a quick mental survey: 'Are there any pubs round here?'

Mrs Taylor mounted an high horse: 'Well ... if you *want* to eat in a pub, that's up to you. It's not wholesome – *they* don't have to comply with the rules and regulations like *we* do. There's The Trident up the road ... but I've never been in there – of course'

Of course not.

Chaite decided to eat at Ruskin House for the sake of good PR: 'No, no, I was just asking, I'd *like* to eat here'

'Right. Seven o'clock sharp. Will you want tomato soup or fruit juice?'

Chaite thought to get her money's worth: 'Tomato soup, please'

'Very good. Here's a key. Don't lose it'

'Of course not. See you later'

By this time, Chaite had managed to make the front door, and was trying to let herself out. Mrs Taylor pushed forward: 'Here – you need two hands'

'Uh-huh'

Mrs Taylor opened the door; Chaite escaped with a smile and a wave; started to walk to Foxworth Manor.

She found herself walking up a broad avenue of limes, with the Manor placed centrally as a backdrop superimposed on rolling hills, but with completely incongruous booms across the road and a Portakabin serving as a gatehouse in the middle distance. An important para-constable stepped out as she approached: 'Good morning, Miss. What can we do for you?'

It was the Foxworth 'we' again, thought Chaite: 'I've come to pick up an application form'

He did the Boyhood of Raleigh act: 'Go over to that door where you can see the sign saying "Reception". That's reception. Ask in there'

'Thanks – see you on the way out'

Chaite walked across to reception, fascinated that all you had to say was 'I've come to pick up an application form' and the whole need for security melted away. An imposing portico; one of the great double wooden doors stood open; she entered, passed through an inner door, and into the Great Hall with its crystal chandelier. Bob Wilkinson had always been adamant that the Great Hall should remain as unspoilt as possible – the only apparent anachronisms were electrical in origin. There was even an hyper-restrained lack of product on show.

'I've come to collect an application form. And some information about the company – and the job'

'Aha! You're the People Person ... [she picked up an envelope] ... how do you pronounce that?'

'Chaite – to rhyme with mighty, and with a hard CH'

'Chaite. I see. I'm Jinny – to rhyme with spinney, and short for Virginia. You're coming in tomorrow, I believe?'

'Am I?'

Chaite questioned in order to clarify. Jinny looked at her diary:

'Yes – ten o'clock'

'Cor-*rect* ... [she looked around] ... I like your lovely home'

'Ummm. Hope you'll come and join us'

Chaite felt she shouldn't say things like that. She picked up the envelope: 'Right, then. See you tomorrow morning'

'Fine. Oh, excuse me ...'

Jinny attended to the telephone as Chaite slipped out of the door.

Exhilarated, Chaite strolled back meanderingly across the lawns, enjoying the arboretal trees, waved at the gateman who was craning up at a lorry-driver who seemed to have taken a wrong turning, and sauntered back to Ruskin House.

Turn the Yale key, and turn the knob. Easier said than done. Normally, you could find a way round, catch one back while you worked the other. She could probably get it with practice, but the knob was too smooth. Mrs Taylor opened the door. Chaite withdrew the key: 'Thanks'

'It takes a bit of getting used to. Needs two hands, like I said'

She still didn't appear to have noticed anything.

'Can we put the Yale lock on the snib while I get the things out of my car?'

'Oh, that's your car, is it? I was just about to take its number'

'It's all right – I know the number'

This was lost on Mrs Taylor. Chaite went out to get her cases. She put one in the hall, went for the other, and locked the car. Surprisingly, Mrs Taylor had taken the first one up to her room, so Chaite went up with the other.

'Thank you'

'That's all right. I expect you'll want to wash and change before tea. It's at seven o'clock sharp. Mr and Mrs Moore are staying as well. You'll be on table two'

Delusions of grandeur.

'Thank you. I won't be late'

Mrs Taylor left the room, and Chaite closed the door. She looked at herself in the mirror. Wash and change before tea, eh? Did she look dirty? Did they dress for dinner here? But a wash would be nice, and she could change her blouse and put on a scarf. But first ... she sat on the bed, opened the WEL envelope and drew out its contents – a folder containing an application form, a copy of the advertisement from the paper and some sheets stapled together headed 'Welcome to WEL'.

Looking round the room for a suitable surface, and finding none, she decided to take the form down to the TV lounge to complete it. But first, she washed and changed as she had promised herself.

Tucking all her papers under her left arm, Chaite descended to the TV Lounge. Mr and Mrs Moore had got there first; she had the choice of withdrawing – which might look rude – or joining them. She joined them, just as Mr Moore switched on the television: 'Time for't regional news. Moost see what's appning'

Chaite sat down: 'Good evening'

'Good evening'

She had no chance of concentrating on the application form, so she chose to look through it and mentally compose her answers. But she must have dozed off, for the next thing she knew was Mrs Taylor coming in, pulling out the plug of the television set with the finality of a true penny-pincher, and announcing: 'Three minutes to seven'

Everyone stood up, and the party made its way to the Dining Room, where soup – or, in Mrs Moore's case, fruit juice – was cooling on the tables. Nevertheless, it was better than she'd expected, as was the shepherd's pie.

Mrs Taylor came in on the attack: 'What about sweets?'

Everyone opted for the cheese and biscuits. Chaite had hardly expected a five-star cheeseboard; the strip of Cheddar and the three selected biscuits per person were as she had predicted to herself. Hard cheese. Say 'mycella' to Mrs Taylor, and she'd think you referred to your underground storeroom. Now she was standing in the doorway:

'Coffees?'

'"Yes, please"' they chorused.

'Additionally' murmured Chaite.

'I'll bring it to you in the TV Lounge'

They herded themselves into the TV lounge.

Mr Moore took up a tabloid.

Mrs Moore produced some knitting.

The coffee came in silence.

Chaite decided to take hers black rather than try to open the little carton of UHT cream.

'Would you like me to open it for you, dear?'

Chaite knew Mrs Moore had noticed. But it was not her policy to be the first to mention it.

She smiled at Mrs Moore: 'No thank you ... I take it black ... [not true, but ... she paused] ... Are you staying here long?'

'Till next Frideh'

'We came last Saturdeh'

'We coom every ye-ar'

'Yes, we bin here, what is it, six ye-ars now, isn't it Bill?'

'Soomat like that. Seven'

'Six. It were seven ye-ars ago we went to Fileh'

'Six, then'

'Mrs Taylor looks after you right royalleh'

God save the Queen.

'That shepherd's pie was very good, wasn't it?'

'Yes. Mark you, t's out o't'freezer. She cukes em individualleh and hots em int'mahcrowave'

'Oh, ah – all mahcrowaves now'

Chaite feels defensive for no reason she can divine: 'Still, it must be very convenient in this sort of business'

'Oh, ah – you've got to move wi't'imes, ah say'

They'd done the food; Chaite tried another tack: 'Foxworth seems a friendly place'

'Oh, yes, it's frenleh – that's why we coom here, isn't it Bill?'

'Aye – that's why we coom ere – mark you, t'place could do wi livenin oop o'nights'

'Yes, where we coom from, we've bingo, and whist drives, and a cinema woonce a fortnight ...'

'... an five poobs'

Chaite wonders at the attractions of Foxworth.

'Our son allus says it's good as Lon'n'

'You've a son in London?'

'Aye, he's a lecturer oop at t'NELP'

'Doon very well for hisself, e as ...'

'As matter o'fact, I'm knitting this for his birthday'

Mrs Moore holds up the pattern – a handsome young man with his family, all clad in immaculate knitwear, all leaning against a tree, all smiles.

'Do you have other children?'

'There's our daughter, Susan. She's trained as a teacher – junior school. She's married to a doctor – they're in Canada now'

Canada ... Australia ... New Zealand ... crammed with teachers and doctors presumably trying to get away from their parents staying in boarding houses back in the Old Country.

'Doon very well for erself ...'

'I don't know where they get the brains from – must be Bill's side of the family. Yer father was clever, was'ne Bill?'

'Oh ah. Mark you, e'd've got further if e'd ad t'opportunities they ave today'

'My sister's been to Canada. But just to do a study for the government. She's a geographer'

'Yes, our Susan studied geography. Did very well at it, too – didn't she, Bill?'

'Oh, aye'

'My other sister lives in Shalthorpe'

'Shalthorpe? There's a zoo there, isn't there? I always say we should go there – don't I, Bill?'

'Oh, aye. Mark you, I'm not shuer I old wi'animals beeng shoot oop. Snot natrl, like'

'No, I don't hold with it, real-leh'

It now became a point of honour with Chaite to get them to follow up just one remark she might make, instead of relating everything to their own experience: 'I took my sister's children to Shalthorpe Zoo. She's got two boys and two girls'

'I keep saying our Susan ought to have children – don't I, Bill?'

'Oh, aye. Mark you, she's got a good job over theer. She'd ave to give it oop if she ad children'
'My sister had her four quite close together – the last two were twins. She got an *au pair* in to help.
'That Mrs Milliken had an *au pair*, din she Bill?'
'Noo ... were Mrs Wilson'
'It was Mrs Milliken – she had one of those spotted dalmatians used to walk along beside the pram'
'I thought it was Mrs Wilson had the alsatian – dalmatian'
'No, it were Mrs Wood ad t'alsatian. I'fact, she ad two on em, cos woon got roon over ont'Good Frideh'
'Oh, aye'
'Noo-o. She were a ... she used to work in t'off licence'
Chaite thought hard. She'd have to pull out all the stops:
'My occupational therapist's called Mrs Wood. I don't know what I'd've done without her after my accident'
'I don't think Mrs Wood with the alsatian was an occupational therapist, was she Bill?'
'Occupational what? Coom to think of it, t'*were* Mrs Milliken that ad t'o pair'
'I thought so'
Chaite gave up. She'd have to go up and fill in her form. She stood up:
'Well, I must be off to bed, if you'll excuse me'
'Tired, are you? Had a long journey?'
'Not too far – from my sister's at Little Bygrave. But I'm going for an interview tomorrow morning, so I want to get some sleep'
'Interview? You're going for a job, like? What do you do?'
Chaite, triumphant, resisted the urge to sit down again – after all, she'd won: 'I'm in personnel management'
Not quite true, but good enough.
'We've got a nephew in personnel management – haven't we, Bill?'
'Oh, aye ... *you* ave ...'
'It's a wonderful career ... [cut in Chaite] ... I expect I'll see you at breakfast'
'Oh, aye. Brake-fast. Eight o'clock sharp'
Was that a twinkle in his eye?
'Good night'
'Good night'
'Good night'
Chaite went up. The knitting needles clicked: 'Poor girl. I wonder what happened to her arm?'

'You ought've asked er, Mildred'

'I were gettin roun to it ... I expect that's what makes her tired'

Up in the tranquility of her room, Chaite prepared herself for bed; arranged the pillows so that she could sit up comfortably; climbed in and started to work on the application form. She was quite proud of her handwriting now. There were no medical questions and she had no qualms about not elaborating under: 'Is there anything else you'd like to tell us about yourself?'

She completed the form, read it through, put it away carefully, turned out the light and went to sleep almost immediately.

The next morning, Chaite put on her business suit – of dark material which looked as though she meant business without being institutional. She sorted out things she might need, and put them in her shoulder bag along with the application form. She went down to the dining room.

Brake-fast passed off quietly. Surreptitiously, Mildred and Bill watched Chaite eating, but didn't get round to satisfying their curiosity.

Having ascertained that it would be OK to leave her things in her room since she had paid the deposit, Chaite went up and took one last look at herself in the mirror: 'I'm going to get a job at WEL today' she said firmly, looking intently at the girl in the business suit. Thank you, Emil Coué.

The walk still took about twenty mimutes. The gateman came out to greet her again.

'Good morning. I've got an appointment with Mr Crowe at ten o'clock'

'Very good, Miss. Come in here and sign my book for me, will you please? While she did that, the gateman was consulting a form. Now he got out a dog-eared telephone list: 'Let's see ... you're for Mr Crowe wasn't it? Crowe ... Crowe ... Crowe ... Ere it is ... 2424'

He drew a telephone towards him: 'What was that number again?'

'2424'

But he was reconsulting his list: 'Here it is – 2424'

He keyed it and waited: 'Oh, hello. Main Gate ere. I've got a Miss ...?'

'Slatterthwaite'

'A Miss Slatterthwaite ere, for Mr ... Crowe. ... Very good. ... Yes, very good. Good bye'

He rose from his chair and led the way outside; Boyhood of Raleigh again: 'If you go across there, you'll see a sign saying "Reception". That's Reception. Go in there, and the receptionist will look after you'
'Jinny. Thank you very much. See you later'
He returned to his hermitage.
Chaite walked across to the Manor, marvelling that, if they knew who you were it was far more difficult to get in than if you were an anonymous stranger. She made sure that she could pull the application form in its envelope out of her bag easily. No fumbling necessary; any ordinary person could fumble; if Chaite fumbled, she looked upon it as failure.

The Great Hall; Chaite received a wondrous smile from Jinny:
'Morning Chaite – to rhyme with mighty'
'Morning Jinny – to rhyme with spinney. I've come to see Ted Crowe'
'I know. He's on a call; I'll tell him as soon as he comes off'
'Thanks. ... [Chaite thinks] ... How long have you been here?'
'Me? About six years – almost longer than anybody else – but then you have to know everybody when you're on the board – mind you, we used to have the old sort like a piano you knit when I first came here, but now it's just pressing buttons which is easier to use when you're busy, which I'm not at the moment ...'
The switchboard emitted an effete noise; Jinny ministered unto it:
'Your visitor's here ... Right. ... [to Chaite] ... Dawn's coming through to get your form – would you like some coffee?'
Chaite felt saturated: 'Not at the moment, thank you'
Dawn arrived, emerging from a corridor: 'I'm Dawn Waters. You must be Chaite Slatterthwaite'
'Yes ... [they shook hands] ... Here's my form'
'Right, I'll just take it through to Ted Crowe. Have you been offered coffee?'
'Yes, thanks. I don't want anything at the moment'
Dawn disappeared down her corridor.
'Would you like to sit over there?'
'No thanks – I'll have a look at the baronial pictures'
There seemed to be a fair amount of activity at the board; names which at present meant nothing to Chaite were flying about; she reflected that in a week ... a month ... she'd be able to put faces to all of them – if she was lucky in the next hour or so. Then her auditory filters picked out her name; Jinny laid down the lightweight headset and leant forward; the Boyhood of Raleigh again: 'Go up that corridor, through the double

glass doors on the right at the end, along that corridor, and Ted Crowe'll meet you there. See you later – and good luck'
'Yes. Right. Thanks'
Chaite set off up the corridor and through the doors, her heart pounding; she knew that Jinny's thoughts were following her. She wondered if Jinny always talked like that, breathless and incessant.

The corridor was very long, with anonymous doors opening off it; it was lit only by daylight filtering through high windows above the partitions from what she supposed must be offices on either side.

Chaite was suddenly oppressed by the hemmed in, déjà vu feeling that long corridors gave her. She tried to capture the feeling, stopping and leaning against the wall, closing her eyes, trying to recall why it happened; what archetypal corridor had initiated the reaction.
She heard a voice: 'Miss Slatterthwaite?'
'Yes'
It was Ted Crowe; they shook hands as he introduced himself.
'Come through here'
He ushered her into an office which could hardly have been more different from what she might have imagined lay behind those anonymous partitions. It was decorated in greens and browns – botanical rather than institutional – and wherever there was a flat surface, there was a plant. Chaite had never seen so many plants outside a display greenhouse – they were on the filing cabinets, on the desk, on tables, on the window sill, on the floor.
She stood, lost in wonder, love and praise: 'What a magnificent *Euphorbia splendens!*'
Ted beamed. It was the signal for a lecture, where this plant had come from, how this one had grown, how they were fed and watered:
'... but do sit down. Would you like a coffee?'
Chaite was now ready: 'Thank you'
Ted, sitting at his desk, picked up the phone masterfully and keyed four digits. A connected phone could be heard to ring not far away. Apart from that, nothing happened. Chaite knew that he was going to peer, cross and puzzled, into the mouthpiece. He did. He tried again. Nothing still happened. He replaced the receiver, wilting, a strong specimen of *Homo technologicus* reduced by its very creation. Chaite affected not to notice.
'Oh well ... [Ted resignedly] ... I'll go and get it myself. How do you like it? It all comes out of a machine, I'm afraid'
'White without – if it does that'

'Yes, I should think so. Have a look at this – I got it last week on the market'

He passed a heavy book to Chaite – a Victorian natural history. It was the moment of truth; she couldn't manage it it in her right hand, and had to bring her left arm into play.

'Oh!' gulped Ted. He went for the coffee. Chaite composed herself and admired the book, wondering what was going to happen next. Ted returned: 'I didn't know about your arm'

'How could you have done?'

'Jinny didn't mention it. Dawn didn't mention it'

'A lot of people don't notice. It doesn't make a lot of difference to me ... [not quite true] ... Anyway, would you have not interviewed me if you had known?'

She gave him the chance to respond.

'Of course. Your form's very impressive – er – your application form, that is'

'Well, I can assure you that my present job ... the job I've just left ... has been a wonderful training – I think I've got the qualities you need ... and I'd be very willing to come for a trial period so that we can get to know each other ... You know, I want this job very much ... [am I selling myself too hard?] ... '

'I can see that. If you're as good an emissary for WEL as you are for yourself, we should get on all right ... But perhaps I'd better interview you, since that's what you've come for'

And so Ted turned to Chaite's application form and the interview proceeded in a more conventional manner – school ... university ... job experience ...

'And you can type?'

'Yes ... I use – used – a word processor in my previous job. To make up all the catalogue entries. I could take a typing test if you like ...'

'If you say you can do it, I'll believe you. I should think you can type better than a lot of people with – ah – two hands ... [Chaite forebore to comment on his assumption] ... When can you start?'

'You're offering me a job? What about salary, holidays, things like that? I need to know before I can accept ... or not ...'

Ted knew that Chaite knew that she was going to take the job anyway. He pulled out a folder; passed her some sheets of paper: 'Here you are. That's the contract. How long do you want to think about it?'

Chaite realised that there weren't queues of people waiting in the wings. She was a bird in the hand – the bird with one hand – so unusually competent that she'd be a talking point. She did not know

that, to Ted, she seemed heaven sent – for he had supported Bob
Wilkinson's unusual advert and, until her call, it had seemed doomed to
failure. Not that he minded failure, but he had been so convinced that
the advert was the right approach ... Anyway, she had offered herself
for a trial period; it would cost him another few hundred at least to get
someone else as competent sitting there. Just because there was
unemployment, it didn't mean that the recruitment exercise was cheaper
– or easier.

'When do you want me to start?'

'How about next Monday?'

'WOW! Suits me fine'

'Right; I'll write. Come and meet a few people ... if you've got time'

So Chaite had signed a confidentiality agreement, and gone on her first
tour of WEL, and been initiated into some of its secrets. The tour ended.
Ted showed her out through a side door, so she had no chance to say
good bye to Jinny. She could go to reception again ... but when she looked
in, Jinny was no longer there, so she made her way back to the B&B on
cloud nine.

How she had landed the job, she was not sure. She could not know that,
as far as WEL was concerned at least, Robert Townsend – he of *Up the
Organisation* fame – had come back into fashion. Bob Wilkinson,
founder and chairman, had suggested to the management (or
leadership) team that they should read (or re-read) the book to see if
there was any wisdom which they could apply; thus had the concept of
the WEL People Person emerged:

*Unless your company is too large (in which case break it up into
autonomous parts), have a one-girl people department (not a personnel
department). Records can be kept in the payroll section of the accounting
department and your one-girl people department (she answers her own
phone and does her own typing) acts as a personnel (sorry – people)
assistant to anybody who is recruiting. She lines up applicants, checks
references, and keeps your pay ranges competitive by checking other
companies.*

Bob, who was almost a member of the old school of personnel
management who could 'tell whether or not a chap's any good the
moment he walks in through the door' realised that this technique
might be good enough for him, but not for his company. So he'd
delegated personnel to Ted Crowe, the company secretary, and Ted had

evolved the system (such as it was) that Chaite was picking up. Ted had three criteria:

- Did the candidate have the technical knowledge needed to fill the vacancy?
- Did it seem as if the candidate would be able to grow with the company and take responsibility?
- Did the candidate present him or herself well and get on easily with people – particularly putative colleagues?

Balancing a number of assessments of these criteria had enabled WEL to make some good choices; now the system needed formalising and organising, and Ted had no doubt that Chaite was the person to do it – according to his criteria.

After he had made his decision, and Chaite had floated on her way, he had spoken to a few of the people they'd stopped to chat with on the Grand Tour. All were pleased to hear that Chaite was joining. None appeared to have noticed anything untoward about her.

As she approached Church Lane, Chaite started to work out ways of opening the front door – but was saved by Mrs Taylor approaching from the other direction with bags full of shopping.
'I've got the job ... [damned if I'm going to let her see how pleased I am] ... so I'll be staying the night. I won't be in till later – going to see a friend'
'Very well. Don't be too late – I go to bed about eleven o'clock myself'
'[So you'll be able to let me in] ... Oh, I should be back before then. See you later'
Chaite made her way to the Market Square and back to Twiney Family Newsagent. She reflected that as time went on she would know every nook and cranny; every jigger, jowler, ginnel, twitten or snicket; every place where one could slip through from one street to another, find a parking place, eat well and economically.

Perhaps she would get accommodation slap bang in the middle. She entered the wonderful world of Twiney. Looking round with fresh eyes she reflected that, whereas every other newsagent's shop in the land was the same as every other – the counter, the racks of magazines, the tobacco, the sweets, the cool cabinet full of tooth-rotting drinks, the greetings cards which never quite said what was required of them, always bought as a last resort – such standardisation seemed to have passed Twiney by.

'Hello, dear. Back again? Find what you were looking for? How can we help you this time?'

'I've got the job I went for ... at WEL – so I'm looking for somewhere to stay. I thought you'd be able to help'

'Job is it? Up the Lectric? That's nice'

'Yes, it is, isn't it? Do you know anywhere?'

'Oh yes. there's some cards in the window, though I think they're mostly the other way round'

'Do you mean I have to look at them from the inside?'

Twiney cackled.

'No the other way round – people looking for rooms, not rooms looking for people, as you might say. Or you could buy the *Telegraph* ... [she pushed one towards Chaite, and scooped up 20p in exchange] ... Or you could try opposite at Primrose Cottage. That's Mrs Primrose. She often takes people in' How ambiguous, thought Chaite:

'I'll go and see if she wants to take me in. Thank you very much. I expect I'll see you again'

'I expect so, dear. They all do'

Chaite emerged into a world that now seemed unreal compared with Twiney's. The market was beginning to wind down. She looked for opposite, and there it was – Primrose Cottage. Why hadn't some greedy developer got his mitts on it long ago? Thankful that he (for it would hardly be a she would it?) hadn't, she set about the task of finding the way in. There was a notice hanging on the railings: 'Go down to basement door and knock'.

Chaite picked her way down the unfamiliar stone steps, wondering if time would be when she would be running up and down them in all weathers without difficulty – in the dark, even.

There was the basement door, nestling under the steps leading up to the front door. It was wonderfully cool. And damp – ferns grew out of the wall. Chaite knocked. She had expected to wait, perhaps even knock again, but the door opened almost at once. Did Twiney have a grapevine? Or a secret tunnel?

'Good evening. Mrs Primrose? I'm Chaite Slatterthwaite and I've just got a job up the Lectric – so I'm looking for a room. They thought over at Twiney's that you might be able to help'

She switched into what she hoped was the vernacular, watching Mrs Primrose's expression: 'The tall lady's stern grey face broke into a charming smile' thought Chaite to herself – my God, that's a real old Sylvie Krin sentence, if ever I framed one.

'Come in and tell me all about it'

Are there any doors that the name of the Lectric won't open in Foxworth?

'Thanks'

Tall Mrs Primrose was pale blue and grey from top to toe. The basement was surprisingly spacious, full of furniture and ornaments – mainly Victorian. It made something to do, dusting everything whether it needed it or not, like painting the Forth Bridge. Chaite was in her element – indeed she recognised some of the pieces as having passed through her saleroom at Sellis's. She was able to launch into instant conversation; Mrs Primrose was clearly a collector rather than an inheritrix. After half an hour or so, during which they had drunk a delicious pot of tea without stopping for any of the pleasantries of sugarwork or milkplay, Mrs Primrose suddenly stopped: 'You're the girl with one arm from Sellis & Toker'

Wincing at the name, Chaite admitted that she was.

'You look different in that get-up'

'I often wore this sort of thing in the office. Oh ... I used to wear a floral overall if I was helping Charlie with the lots'

'What are you doing up the Lectric, then? ... [Mrs Primrose normally calls it WEL, but thinks she's pleasing Chaite; thus can myths spread] ... You were looking for a room?'

'Yes. they said in Twiney's ...'

'Well, you're in luck. Mr Mason's already moved out, so we'll be able to talk about antiques. Come and see'

Chaite didn't feel she'd been given much of a chance, and wondered how much antique talk would be required; interesting as it was, there were other topics up for grabs, and she wasn't sure that Mrs Primrose could sustain them.

She suddenly felt some unaccustomed alarm at the fact that there appeared to be no television in the Primrose sitting room. They climbed the narrow stair from the basement to the ground floor, and were confronted by a stripped pine door; a brass card-holder announced: 'E Mason'. Mrs Primrose knocked, more from habit than expectation. There was no reply. She got out a key and led the way in.

It was a most magnificent room stretching from the front to the back of the house, the bay window at the front looking out across the Market Square, and the French windows at the back leading to an enclosed garden sloping up to an old wall of red brick. The furniture: a comfortable-looking three-piece suite, bookshelves in the alcoves beside the blocked-up fireplaces, a polished mahogany table, and a large sideboard. To the left of the French windows a door which Mrs

Primrose now threw open; from a small vestibule there was the kitchen to the right; to the left, stairs leading up. Chaite noted with secret approval that none of the doors except the entrance had handles; all were fitted with ball catches. She followed Mrs Primrose up the stairs to a bedroom containing a not-quite-double bed, built-in wardrobe, and a view over the Market Square from an even higher vantage point. Opening off the bedroom was another door to an enormous bathroom equipped with everything anyone might ever want in a bathroom, including an exercise bicycle.

So far, Chaite had said nothing. She was overwhelmed:

'How much of this belongs to Mr Mason?'

'Nothing. He's gone. That's *my* exercise bicycle – but I don't use it. Just having it makes me feel better. Do you ride?'

Chaite laughed: 'Exercise bicycles, yes. Horses no. I can't believe that I can possibly afford to live here. How much are you asking?'

'Thirty-eight pounds a week'

'WHAT?'

'I could come down a bit if that's too much'

'No ... no ... I thought it was very reasonable. I'd love to take it'

Chaite suddenly became conscious of being in someone else's house – stupid, she told herself, since she was about to take it on. She led the way downstairs, entering the kitchen for the first time, pulling open cupboards from that obscure impulse to which we are all liable to succumb – perhaps in the hope that some arcane secret will be revealed – and turning on taps.

Satisfied that everything worked – and quite prepared to accept anything that didn't on the grounds that it could be fixed – Chaite returned to the basement, Mrs Primrose following her.

She got out her chequebook: 'A month's rent in advance?'

'Don't worry about that, dear, and don't be afraid that I'll let it to anyone else – you're Meant; the cards said so'

Chaite asked no questions, but felt Meant. She prepared to go: 'May I move in tomorrow?'

'Of course you can. I'll be in all day ... I'll tell you what – here's your key. You can come and go as you please'

'Thanks ever so much. I'll look forward to seeing you tomorrow, then'

She took her leave, wondering why she attracted – deserved – so much good fortune.

Chaite emerged into the lengthening shadows. She looked round Foxworth – 'her' Foxworth. She had a job and the most magnificent flat.

She was part of a new something – all on her own merits. 'The girl who's tired of Foxworth is tired of life' she said to herself. She wondered where the cosmic catch was.

Bursting with her news, she found a phone box and telephoned Mercia. Then she returned to Ruskin House. She performed the door-opening sequence she'd been practising mentally; it worked. Mrs Taylor came bustling out of the innards: 'You're back early. You don't want to eat, I hope'
'No ... in fact, I'm very sorry, but I've just rung my sister ... I've got to get back to her ... family matters ... I'll pay for the night' [she pulls out three prepared fivers] ... that's seventeen pounds with the deposit ... hope that's OK'
Looking disdainful, Mrs Taylor accepted the notes in silence. Chaite smiled uncertainly: 'Right ... I'll just go and pack my things, and then I'll be off'
She went upstairs and flung everything into her cases as fast as she could, carried it all downstairs in two trips, managed to open the front door, loaded her car, left her key on the hall table, called a desultory goodbye to Mrs Taylor and left Church Lane and Foxworth, looking forward to whatever celebration she and Mercia would surely have that evening.

15
Tuesday 23 July 1985

Good turns sour; out of evil comes forth good.

Chaite was having to find a new job because of the objectionable behaviour of Kevin Toker. Chaite had not wanted to work with him – let alone *for* him – she had quite enough to do looking after her own side of the business.

She recalled her first day at Sellis & Co, Auctioneers and Estate Agents – long before Kevin had appeared on the scene – when she had arrived to bring James Sellis's dreams to reality. The Sellis family had been in the business for over a century; James had been brought up with it; there were few farms, holdings, plots in the area which had come to auction in the previous decades without falling under his hammer.

Now, with the decreasing movement in sheep and cattle, and the increasing demand for sales of bygones – some would call it junk – James wanted to start a regular auction: 'go domestic' as he said.

Serendipity came into play; it was at tea in the vicarage garden on the day of the Rusham village fête that James Sellis had enthused about his plans to a beautiful girl in a floral tent.
'You ought to talk to my sister ... [Cepha had said] ... she's got a first in history and fine arts, and she and her husband have been doing up a cottage for the last year. I think she may be looking for a job ...'
James Sellis was fascinated:
'I'd certainly like to meet her. We can't afford to pay much, you know ... [like hell you can't, thought Cepha] ... but ... well, let's see'

So Chaite had seen; had seen an opportunity for learning, for turning her considerable knowledge to good use, perhaps for indulging her love for collecting; for finding out about the trade from the inside; maybe, one day she'd ...

That was in the future. Chaite joined Sellis & Co, and threw herself intensively into market research, visiting as many sales as she could, antique/bric-à-brac/junk shops ... until the week when James Sellis was asked if he could clear no fewer than three houses. He held a hurried conference with Chaite, who gave him the confidence to say 'yes'.

They had a marquee erected over the old cattle pens, and got the old sheds beside the pens patched up in a remarkably short space of time. Chaite started to classify and catalogue all the items as they stood so that they could be taken to the makeshift salerooms in order.

They held two sales – the first of furniture; the second of more esoteric items. From then on, that side of the business was made; Chaite virtually took it over, advertised a regular monthly sale; people started to bring lots in; the business thrived. Thus was James Sellis's dream realised.

As far as business was concerned, Chaite's accident had been an unfortunate hiccough. She had an excellent assistant in Claire, and she recovered so robustly that she missed only two sales. Far more devastating to her saleroom career was the arrival of Kevin Toker.

When Chaite returned to work after her accident, she had thought it a good idea to meet the paragon Kevin Toker, whom James had met at some professional dinner. Kevin had visited the office a few times, and Chaite had at first found him pleasant; neither attractive nor repellent; clearly competent from the sorts of questions he asked, and the suggestions he made.

It was not until he joined the firm that he started to reveal himself in his true colours – though Chaite could never quite bring herself to believe that he was really like that.

James had asked her to help Kevin find his feet. But it was then that he'd started to niggle and twit away at her, insinuating that she couldn't be much good at her job because she had only one hand and must therefore be half-witted. His extension of this was that James must have had some dark motive for taking her back after the accident. True, Chaite and James had built up a very close working relationship, and were very dependent upon one another's work, but their relationship seemed to be something that Kevin couldn't comprehend.

Chaite was competent and efficient, and saw herself as part of the firm, helping James to build up the saleroom; make it successful. Kevin could not understand this relationship based on mutual trust and respect – he was convinced that there must be something more sinister going on, but was puzzled that he could never (of course) find any evidence to support his conviction.

The seeds of Chaite's downfall were sowed thus. It was late one Monday evening; Chaite stayed on to type an urgent letter for Kevin – although it wasn't her job – then took it to him, with stamped envelope at the ready, for him to sign. The letter – and the document to which it referred – had to arrive the following morning if the transaction to which it referred was to proceed. Chaite had wanted to suggest that some other means of delivery might be preferable, but Kevin's look shut her up. She didn't know why she bothered.
'OK, Fatima – you can go now'
Chaite left quickly; retired to the fastness of the ladies loo to cry her eyes out. She could not know for certain, but she was pretty sure that Kevin called her Fatima in some tortuous reference to the penalty of Shariah law ... and since she was neither a shoplifter, nor a Muslim, it was hyper-cruel, as well as being grossly unfair ... and as for 'you can go now' ... who did he think he was? A prime candidate for the Rub' al Khali. But she'd have to fight her own battles; it was no good burdening James Sellis with this one – he wouldn't have a clue what to do.

Tuesday morning; the phone rings; the letter and the document haven't arrived. Chaite tries to reassure the client: '... Well, it should've

144

caught last night's post ... I prepared it myself – yes, I'll put you through'

She can hear Kevin in his office: '... is that what she said? Well, I'm very sorry. Actually, the silly bitch has only got one arm, so I'm not surprised ... Hello?'

Chaite sees red. With tears of rage, she cuts off the call and storms into Kevin's office. She feels as angry now as she did on that Cup Final Saturday. Kevin freezes when he sees the look on her face, stands up quickly, not knowing what's going to happen. He laughs nervously: 'Look, Chaite ... I didn't mean ...'

In her rage, Chaite forgets that she is no longer left-handed; she steps forward and slaps Kevin's face, sees him reel away and fall as the solidity of her artifical arm catches him across the side of the head.

As happened on that previous occasion, her victim lies quietly on the floor, not daring to move for fear of what might happen next, Kevin's coat hangs on the back of the door; acting on a hunch which proves to be correct, Chaite finds the missing document – along with some other items which ought to have been posted – in the inside pocket. She pulls everything out; throws it down on his desk. Still he doesn't stir. She picks up the important envelope, and goes back to her office. She rings the client – who is covered with confusion – apologises for their having been cut off, and promises to send the envelope by messenger.

Having arranged that, she feels much calmer; she goes in to James's office: 'I've come to give you my resignation'

'Nonsense ... why?'

Reluctantly, she explains what happened, and the innuendoes leading up to it. One of them has to go, and she's the one. She doesn't mind now; if James Sellis, whom she respected, thinks Kevin Toker fit to join the firm, there must be something wrong with his judgement.

James, who knows exactly what to do as long as everything is going smoothly, and is all at sea if it isn't, can only agree with Chaite – yes, he can quite see the problem – but he can't think what to do for the best.

All her respect for him has by now evaporated; the fact that he is not entreating her to stay strengthens her resolve to leave; her pent-up rage blanks from her mind the perfection and excitement of her job, in which she once saw such a limitless future; makes it easier for her to leave.

She goes back to her office and clears her personal belongings out of her desk and her cupboard. What was private and homely becomes once more impersonal: containers of wood and grey steel. She purposely leaves a few treasury tags, paperclips, spent pens and other trivia in the drawers; to clear them properly would be to stamp her personality upon them; now, they are like 'empty' drawers in a million other desks.

She is still shaking with a mixture of emotions as she says her goodbyes to some very good friends, makes her way home, packs a case, and departs for the comfort of Mercia once more.

16
Sunday 22 May 1983 *et seq*

Her crushed wrist having been cleaned, her wedding ring having been removed, X-rays having been taken, and dressings having been applied, Chaite is taken to a room off the corridor leading to the orthopaedic ward where an orthopod comes to see her – or rather her wrist.

She – or rather her wrist – is no candidate for microsurgery. There's nothing to do but wait and see if it's viable.

Chaite's night is far from comfortable; her left arm elevated, a drip dripping, a miasma of pain. Night turns into day. Chaite is dimly aware of activity around her; her heightened hearing receives squeals, pistol shots, the clangour as of a campanile, people shrieking at the tops of their voices – in reality, they're just going about their ordinary business in the ordinary way.

Nurses appear and disappear, bedpans slip in and out, she is fed, she exists in a half world where nature seems dead; where there is no proper distinction between day and night; visions constantly change, her dead parents come and see her, in the room the people come and go, murmuring at and about her.

But above all there is the nagging pain, the pain that will not ease for one moment, the pain that first visited, excruciatingly and exquisitely, on Saturday afternoon.

It is Monday morning; apprised by telephone, Mercia is sitting by Chaite's bed. In comes a young doctor: 'Good morning ... this is your sister, I understand?'
'Yes ...?'
'I'm Dr Bendall, Mr Moreton-Smith's registrar. I'd like to take a look at her ... Would you mind ...?'
'Of course not ...'

146

Mercia gives Chaite's right hand a squeeze, goes out into the corridor, wanders aimlessly up and down, admiring the view from the window – a vast expanse of brickwork. Eventually a nurse appears: 'Would you like to come back in?'

'Thank you ... who's Mr Moreton-Smith?'

'He's our orthopaedic consultant. He's looking after your sister'

Mercia returns to the bedside: 'How ...'

'Your sister's wrist isn't going to get any better – the bruising's massive; the blood supply to her hand seems to be very poor. We could wait another twenty-four hours, but I'm afraid there's probably only one thing we can do'

Mercia thinks she can guess what that is. Can Chaite?

'Please ... please ...'

Mercia is shocked: 'Are you sure?'

'Even if we can save her hand, she'll not he able to use it. She'll probably be in constant pain. It'll be much better if ...'

'But you think it might improve in the next twenty-four hours?'

Dr Bendall avoids the truth: 'We'll have to wait for Mr Moreton-Smith's opinion'

'Are you sure ...?'

'If we are able to save her hand, it'll be useless to her ... whereas she · could have a very useful artificial one ...'

'But ...'

'... They can do marvellous things these days ... putting men on the moon ... they can certainly fit your sister up with a new arm ...'

'Arm?'

'Well ... hand; it'll fit on at the elbow, and it'll be far better than what she'll have now. Perhaps you could talk to her ...'

He goes out.

'Chaite?'

'What?'

'Can you hear me? Did you hear that?'

'They're going to stop the pain'

'Yes ... yes, that's what he said'

'And make it as good as new'

Mercia thinks that Chaite understands more than she does.

The registrar returns: 'We'll have to ask her to sign a consent form for the operation'

The form is on a board, with a pen; he gives it to Chaite: 'Read this ... [he pauses all too short a short while; Chaite sees no point in trying to read it] ... Do you understand it?'

147

'Yes ... yes'
Now Mercia isn't sure: 'What if she *doesn't* understand it?'
'Then her next of kin will have to sign on her behalf'
'You mean I'll have to ...?'
'Is she married?'
'Well ...'
'Then her next of kin will be her husband'
Mercia comes back hurriedly: 'That's all theoretical. You do understand it, don't you, Chaite?'
'Ye-es'
'Right. Could you sign here, please ... [why does he shout so?] ... you'd better use your right hand ... [I can't use the other hand, stupid] ... just here'
'I'm signing so that you can stop the pain?'
'Yes'
Liar.
Chaite makes a Chi and a squiggle.
'You've signed with an X – ha-ha'
What the hell's he laughing at?
'It's a Chi – a Greek Chi'
'Oh, very good ...'
He's not listening, is he? He nods and leaves the room.
A nurse hovers.
Mercia bends down and kisses Chaite: 'Bye bye for now... I'll see you ... later. Good luck'
Mercia can think of nothing else to say. She leaves with tears in her eyes. At the door she turns, but Chaite doesn't seem to be looking. Mercia blows her nose noisily into her handkerchief; leans against the wall of the corridor for support, head a-swim.

'Come and sit down'
'Oh ... thank you'
She allows herself to be steered – with her eyes shut – into a staff room with a kitchen unit and institutional easy chairs; she sits.
'Can I get you a coffee?'
'Yes please ... black, no sugar'
She hears the kettle being filled, the sound of the coffee jar, the tintinabulation of spoons in mugs.
Her saviour sits down while the kettle boils; she wears a label:
Nione Wood – Occupational Therapist.
Mercia points: 'How do you pronounce that?'

'Ny-oh-knee. Have you been visiting?'

'Yes – my sister Chaite. She's just signed a thing ... to have her hand ...'

'Ah yes. It'll be the best thing. I've seen Chaite; I'll be looking after her when she gets her new hand'

'If it comes to that ...'

The kettle switches itself off; Nione makes coffee; hands Mercia her mug; sits down. Mercia feels that if anyone is going to make things better, it's Nione. If Mercia were a newly-hatched chick, they'd call it imprinting.

'Have they explained what they're going to do?'

'Well ... just that they're thinking about amputating Chaite's hand to stop the pain'

'It's not just to stop the pain – even if her wrist healed, it wouldn't be much use to her. Do you know how it happened?'

'No ... I just got a phone call from Roy – that's her husband – and he said that Chaite had had an accident, and told me where she was – here – and said he was going away for a bit. Then he rang off'

'I see. It happened at home, do you think?'

'I don't know. I can't imagine *how* it happened ... I just don't know. Will they – you – *really* be able to give her another hand?'

'Oh yes ... we can give her a hand which'll enable her to do things ... and it'll look quite good'

Mercia's vision of Chaite's new hand is different from Nione's – utterly bionic; an almost perfect replacement. Talking about it in such a matter-of-fact and positive way is making her feel better; calming her down; making it a little easier to accept the earth-shattering loss her sister is suffering: 'Did you know she's left handed?'

'What? No. I haven't got that far. But she'll easily learn to write with her other hand'

'She'll be forced to, won't she?'

'Well ... you can write with an artificial hand, but you don't get the fine control ... what's her job, by the way? She said something about a saleroom'

'She looks after James Sellis's auctions – you know, the auctioneer and estate agent. She really got it going, really'

'Does she need two hands for that?'

'No-o-o ... it's quite supervisory, I think. But they might not want her back'

'Ah. There's no reason why they shouldn't ... she could start back in a couple of months – if she's strong. If she can take it slowly'

'She's strong – I think. When will she get her new hand?'

'Well ... that might take a little longer ... but ... three or four months, perhaps'

'And when will she be out of here?'

'Oh ... certainly in a couple of weeks, I'd say'

Nione can see that Mercia is in a more hopeful state than when she found her. She looks at her watch: 'I'm awfully sorry, but I'll have to go soon. But we'll meet again. Who's going to look after your sister when she's discharged, by the way?'

'Well ... I've no idea what's happened to Roy. And Cepha – that's our other sister – 's got four young children. I guess it'll have to be me. I can do it. Luckily, I've got time'

Nione rises; so does Mercia. They shake hands squeezingly.

'Thank you for being so kind. I'm fine now. We'll meet again'

Nione starts to tidy up as Mercia leaves the room, turning in the doorway with a smile and a thank you.

Mercia decides against going back to see Chaite. She does not know that she's just missed Chaite passing down the corridor on her way to theatre; Mr Moreton-Smith has decided to operate. Mercia turns towards the lifts. The doors of the lift bearing Chaite upwards close just as Mercia arrives in the vestibule.

Mercia arrives home; immediately rings Cepha:

'Hello'

'Oh, Cepha ... [Mercia's voice trembles] ... I think Chaite's going to lose her hand'

'WHAT? Say that again'

'I said Chaite's going to lose her hand. They won't be able to save it, I know they won't'

'They can't do that to her. I won't let them – what's the number? I'll ... soon ...'

'CEPHA. Don't be silly. Her hand's all dead, and so will she be if they don't ... anyway, she's in terrible pain, and she's signed the form'

Mercia sees the scene from above, like a split-screen film – Chaite's elder and younger sisters holding their telephone receivers, discussing her fate, regardless of the fact that the great Juggernaut Hospital has it all under remorseless and irreversible control.

'When will she be out again? And where will she go?'

'In a couple of weeks – so Nione Wood says – she's the occupational therapist I met who'll be looking after her. She'll be able to come and stay with me – luckily, I've got the time at the moment, and I think I can keep it that way while Chaite needs me'

'Poor little Chaite ... what'll happen to her?'
'She could be back at work in a couple of months – Nione says. And they'll be able to give her a new hand so that she can do things – Nione says'
'Right. So what's to be done now?'
'Well, I'll ring James Sellis ... And I'll ring the hospital this evening, and let you know if there's any news'
'OK then. Chaite ... I just can't get over it ...'
They talk a little more; then sever the sororial link.

Now Mercia rings James Sellis: 'It's Mercia here – Chaite's sister'
'Oh yes? How is she now?'
'I'm afraid she's going to lose her hand'
'Oh ... that *is* bad news. Poor girl. Is there anything I can do ...?'
'Well ... I'm not sure ...'
'When will she be able to come back to work?'
Mercia's heart leaps: 'Oh ... Mr Sellis ... you won't be getting someone else?'
'Replace Chaite? Impossible – even if ... No, you tell her I want her back just as soon as she's able to come. That'll give her something to look forward to'
'That's really good news, Mr Sellis. I've been talking to the occupational therapist, and she thinks Chaite might be able to get back to you in a couple of months. Perhaps. It all depends'
'Two months. June, July ... it's usually quieter in the Summer. We'll manage until she can ... tell her not to worry. When can we come and see her?'
'I'm not sure ... I'll let you know when she's ready for visitors ... I'll keep in touch'
'Thank you, Mercia. Now, is there anything else I can do ...?'
'Not that I can think of ... Keeping Chaite's job open is ... If there's anything else, I'll certainly ...'
'Right. Good bye, then – and give Chaite all our best wishes'
'I will – good bye'
'Good bye'
Mercia hangs up. Ending a conversation with James Sellis can be very difficult.
    She goes to the kitchen, makes herself a sandwich and a coffee, using one hand as far as possible. She can see that it's not going to be too easy for Chaite. But she can also see how she'll be able to help.

Then she forces herself to her desk and tries to concentrate on editing the next chapter of *The physical and economic geography of the EEC*. But she can't concentrate, and decides to go for a walk round the common.

Mercia is sitting on a bench on the common watching the children playing on the roundabout and swings. All the time, she is thinking of Chaite; wondering whether there's a chance that they'll be able to save her hand; whether perhaps it's all a bad dream.

Her mind turns to the operation; she has some vague vision of the central figure of Mr Moreton-Smith, surrounded by lesser mortals, crowding round Chaite; everyone and everything swathed in green sterility. The anaesthetist sits, caringly professional; Mr Moreton-Smith calls for various instruments and implements of which she doesn't like to think; the clink of stainless steel trays and bowls, professional murmurings ... the scene changes to a comic shadow operation, strings of sausages being removed, hammers, pliers, saws ... saws ...

Drain and sutures; gauze and padding; splint and bandages.
The green anaesthetist administers a brachial plexus block:
'That'll keep her arm numb for twenty-four hours ...'
Chaite is moved to the recovery room.

Mercia looks at her watch. It's nearly half-past five; where has the day gone? And tomorrow ... Did Mercia but know it, Chaite has been out of theatre for nearly an hour; is now on her way back to the orthopaedic ward.

Now Mercia feels a great relief on Chaite's behalf; she believes it's telepathic, and sees Chaite out of pain and sleeping cherubically, a Mona Lisa smile. Unable to bear the suspense any longer, she trots home and rings the hospital.
'Orthopaedic Ward, Staff Nurse Potts'
'It's – I'm enquiring about Chaite Slatterthwaite – it's her sister here'
'Ah ... She's just arrived back on the ward ... The amputation went well, and she's comfortable'
'The WHAT? I thought they hadn't decided ... They were going to decide tomorrow. If they decided to do it at all'
'No ... Mr Moreton-Smith had her on his list for this afternoon'
'Oh ... oh ... When can I see her?'
'I don't think I should come to-night ... I should ring tomorrow morning; you ought to be able to come in any time after ten o'clock'
'Right ... give her my love, will you?'

'Yes, I will. What's your name again?'
'Mercia. Thank you, then. Goodbye'

Chaite stirs in the night. A nurse is looking down at her. Chaite looks
up. Her left arm feels as though it's gripped in a vice: 'These bandages
are awfully tight'
The nurse smiles professionally: 'Don't worry – it'll wear off'
'Seriously, can't you loosen them a bit?'
'Not yet. Try to get some more sleep. It'll get better, I promise you'
Chaite feels too tired to argue. She knows she's reached some sort of
turning point in her life, but can't quite think what it can be. Somewhere
a telephone rings. She hears the nurse moving away. Her whole body
feels as though it belongs to someone else; she has no motor control; she
can think about moving, but is too weary to put the thoughts into
practice. With a superhuman effort, she moves her right hand to
explore those tight bandages. The bandaging seems enormous. Now
everything springs sharply into focus – 'like black crenellations against
a cloudless sky' she thinks. Where is her left hand? It couldn't be ... she
wiggles her fingers inside the tight bandage ... No, that's all right. She
drifts off to sleep again.

Tuesday morning; Mercia rings the hospital to find that Chaite has had
'a comfortable night' and that she can come in at ten. So at ten o'clock on
the dot Mercia emerges from the lift, fearful of what she will see. But
she must be strong – she's Chaite's sister, and she's going to look after
her when she comes out of here.
    Mercia makes her way to the room where Chaite was yesterday;
her heart misses a beat, for the occupant of the bed is in traction ... but
it's not Chaite; it's one of those old ladies with wispy white hair and
pale sunken cheeks who seem to exist only in institutions. Mercia tiptoes
away; finds a nurse: 'I've come to see my sister – Chaite'
The nurse points: 'That room there'
It's a four-bed unit; only one bed is occupied.

Mercia kisses Chaite on the forehead. She is surprised at how small
Chaite looks – as though they've put her into an enormous bed for a joke.
She can't help looking at Chaite's left arm, hugely swathed in padding
and bandages, supported on a board ... it looks ... perhaps they've been
able to save her hand after all.
Chaite wakes.
'How are you?'

'Fine – but the bandages are a bit tight. I'll be out of here soon'
Mercia doesn't want to remind Chaite of her condition, but wonders whether the pain has gone with the hand: 'How do you feel ... in yourself?'
What the hell does that mean?
'As I said, fine, except that the bandages are a bit tight. I asked the nurse to loosen them, but she said it was best to leave things as they are for the moment'
'I met Nione Wood yesterday. She's the occupational therapist who's going to help you with your new arm'
This means different things to Chaite and Mercia.
'Good. Perhaps *she*'ll be able to loosen the bandages – I can wiggle my fingers again now – the pain's gone'
It dawns on Mercia that Chaite has chosen not to accept what has happened. She's at a loss for words. Chaite continues: 'It's marvellous what they can do these days – I should be back to normal ... very soon'
Mercia gulps: 'Good ... and I've got some good news for *you*; I spoke to James Sellis yesterday, and he's looking forward – very forward – to you getting back to work as soon as you can. He'll probably come and see you this weekend'
'What day is it today?'
'Tuesday'
'Tuesday. How long have I been here?'
You came in on Saturday. This'll be the ... third day'
'Oh. Well, I'll be out tomorrow, I expect. Or the next day. And back to work next week. That's not too bad'
'I'm not sure ...'
'There's nothing wrong with me, you know – once I get these bandages off'
'Ah. Well ... er .... would you like to come and stay with me for a bit when you *do* come out? I'd like to help you ... help you to get really properly better'
Chaite smiles: 'Thanks – I'd like that ... little sister'
It's years since she's called Mercia that.

'How are you Chaite?'
It's Cepha.
'Fine; I'll be out of here very soon'
'Well ...'
'They'll be taking off these bandages any time now, and then I'll be able to go home'

'I'm not sure that it's as easy as that'
'Nonsense. There's nothing wrong with me, you know ... once I get these bandages off'
'Chaite ... they weren't able to repair your hand'
'Yes, they're awfully clever at that sort of thing'
'Chaite, Humpty, THEY CAN'T PUT YOU TOGETHER AGAIN. I'm afraid you've got to face it – YOU'VE LOST YOUR HAND'
'Don't be silly; it's under these bandages'

It's so easy to be ill in hospital. Chaite loses track of time: eating, dozing, Nione Wood, visitors coming and going, especially Mercia. Doctors and nurses. Curtains drawn round; dressings removed, drain removed; new dressings; drip removed; doctors' rounds; physiotherapist keeping her shoulder and elbow working. Chaite's body focuses on the time of the next blessed injection; she becomes an instant junkie. Her mind focuses on the routine, trying to eliminate the time until the next spell of relief; she has no cognisance of life before – or after – pain.

It seems to go on for ever, but in reality it's Friday morning when Chaite awakes and comes to terms with what's happened.
'Ah-ah-ah-ow-ow-ow-oo!'
She rings the bell. A nurse comes silently and swiftly.
'My hand's gone'
'Yes ... Mr Moreton-Smith thought it was the best thing'
'Why didn't he tell me?'
Defensive nurse: 'I'm sure Mr Moreton-Smith and Dr Bendall both discussed it with you. And you signed the form'
'Did they? Did I? Did my sister know?'
'I ...'
'I want to see her. I want to see my sister Mercia – when's she coming?'
'She'll be in this afternoon as usual, I expect'
Mercia arrives; is intercepted by the nurse: 'Your sister's been asking for you. I think she's ... sitting up and taking notice to-day'
'That's good. Is Nione coming in?'
'She usually comes round in the mornings, but I'll give her a ring and see if ...'
She dematerialises; Mercia finds Chaite sitting in a chair by the bed, her bandaged stump propped up on a pillow. She wishes she could think of something to say other than: 'How are you today?'
Chaite ignores the question: 'Did you know my hand had gone?'
'Yes ... we talked about it with Dr Bendall ... on Monday ...'

'Did we? Did we? Why did you let them do it? How am I going to ...?'
Chaite bursts into tears. Mercia tries not to feel guilty at suppressing
information she suspected all along that Chaite had not possessed.
Suddenly, Chaite stops crying. She has clanged the past into one of her
safe deposit boxes; welded the lid firmly shut.

The registrar arrives: 'I'm Doctor Bendall, Mr Moreton-Smith's
registrar'
The nurse explains that Mercia is Chaite's sister, and will be looking
after her when she's discharged from hospital.
It's almost as though everyone has forgotten Monday's conversation.
'Oh, that's very good news. Your sister's coming along fine, just fine.
We'll soon have her back to normal again ... [Will you? How?] ... You
can take her over to see my colleague in ALAC next week – staff nurse'll
make an appointment. He'll fit her up with another arm and she'll be
as good as new'
'What, next week?'
'Well ... it'll take a little longer than that, but he'll soon have her back
to normal. Yes. Is there anything she wants to ask me?'
'Well ... you'd better ask Chaite that. I think she's with us'
Chaite can pick up the mockery in Mercia's voice; it's lost on Dr
Bendall.
'There *are* two things'
Dr Bendall turns to Chaite in surprise: 'Oh? What?'
'Why's my arm so short? I thought it was only my wrist that was
damaged'
'Well ... we're going to fit you up with a new arm'
'So?'
'So there's got to be room for the wrist mechanism in your new arm. You
only need a short stump – just enough for the muscles to work. Fourteen
centimetres below the elbow, that's best. You won't need any more'
'Oh ...'
'What's the other thing you wanted to ask?'
'Er ... What's ALAC?'
'ALAC? Oh ... ALAC ... the Artificial Limb and Appliance Centre. It's
in another building on the site. Your sister will be able to take you over'
Dr Bendall moves away to spread more sweetness, light and misplaced
hope. Chaite murmurs: 'Take me over'
Mercia whispers: 'It's a take-over'
They giggle together; it turns the clock back.

On Saturday, Chaite wakes with a palindrome churning in her head; now she's awake, she can't quite get it right. She thinks hard ... what is it ... ? A man, a plan, a canal – Panama! That's it ... Ferdinand de Lesseps ... but why did she have it on the brain ... ?

Something to do with ALAC ... yes ... Alas, alack ... where does it go from there? What is it backwards? CALA, sala. George Augustus Sala? Perhaps it's a palindrome after all. No, it was a pun ... a lass – Chaite; a lack – Chaite's hand. She wonders if the staff have seen it that way.

The weekend passes tiringly; the clinical function of the hospital grinds to a halt, to be usurped by streams of visitors bearing flowers, fruit, get-well cards, bottles of squash and the detached concern of those who can get up and walk away whenever they choose.

Chaite receives Mercia (of course), Rupert and Cepha, James Sellis, her assistant Claire, Claire's assistant Debbie, Charlie the porter and Norman Bland the auctioneer. Her bed area turns into a veritable florist's shop.

When Mercia visits on Monday, Chaite is about with her stump much more lightly bandaged.
'Hi'
'Hi ... I went to the loo all by myself this morning. And washed myself'
'Well done ... how did you feel?'
'Woozy ... but I felt jolly proud ... Did you say that you're going to look after me when I come out? We'll have to talk about that'
'When you're ready. I think we'd better talk to Nione as well – I hope she'll be coming along soon'
'Good. And do you know what else?'
'No?
'Doctor Bendall ... "Mr Moreton-Smith's registrar" [they say it together, with giggles] ... says I'm ready for the take-over to ALAC tomorrow ... will you be able to come?'
'Of course; what time?'
'The appointment's at eleven ... it's a Doctor Meadmore, the Medical Officer. Apparently, he prefers people to visit him rather than him coming to see them'
'Sounds very important'
'Yes. Reading between the lines, he sounds very odd. I'm looking very forward to meeting him – as James Sellis would say'
They fall to talking of other things.

Chaite shows Mercia her attempts at writing right-handed; Mercia is impressed. Chaite does not tell Mercia that she can feel a pain in the hand that isn't there almost as bad as it's ever been.

The following morning, Chaite is sitting by the bed; Mercia arrives to take her to ALAC.
'What's the time?'
'Oh ... twenty to'
'Retter get ready'
A nurse brings a wheelchair: 'Can I give you a hand?'
'Yes PLEASE'
Everyone blushes in silence; Chaite sees there's going to be a lot of this. How can one train oneself not to blush? She'll have to practice with Mercia. Now she's in the wheelchair, cradling her stump in her right arm, as it were a lost child.

They make the journey in silence. Chaite realises how vulnerable she is; how weak and institutionalised; her first thought is that she wants to get back to the ward; then it suddenly comes to her that *this* is the real world; then she longs for her release, for her independence – even if it's independence with Mercia behind her – as she is now, pushing the chair. There seem to be few people around at eleven o'clock; those that are are hospital oriented; Chaite doesn't feel stared at.

The doors open automatically as they approach the ALAC building; the huge reception area seems to be empty ... but it's not – there is a young Asian receptionist in a beautiful sari retrieving something from under the desk. She bobs up like a jill-in-the-box: 'Good *morr*ning; can 1 help you?'
'Yes ... we've come to see Dr Meadmore'
'And yourr *name*?'
'Chaite Slatterthwaite'
She consults a list: 'El*even* o'clock'
'Yes'
'Would you wait *over* there please? Until you hearr yourr *name* called'
The girls go to the waiting area where two motionless pensioners sit back to back, contemplating the knocked-out carpet tiles.
Chaite and Mercia are trying to work out which limbs might be missing, without success, when the call comes: 'Miz Slatterthwaite ... [she points] ... Go down the *corri*dorr herre, and you hwill *see* Dr Meadmorre's dorr open -- he is ex*pect*ing you now'
It all falls pat, just as she tells them.

Dr Meadmore sits in a white coat, hairy suit beneath, looking over his half-moon spectacles: 'Come in – you must be Miss Slatterthwaite – and you are ...?'

'I'm Chaite; this is my sister, Mercia'

'Hmm. Unusual names. Unusual names, aren't they?'

'We're used to them'

'Our eldest sister's called Cepha. That's pretty unusual, too ... and there's Nione ...'

'Hum. Is Miss Wood a relation too?'

'No, it's just an unusual name'

'Yes. Put her here, please'

Oh, dear – he's in 'Does she take sugar?' mode.

Chaite is now sitting in her wheelchair on Dr Meadmore's side of the desk at least she's not on the other side – that would be just too WF Yeames: 'And when did you last see your arm?'

Mercia deliberately withdraws to an inconspicuous distance.

Dr Meadmore prepares to make notes: 'Now ... it's Chaite Slatterthwaite? And her date of birth?'

'Fifteenth of July nineteen-fifty-eight'

'So she's ... twenty-four – twenty-five in July'

Chaite nods. Well ... it all helps to pass the time.

'And ... [he cocks his head towards Mercia] ... what did she do for a living?'

Mercia refuses to be drawn in.

Chaite refuses to talk in the past tense: 'I work at Sellis's ... the auctioneers and estate agents. I'm in charge of all the saleroom activities'

'Yes ... [how can he find so much to write?] ... And what did this entail?'

'Well, we have a sale on the third Friday of every month, and I look after the advertising, and cataloguing and arranging the lots as they come in, and on the day make sure that the sale goes smoothly and all the records are kept up to date ...'

'Do you do all this singlehanded?'

Chaite gulps: 'No, I've got ... [she goes to count with fingers that aren't there and is doubly confused] ... I've got up to four people in the firm to help me – one permanent assistant – that's Claire – and the others have other jobs except for the run-up to the sale. And there's the porter, Charlie – and Norman the auctioneer'

Has he stopped listening? He lifts the phone and buzzes for his nurse: 'Now ... let's have a look ...'

Chaite extends her arm; turns away her head. Mercia peers curiously, seeing for the first time – with a mixture of compassion and revulsion – what has happened to her sister as Dr Meadmore's nurse removes the bandages so that he can examine the stump: 'Hmm ... still quite swollen ... but it's healing nicely ... that's a good six inches ... one of Moreton-Smith's best ... Bend ... Straighten ... Any pain?'

Chaite lies: 'No'

Dr Meadmore produces what passes as a smile: 'Good ... Right, nurse!'
The nurse re-applies bandages.

There is a sound in the corridor. Dr Meadmore calls: 'Mr Redman, please ... [enter Mr Redman] ... This is Miss Slatterthwaite ... [an exchange of nods] ... who'll be needing a new arm. Redman is my arm man. He'll be fixing you up when the time comes ... Thank you'

Mr Redman leaves.

'And when *will* the time come?'

'Probably another six weeks or so. It depends on the healing process ... now, has anyone explained the options to your sister?'

Mercia keeps silent.

'What options?'

'Prosthetic options'

I don't believe it: 'As I understand it, I can have a new hand which I can do things with and a lighter one which looks more plausible'

Dr Meadmore smiles broadly, as if rewarding a child: 'That's right. You can have an arm with a variety of terminal devices – a cosmetic hand, a functional hand, a split hook ... [this is the ... *round* window, and this is the ... *square* window] ... You'll soon learn how to use it'

'Oh? And what happens if I don't?'

'My dear young lady – I can assure you that you should find little difficulty in using it. But I grant you that many people who are born upper-limb deficient never use a prosthesis'

WHAT?? Chaite catches Mercia's eye: 'Oh? Why not?'

'Because ... they learn not to'

What tortuous reasoning is this?

'They wouldn't have to learn not to, would they? Are you suggesting that I should learn not to?'

Dr Meadmore is tetchy: 'No, I'm suggesting that you'll have no difficulty'

This could get very hairy; the girls exchange glances again.

Dr Meadmore clears his throat, leans forward, and pushes Chaite's chair back slightly so that he can open one of the drawers of his desk.

To Chaite, it looks like a dolls' hospital in there: 'Ha-ha – looks like a dolls' hospital in there'

'Yes – very good ... [he extracts a small leg from the tangle] ... Now, this is a leg ...'

From the corner of her eye, Chaite can see Mercia silently shaking. This session with Dr Meadmore is the best medicine she's had yet.

'Yes – that's a leg. I've got two of them already. Anyway, that one's too small. How about an arm?'

'I'm coming to that ... [Dr Meadmore extracts an equally small arm] ... Here we are; this is the sort of thing we can give you'

He hands it to Chaite; by a huge effort, she avoids stretching out the wrong arm to take it. It seems very hard and unyielding. She lays it on the desk, orients it, and offers it up: 'It's a bit small ... like the leg'

Mercia emits a strangled snort.

'It belonged to one of my patients. You'd have one the – er – proper size. Of course'

'Of course. How does it work?'

Dr Meadmore reaches for the arm so that he can demonstrate:

'This is a supracondylar arm of the sort we'll give you ...'

'It fits ahove the knuckle?'

'Knuckle?'

'Kondylos. It's Greek for knuckle. And supra is Latin for above. It's a mixed derivation – like "television". But I assume you're talking about the condyles of the humerus'

Dr Meadmore's technique with those who display any knowledge of their own is to ignore them and treat them like the mentally underprivileged; he continues to demonstrate the arm as though nothing has happened, but to Mercia; Mercia is interested in the hardware, even if the presentation leaves something to be desired; she has come to look over Chaite's shoulder – partly out of pity for Dr Meadmore – and it is to her that he demonstrates: 'Now, the stump will fit in here ... [I'd never have guessed] ... and this is where the knobs of the funny-bone go ... [you bum!] ... then a simple harness passes over the sound shoulder fitted to this cable attachment ... here. Pulling on the cable opens the terminal device ... like this. When it's all fixed up, the patient can pull the cable by moving his sound shoulder and pushing his stump forward ... [What if he's a she, Chaite forbears to ask] ... and then the thumb and these two fingers open ... like this ... [he demonstrates] ... and he can pick things up ... You've got quite a grip there ... feel'

Mercia breaks her vow of silence: 'So this is the sort of thing Chaite'll have?'

161

'Yes – it's very lifelike ... She shouldn't have any difficulty with one of these'
Fascinated, Mercia retires again. Chaite decides to test the water:
'It'll have to be a bit larger than that if it's going to match this one ... [she holds up her right hand] ... How do you change the hand?'
'Oh – the hand comes off ... like ... this ... Oh, well, it's a bit tight ... [he struggles with it using both hands; the girls imagine the one-armed child to whom it must have belonged giving up and throwing it to the dog] ... Anyway, Redman has a whole range of terminal devices the patient can plug in ... but most people settle for two or three – the hand, the split hook which is opened in the same way, and perhaps something else according to the individual's needs'
Chaite knows what she needs – to turn the clock back a fortnight and start her life again from there.
Dr Meadmore returns to the drawer: 'Here's a cosmetic hand – you'll feel that it's much lighter'
He passes it to Chaite; she forgets and stretches out the wrong arm; the hand falls to the floor.
'Ooops ... sorry'
Dr Meadmore stoops and picks it up; returns red-faced and puffing:
'Ah ... are you ... were you, by any chance ... left handed?'
'By Jove, Holmes, how did you guess?'
Dr Meadmore takes it crossly: 'You didn't tell me – I had to guess'
'I said I was sorry'
The telephone rings; Dr Meadmore barks: 'Yes ... mmm ... I'll be about ... [he looks at his watch irrelevantly] ... five minutes. Mmm. Thank you ... [he turns back to Mercia] ... Well, I hope that's been helpful to your sister'
'Extremely helpful, thank you. I expect we'll meet again'
'Yes. And if there's anything else you want to know, just make an appointment. Goodbye'
And so the girls are ushered verbally out.

Mercia trots out pushing Chaite at top speed; the old boys are still playing book-ends; the girls throw a goodbye over their shoulders at the receptionist as the doors roll apart to let them out. Mercia keeps up the pace until they reach a wooden seat under a cedar tree given in memory of someone's old dad, who loved to sit there. Chaite reads the engraved plaque: 'And what did he sit on before they gave the seat in his memory?'

It's too much for both of them – the seat, the book-ends, Dr Meadmore and his dolls' hospital. They howl with laughter for a long, long time. That interview will keep them going for weeks.

Rupert and Cepha are waiting to talk to Chaite; they're all sitting in the day-room; Rupert is looking official: 'Now, I expect you realise that Roy has ... gone away'
Chaite is wanting to shut the compartments in her mind, but: 'What about Roy?'
'You don't have to worry about him any more. He's not worrying about you'
Chaite took that in: 'He's really gone away? For ever?'
'As far as I can make out. He left this note for you on the television. I read it, of course, because I needed to gather any information which would shed light on the circumstances of the last few days'
Cepha loves her husband dearly, but sometimes wonders if he should have been a lawyer rather than an accountant.
Chaite makes an effort: 'What does it say?'
'Just that ... here, you read it'
It is addressed to Chaite, after all.
Chaite reads it. Then: 'I see. So he's ... gone away ... [she bursts into tears] ... I wish I could feel something ... anything ... I ought to be sorry, but I'm just ... numb. Roy and my arm ... they seem to have gone away together ... I just can't ...'
Like most people, Rupert is at a loss when faced with a grief he cannot share:
'He suggests that you can sell the cottage if you want to. Don't you want to live there?'
'No ... NO. I don't ever want to see it again'
'What about all your things? Furniture ... books ... ?'
'There are some things I'd like to keep. But rest can go in one of our sales. Would you mind ... could you look after it for me? I know it's a bit of an imposition ...'

Over the next few days, Chaite wanders mentally through the cottage, room by room, time and again, discussing the contents with Mercia, who gradually compiles lists of the things to be kept and the things to be sold. Then they all discuss it – Chaite, Mercia, Cepha and Rupert. Chaite signs a list of things she definitely wants to get rid of; Rupert promises to deal with it: 'I've got this document from Roy's solicitor now. He – Roy – relinquishes all his rights in the goods and chattels

which might be deemed to be jointly owned. But he does appear to have cleared out the workshop – Roy, that is'
'Well, it was all his stuff in there'
'He doesn't seem to have taken much from the house – except for his clothes. All the drink seems to have gone ... what's the matter?'
'Oooh ... terrible pain ... I don't want to talk any more ... no, I know you're being very kind but ...'
'That's all right – I'll look after everything for you'

By the end of the second week, Chaite is getting very bored. She has shut her mind to the past, accepted herself as she is now, and wants to get on with the future. She wanders about the ward and the corridors like a lost soul waiting for the pearly gates to open so that it can proceed with the next stage of its existence. She goes to the loo and washes herself more than is necessary, just to practise.

After two-and-a-half weeks, Chaite receives some eagerly-awaited intelligence: 'Good morning, I'm Dr Bendall, Mr Moreton-Smith's registrar ... [doesn't he recognise me yet?] ... how are you today? ... Let's have a look ... Hmmm, yes ... How are you sleeping? ... Any pain? ... RIGHT! I think we'll discharge you on Friday'
'You make me feel like a piece of artillery'
'What? Oh, ha-ha, very good!'
Chaite experiences a mixture of elation and sadness. In hospital, all your thinking is done for you. It's as near as you can get to the royal jelly. Outside ...
Mercia's elation is tempered with trepidation. Will she really be able to cope, as she's always promised?

Thursday afternoon; enter Nione Wood: 'I hear you're going home tomorrow'
'Yes ... I'm not sure whether to be glad or sorry'
'I should be glad, if I were you ... if I had a sister like your Mercia'
'Thanks, I'll tell her. I know she's a bit worried ... no, you can tell her yourself – hello Mercia'
'Afternoon all. What's she saying now?'
'She's saying she wants a sister like you'
'Oh yes ... what'she want?'
'Nothing, nothing ... I've just come to give Chaite one or two farewell presents ...'

Nione produces a Dycem mat to stop things from slipping about on the table, and some Theraband elastic webbing for Chaite's stump exercises; they discuss bandaging, and various tasks for Chaite to get her teeth into.

Chaite spends much of the night with her mind churning over and over, rehearsing ways of doing things. She tells no one about the pain in the hand that isn't there; she tries to shut her mind against it.

Friday comes, and with it Mercia with outdoor clothes for Chaite and cases to carry all the things Chaite has amassed during her three weeks in hospital.

Chaite has been mentally preparing herself to walk down to Mercia's car, but is glad she hasn't told anyone because when it comes to the point she realises how weak she really is. She says her good-byes to the staff, and the other patients. Mercia takes her to the lift in a wheelchair. Down they go, and out to the car.

Chaite suddenly realises that she's in the real world. In hospital, people are not surprised if you're ill, or heavily bandaged, or enclosed in some grotesque apparatus; in the real world people stare – and even if they don't, you think they do.

Chaite feels a great revulsion for herself, and for this real world she's been longing for ... but it passes; as the birds sing, and the sun shines, and Mercia smiles at her lovingly as she helps her into the car, Chaite is righted, and almost looking forward to the challenges to come.

Extracts from Chaite's journal:

Monday 13 June: V good to be out & about. Amazing how fast motor cars seem to travel. Good weekend; too much TV. Practising writing and M's word proc. Walk Sun pm, people don't seem to notice.

Thursday 16 June: Complete bathing and dressing unaided now; deep joy in getting hang of toothpaste!; could be almost back to normal. Eating always easy! Tried M's electric tin-opener & helped her make cake. NW Tuesday.

Tuesday 21 June: Back to NW this pm; worked at keyboard with *Typing exercises for one-handed people*. Look fwd to practising this. NW offered me a game of table tennis with bat strapped to stump; good therapy she said, but I tht it unnecessary – I didn't play before! Appt with Dr M a fortnight today.

Tuesday 5 July: Dr M this pm; says stump will be ready for cast in four weeks – possy before, but he's giving a paper at some international conf in Stockholm – whatever that's got to do with it. Hope they all enjoy it – perh he'll take his dolls' hosp.

Tuesday 12 July: NW again today; typing coming on well; got me using stump for space bar but I don't really need to.

Sunday 17 July: M took me to disused aerodrome & let me drive car. Not V good at changing gear (!) but don't see why I shdnt drive an auto. Cd join IAM. Rang Rup – he 'knows a man' & will see what he can find. I fancy a mauve Metro. C&R said I can have their granny flat when I'm ready. Whooppee!

Saturday 23 July: Went thru wardrobe with M. I suppose short sleeves are out also anything too tight, NW says, if op cord for new hand is to work comfortably. V sorry to see some things go – sat in garden & let M go to Oxfam alone.

Tuesday 2 August: Saw Mr Redman who's called John & comes to life without Dr M. Since Dr M didn't turn up anyway, why the delay? Perh he just wtd to boast he was going to a conf. Grrr! JR spent long time measuring my R hand; I didn't make obvious rude comment! Then he made plaster cast of stump. Back in 3 weeks. Meanwhile, replica me being made in Nottingham. Feels V odd.

Friday 4 August: Must think about going back to work soon – sure I can cos JS says I can start part time & make my own hours. C&R say granny flat is ready. Big Snag – leaving M. We've had a good time – she's almost as dependent on me as I am on her, but she must get on with her work too. Went shopping for new business outfit with suitable sleeves; found it at Walker's; assistants all pretended not to notice. Problem: what to do with flappy L sleeve – could tuck it in pocket, but can use stump for some things. Turning back the cuffs seems to be an answer.

Saturday 13 August: M moved me to granny flat today, settled in with load of fungibles & looking fwd to being on my own again – with big sis there if I need. Going to try JS on Mon.

Monday 15 August: Spent weekend practising living alone. Today back to JS. Felt everybody was staring, but no one said anything except nice to see me etc – apart from Debbie who wanted to know all about what it's like losing an arm – bit of a relief, cos they all wanted to know really. Took most of the day to catch up with what's going on – sale Fri – saw some of my things on show but pretended they were someone else's. JS V affable.

Friday 19 August: Sale went well; forced myself to help Charlie so that I cd get used to public appearances; only one mistake reaching with wrong hand but nobody saw (I hope!)

Tuesday 23 August: Back to JR; they've moulded a little plastic cup from cast of stump; bent elbow and it slipped on; straightened elbow and it couldn't fall off – felt funny but now see why it's called supracondylar & how it works (which had worried me). Now they've got to make it into an arm. I'd almost got round to telling them that I wasn't going to bother, but it'd be silly not to try. NW said you look more natural if you're wearing an arm cos you move more balanced and fluently, and people don't notice so much.

Also saw vid of arm wearers doing things & met Cathy (girl who starred in it); she also said most people don't notice her artificial arm; believe that when I see it, but she should know. They seem to notice me at the moment. She also told me re simple running repairs – can use a G-string (guitar!) for op cord.

Friday 26 August: Got into trouble today from horrible hairy farmer who wanted 'a hand' to unload heavy sideboard; the one time when someone might have noticed he didn't. Charlie came & got me out of it; was quite blunt.

Tuesday 13 September: Got new arm for next sale! Back to see JR who produced arm with flourish; better match (size, colour) than I'd dared hope. Just bent elbow & it slipped on; felt as if I was in shoe shop. Straightened elbow and it couldn't be pulled off – magic! JR fixed op cord & adjusted it; Dr M hustled in with his 1/2 moons, took 1/2 a look and said 'very good, off you go to OT, mind you wear it all the time' and disappeared again. Peculiar man; I'd wanted to ask how Stockholm was (be nice to Dr M week) but no chance.

JR got me opening and closing fingers by adjusting tension on the op cord. Gave me split hook and said NW would show me how to fix it on. Got hang of working hand by the time I got down to NW; she was pleased and amazed; she produced board with pegs and shapes for me to try manipulating. Wasn't all that easy cos I cdn't see what I was doing (hand got in way) so she showed me how to remove hand and plug in split hook – really yukky but V good for pick and place game & it's lighter and takes much less force to open (depends how many little rubber bands you put on) so less tiring than hand. Don't like look of it at all, but I'm going to try it. NW said Dr M is a bit strong on advice – shd take arm off when it gets tiring – get used to it in small doses.

Wednesday 14 September: Back to JS complete with arm. Several customers came into office, but nobody seemed to notice. Arm a bit hot & heavy but heaps better than nothing now. M came round, I cooked evening meal with help of hook. Took quite a long time, M watched but didn't help.

Friday 16 September: First sale with arm; I made up the book; only people who noticed seemed to be those who remembered from last time – hardly any.

Sunday 18 September: Dream: Roy brought my hand back – was it retribution? Told him where he could go cos I'd got a new one, but still awoke grieving. Went with family to zoo; V good day apart from nagging dream.

Tuesday 20 September: PM with NW; tried typing TD (as they will call them) V helpful, much lighter than hand, even more yukky than hook. Easier to come to terms with it in OT dept where you expect people to be like that. Did blocks exercise again with hand and hook. Long session with NW, spent a lot of time talking about cats and travels in Europe.

Monday 3 October: Arranging today for viewing tomorrow; hook V useful; Charlie said I was 'Very dextrous', I said it was more like sinister but finer meaning got lost. Lie in bed thinking of ways of doing things. V good in kitchen now. Seeing NW tomorrow (another cat session?) don't think there's much point in going to see her any more; she says I can ring her if I've got a problem. Don't like having to drag M along to give me a lift, except we both enjoy the days out.

Thursday 20 October: Appt for 2nd arm cast 15 Nov. When I've got that one they'll wait a bit until stump has shrunk and then re-do this one. Makes me feel like the Forth Bridge! JS introduced me to Kevin Toker – he met him at a professional din. Thinking of joining the firm – cd be a gd idea – let JS take things a bit easier. KT eligible ...?

*　*　*　*　*

Nione Wood goes to her record cards; S ... Slat ... She pulls out the card; takes up her pen; writes:
'Wish all my patients were like Chaite!'

17
Cup Final Saturday 21 May 1983

The last straw had been Roy the Slob. True, he could be loving and attentive – that was, after all, why Chaite had married him.

Roy, for his part, had not exactly married Chaite for her money ... but he had certainly been cognisant of the comfort it would afford them. The start of Chaite's third year at college had been shattered by the death of both her parents; this had not only left her with a third share of a considerable estate (making her, in her better moments, feel like something out of Jane Austen) but had driven her into the arms of Roy, a third year, third class, social scientist ... that Chaite had gained a first class degree in history and fine arts was no small achievement in the circumstances.

Chaite kept the exact amount of her fortune to herself; she thought that it should make no difference to her and Roy; she could support them both while they took their time to find jobs they would enjoy. Roy made no excessive demands; they bought an old cottage with a few acres of land at Stanfield, and spent a year or so living very simply, pottering about, doing it up.

In a desultory way, Roy had tried to find a job without wanting particularly to succeed in the quest. Chaite had joined James Sellis in the Autumn of 1981, and revelled in the long hours of hard work while Roy was still (she thought) trying to find a job in between slow reaches of home improvement.

After a year or two of hard work with James Sellis, it began to dawn on Chaite that Roy's habits were deteriorating; he lay in bed until all hours, he gave up washing much, drank more and more – in fact, he seemed to

169

spend most of his time at home either in bed or getting drunk and snoring in front of the television.

Today, it is the Cup Final. Chaite has been drudging in the washhouse, and has just hung out a load of washing. The line has snapped. Chaite has snapped. She's absolutely livid with everything, not least Roy to whom she runs, interposing her body between him and the television, standing consciously like a fishwife, arms akimbo: 'Now the bloody clothes-line's broken, and your fucking shirts are all in the dirt. You'll come and mend it NOW; otherwise ...'

Roy is slumped in the chair with his can of Newcastle Brown; he glares at Chaite balefully and says not a word as the television chants and roars.

Chaite runs out to the kitchen; goes into slow motion. The crowd chants and roars; she hears the snap and hiss as Roy opens yet another can.

She picks up the German cook's knife Cepha and Rupert brought them from a trip abroad; she grasps it tightly in her left hand until the knuckles become white; then, looking at it as though it were something she was nothing to do with, and keeping her eyes on it as if she were guiding it by remote control, she walks slowly, zombie-like, to the room where Roy sits drowned in *that noise*.

How she hates *that noise*, and all it seems to stand for for. This is where it's going to STOP. She enters the room and, just as Smith scores the first goal for Albion, she STABS the knife through the back of the chair – surprised at how easily it goes through; she pulls it out and stabs again ... and again ... and again ...

Roy slumps forward on to the floor. The can falls; Newcastle Brown fizzes into the carpet.

The television chants and roars frenetically, but Chaite hears it no more. Still staring at her hand grasping the knife, now in horror, she turns and blunders from the room, through the kitchen, into the garden, dodges into the workshop. There she stands, gasping for breath, her heart pounding: the only thing she can see is the knife grasped in her left hand, the only thing she can think of is that she is a murderess, and that the murder weapon has somehow fastened itself to her.

She knows that she has to get rid of the knife, but she can't. She is a murderess, and her hand just won't open and release the knife. She stands in a plane of sunlight beaming in through the slot between the doors, which are slightly ajar. She stares at the knife in fascination.

Inside the house, Roy rises slowly from the floor, stone cold sober; he turns off the television. SILENCE! What does the Cup Final, or its result, matter now? What has got into Chaite? Where is she? What will she do next?

He tiptoes gingerly from the room in case Chaite is hiding somewhere, sees the open door to the garden, sees the door of the workshop ajar ... and sees, reflected in the greenhouse as it were Pepper's Ghost, Chaite standing catatonically inside the workshop still grasping the knife.

Then, to her disembodied amazement, Chaite sees the dead Roy coming from the house; he looks around cautiously – as well he might; he is not to know that all Chaite's anger and force are spent; all he knows is that she must be madder than Lady Macbeth. First he must secure her, then fetch help.

He stands, unsure whether to call out or to remain silent; whether to move slowly or fast. And still Chaite stands, powerless to move.

Now Roy lunges forward and slams the workshop door shut. His sudden movement unfreezes Chaite; as the door shuts, she springs towards it in an attempt to escape, trips, falls flat on her face. The heavy door closes, crushing her wrist. Chaite yells and passes out.

Roy does not notice what has happened. He flicks the hasp and drops the podger through the staple, feeling nothing but immense relief that Chaite is safely – he thinks – contained inside the workshop. He has no idea what has come over her; he will leave her to cool off ... or should he call a doctor to calm her down?

No ... people ought to be able to work out their own problems, not go running for the doctor at the drop of a hat. Yes ... he'll wait for Chaite to cool off – judging from the silence, she seems to have calmed down – later, he'll go and let her out, and they'll go to the pub and have a few drinks and carry on from where they left off – except that he'll change his habits ... a bit – after all, the football season's now over (apart from the replay, in which he'll take little interest).

In a daze, Roy wanders back to the kitchen. His thoughts turn to Newcastle Brown, but he finds the idea revolting. He decides to leave Chaite for half an hour or so – unless she starts to call out.

But after a few minutes he can bear it no longer; he walks slowly and quietly to the workshop and taps on the door.
No reply.
He tries to see through the window, but the angle of vision is inadequate; the interior too dark.
He knocks more loudly – still no reply.

He throws open the door.

Chaite lies unconscious.

Roy has some idea that you don't move people when they're unconscious.

He picks up the knife, and tosses it out of sight; then he dashes back to the house and phones for an ambulance.

All this is happening in methodical slow motion, in a dream.

In no time, and in infinite time, he hears the sound of the ambulance, and a loud knocking on the front door. Although there are but two of them, the ambulance men seem to fill the house.

'There's been an accident ... [he said] ...

She's in the garden. In the shed'

They go through and size up the situation.

They kneel by Chaite with a first aid kit; then return to the ambulance for a stretcher.

Roy takes some comfort from their calm; 'they've seen the lot' he thinks.

The bandaged Chaite is laid on the stretcher; carried to the ambulance; inserted.

'Perhaps you'd like to travel with your wife, sir ...'

'My wife ...'

Roy locks the house and climbs into the ambulance.

Roy is too shocked to think of anything apart from the fact that the only way to travel in a speeding ambulance must be lying on a stretcher ... before he falls to irrelevantly wondering about the state of cleanliness of his underpants.

They arrive at the hospital.

Chaite is taken away on her stretcher. Roy is led into a cubicle.

He starts to shiver and weep uncontrollably, unashamedly.

He has failed miserably.

His marriage has failed miserably – has not his wife tried to murder him ... and is she not now going to die?

It's all his fault.

A nurse comes and peers at him; a doctor comes and feels his pulse, looks at his pupils with a pen torch.

He still shakes and weeps.

A nurse comes in with a clipboard and tries to extract details of names, addresses, dates of birth, religions ...

Who's his doctor?

What's his hospital number?

What's his wife's hospital number?

Why the hell does this matter at the moment – or, indeed, ever?

They make numbers seem like the most important thing in the world.
It all seems to lack relevance; he can almost remember who he is – but why should anyone else be bothered?
The nurse bustles in commandingly with a little plastic cup: 'Drink this'
Roy sits up, slurps, falls back with a sob and a sigh.
In another cubicle, the casualty officer has called the consultant; they are examining Chaite's wrist.
There's some remote chance of repairing her.
Quickly, yet unhurriedly, she is undressed and prepared; the crushed wrist cleaned; the wedding ring removed; X-rays taken; dressings applied.
Chaite is delivered to a room in the orthopaedic ward.

Roy feels better when he wakes up.
What happened? He was watching the Cup Final on the television ... she crept into the room and started to stab the back of his chair piercing the cushion repeatedly, but he was untouched. Was she mad? She couldn't really have wanted to kill him ... or could she? Was she really that fed up with him? He could never really believe that she hated football as much as she said she did. And yet she had, apparently, tried to kill him.

That's it! He had stopped her vicious onslaught by pretending to die, toppling forward off the chair and lying motionless on the floor, waiting to see what would happen. E'en now, he could hear the Newcastle Brown fizzing into the carpet, taking complete precedence over the Cup Final, in which he had lost all interest. Presumably his act had put an end to hers; she'd left the room ... and now he remembers what happened after that ...

Enter a casualty officer, white coat and stethoscope flying: 'Feeling better?
... [He goes through a gamut of doctorly motions] ... How did it happen?'
'How did what happen?'
'The lady whose hand was injured?'
'Will she be all right?'
'*She* will, but I'm afraid I can't guarantee her hand ... [Roy's faith in the medical profession ebbs] ... I'm afraid we'll just have to wait and see'
Roy sinks back; his eyes fill with tears again.
It feels like the end of the world.
'Can I see her?'
'I'll ask nurse to find out'
Delegating thus, the doctor leaves the room assertively.
So Roy lies on the bed, the charade, and what he *ought* to have done churning round in his head.

Perhaps he should have risen up and fought her for the knife ... but there had been so much fighting.

It hadn't been what he had expected of marriage.

Perhaps he should have ... things should never have reached that pitch.

The doctor reappears: 'Your wife's asleep – and she's going to be drowsy when she wakes up. It'd be best if you could come back tomorrow'

Roy now discovers that he doesn't mind not seeing her.

He cannot think what he would say to her.

He's glad not to have to force himself to speak to her – and not to have to suffer all that she might say – or not say.

Traumata might draw some couples together, enabling a fresh start. Roy realises that this is the end of their road.

He finds the public telephone and calls for a cab.

He waits for what seems an unconscionable long time; black eyes, bloody noses, limping limbs, a passing show of damaged humanity moves before him, accompanying friends and relations sit whispering or staring vacantly into space.

He is both appalled and relieved that he feels numb and neutral – if not positively negative – about her.

He tries to think himself into a different frame of mind, and is ashamedly overjoyed to find that, try as he will, he can't.

The cab appears, the driver mercifully silent.

Roy arrives home, pays off the cab, goes indoors.

He moves slowly round the house, looking at everything as though he hasn't seen it before.

He goes to the workshop and examines the door, clears up; soon there is no sign that anything untoward has happened.

He retrieves the knife, wraps it heavily in several newspapers, seals the bundle with sellotape ... and wonders what to do with it. He decides to hide it in the rafters of the workshop – for the time being, at any rate.

He goes back to the house.

He has already determined that nobody will know what happened unless she tells them.

In the living room, he takes the stabbed chair; puts it outside ready for the dustmen who will come on Monday.

He clears up the tins and deranged newspapers, runs the carpet sweeper round the room, arranges the furniture.

He finds a torch, goes up into the loft, and brings down some suitcases.

He packs all his clothes and the few belongings which are really his and about which he cares.

He goes to the kitchen, turns on the radio for company, and makes himself a desultory omelette.

He eats it slowly, washing it down with neat Cinzano, his mind a complete blank.

He drinks most of what's left of a bottle of whisky and snores the night away cramped on the sofa.

He awakes feeling like nothing on earth.

Suddenly the events of the previous day hit him; he goes to the lavatory and is sick.

Now he's sure that his world has come to an end.

He showers, changes his clothes, and writes a note to her, which he leaves – ironically, he thinks – on the television.

He thinks that he'll have a couple of days to try to get back to normal – if there is ever to be another normal.

If he decides to return, no one will ever know that he once contemplated leaving.

If he doesn't return, that will be that; the note on the telly will explain it all.

He loads his suitcases into his car.

He secures the house.

He gets into his car, starts the engine and drives away.

And he will never see her again.

Notes

Interactive index

(See page viii)